THE IVORY SWING

Janette Turner Hospital

SEAL BOOKS
McClelland and Stewart-Bantam Limited
Toronto

For Clifford, Geoffrey, and Cressida

*This low-priced Seal Book
has been completely reset in a type face
designed for easy reading, and was printed
from new plates. It contains the complete
text of the original hard-cover edition.*
NOT ONE WORD HAS BEEN OMITTED.

THE IVORY SWING
A Seal Book

PRINTING HISTORY
McClelland and Stewart Limited edition published September 1982
A Selection of Literary Guild Book Club, 1982

*The epigram was taken from a Bengali song in praise of Krishna,
translated by Edward C. Dimock, Jr. in The Place of the Hidden
Moon (© 1966 by The University of Chicago. All rights reserved),
and is produced by permission of The University of Chicago
Press.*

Seal edition / October 1983

ISBN 0-7704-1823-6

PRINTED IN CANADA

COVER PRINTED IN U.S.A.

U   0 9 8 7 6 5 4 3 2 1

ACKNOWLEDGMENTS

A chapter of this novel, in slightly different form, was published in *The Atlantic Monthly*, as the short story "Waiting." It received an "Atlantic First" citation in March 1978.

Another section, again in somewhat different form, appeared in the *Kingston Whig-Standard Magazine*.

Grateful acknowledgment is made to Harvard University's *Center for the Study of World Religions*, a fondly remembered home and the source of my family's long-standing preoccupation with India.

Also to the *Shastri Indo-Canadian Institute* which sponsored my husband's sabbatical research in India in 1977-78.

Special thanks are due to Professor Wilfred Cantwell Smith (formerly of McGill and Dalhousie Universities, and now of Harvard University) for his reading of, and early support for, this manuscript. His points of concurrence and his wondrously detailed disagreements with me will always remain the greatest of intellectual compliments.

To Blanche Gregory, literary agent *extraordinaire* and much loved friend, my warm thanks.

Also to Ellen Seligman, my editor at McClelland and Stewart, with whom in a few intense and frenetic weeks I have shared conflict and insight, exhaustion and hilarity.

I am forever blessed!
For I am his own breath, within his flute!
And if that breath is used up, in one song,
I shall not mourn.
The joy of all the worlds is in his flute,
and I his breath!
Let my song be good or evil,
let it be played with joy or sorrow,
I will sound it in the morning,
and in the evening it will sound,
and I will play it, softly muffled, in the night.
I will play it in the spring,
I will play it in the fall,
and when his breath is used up, in his song,
I shall not mourn.
My song will be the loveliest of songs.

1

They did not quite know what to make of each other, Juliet and the boy. They were very strange to each other.

Every morning just before sunrise the sound of his flute would sift like birdsong through the coconut palms. She would be startled from a sleep teeming with a confusion of remembered faces in unfamiliar settings, her past jolting by on buffalo carts, green mold and jungle vines sprouting from the eyes of old lovers, jackfruit and mangoes pressing against the windows of the house with snow on its roof. She would stumble to the storm door.... No. Not that house, not that door. Not a door at all really. She would stumble to the front grille and unlock it, blinking out into the coconut grove already alive with the tending activities of Shivaraman Nair's servants.

The boy would offer the little vessel.

"Milk," he would say proudly, in the English learned from her children.

"*Pahl*," she would confirm, taking it to the kitchen. "*Uba-garam*."

"Thank you," he would repeat.

That was the full extent of his English vocabulary, but since he was illiterate in his own tongue, proportionately he was doing better than she. Still she would think with wonder: here I am in a South Indian village conversing in an obscure dialect at an hour when I would prefer to be in deep sleep.

She would take the milk to the kitchen, transfer it to a cooking vessel, light a fire in the small clay pit, and balance the pot over it. After the milk boiled she would skim the clotted cream off the top, set aside the portion for the day's yoghurt, and pour the remainder into an earthern pitcher on a cool stone slab. While she boiled the water for coffee the boy would begin his sweeping. She would go back to the bedroom to dress and to wake her husband.

The first time it happened she was outraged. The boy quietly opened the door and began to sweep. She was standing naked, too astonished to move. He watched her as he swept, neither embarrassed nor interested.

"*Po!*" she said angrily. "*Po! Po!*" Go away!

He left, puzzled.

There were constant misunderstandings. That they had a "boy" at all was one of them. On the first day, Mr. Shivaraman Nair had shown them over the house. It looked cool and gracious as a palace under its umbrella of coconut palms.

"It is fit for a maharani!" Juliet had exclaimed.

Mr. Shivaraman Nair had asked: "How many servants are you needing?"

"None." She was blithe about it, being preoccupied with the exquisite tilework, sensuously conscious of the marbled floor cool under her bare feet. She did not understand that the kitchen was of a different order, that it was intended only for servants with skills more ancient than her own, that it came equipped with a knee-high sink, a stone mortar and pestle, and a cooking pit.

"I don't need any servants."

Mr. Shivaraman Nair sniffed with contempt. She had lost face and caste. All Westerners were wealthy, and wealthy people should behave as befits wealth. Just as Nairs should behave as befits the superior status of the Nair caste. The quality of his tenants reflected on his family.

"Then I will send only the sweeper each day," he said coldly.

"A sweeper! I can do my own sweeping. It is nothing."

This was because she thought she knew what a broom was. She had not yet seen the little hand-held tuft of palm leaves. She had also been taken aback by his anger.

"It is your affair that you are being yourself your own cook-bearer. It is my affair who is being sweeper on my estates. This is the task of servant peoples. No other persons are sweeping on my properties. And so we are only awaiting the auspicious time for you to commence living in my house."

"Auspicious time? But we have already rented the house for this month. We were expecting to move in today."

"No, no, this is not possible. The astrologer has been consulted. The auspicious day for visitors to move into my house is next Tuesday, in four more days. On that day, I will send the boy to the hotel to communicate the auspicious hour."

So it was settled. On the auspicious day at the auspicious hour they took up residence. And the boy brought the milk each morning and swept floors and courtyard. He was called simply "the boy" by Shivaraman Nair; or sometimes "the *peon*" or "my *peon*."

In the first week, when he arrived with milk and morning mists, Juliet had spoken to him in Malayalam. "What is your name?"

He was thrown into utter confusion. It was not a question he was used to being asked. He blushed and stammered. Eventually he managed to say: "Prabhakaran."

How old was he? she asked. He did not know.

"You cannot be more than twelve," she said. "I think you are twelve. Just a little older than my son."

He nodded rapidly, smiling, happy to accept her judgment.

"Jonathan is ten," she explained. "And Miranda is eight."

You are all only children, she almost added. And yet the boy was a full-time laborer, a bonded servant of Shivaraman Nair.

"Jonathan, Miranda, *minna*?" he asked.

She knew the word.

Already he had taught her children to fish for *minna* with

cupped hands in the irrigation ditches between the coconut palms and in the muddy water of the flooded rice paddy. She was afraid of malaria – there had been an outbreak at Cochin, not far north – and of hepatitis.

"Later," she said. "After the school lessons."

He smiled and nodded again. They continued to look at each other, anxious to please, willing to be friends, not knowing what to say.

Then, somberly, he produced the little wooden flute that he wore tucked into the waist of his *dhoti*. He played a short strange song, alien to her western ears, bittersweet. She perceived it as some sort of gift, and brought her hands together in front of her face in the traditional way of thanks.

They both made *namaskaram*, bowing slightly towards each other. It was not, Juliet knew, the way one was supposed to greet a servant.

2

"India!" Jeremy had said slightingly and incredulously. "It makes me think of dust and mosquitoes and bananas gone overripe and rancid."

She was crushed. She had expected him to be envious and excited. She had expected that she would be sustained under the equatorial sun by her fantasies of his fantasy of a nut-brown Juliet smelling of the tantalizing tropics with a hibiscus in her hair.

"You must be crazy!" he said. "For a whole year! It's like being buried in a swamp. You'll be pining for snow and books and rationality, whatever the wanton tropical inclinations of your body."

It was a slip, a forbidden word. Her body. One of the unspoken rules of the complicated game they played was that they never alluded to the fact that they had once been lovers.

They both looked silently at the table between them. The fingers of Jeremy's left hand drummed a light rhythm. Juliet studied, mesmerized, the distance between her right hand, resting lightly beside her glass, and Jeremy's fingers.

"I suspect you're not admitting to yourself your real reasons for going," he said.

Another error. Another impasse. He thinks I'm going because David requires it, Juliet decided. She was annoyed and defensive. What would Jeremy – with no children and two

13

divorces behind him – know of the complex adjustments of marriage and family life? It was another rule that they never spoke of their marital states or living arrangements or current partners.

She was irritated with herself for having called him. These things happened occasionally. There was a blurred borderline crossed by accident at certain moments. Randomly. Sometimes events were safely pliant in her mind. Sometimes Jeremy was actually there, tangible, disruptive, in the precarious terrain of slithering reality.

"Hello," he had answered.

"Hello. Jeremy?"

"Juliet!" She heard the note of pleasure. And caution.

"I'm going to India for a year. Just calling to say goodbye."

Ridiculous thing to say since she hadn't seen him or spoken to him for about a year anyway.

"Good god! India! Why India?"

"For David's sabbatical."

"India," he said again. There was a pause. "Can you get here for a day before you leave?"

Typical, she thought. Now he feels safe. When acceptance will be difficult or impossible, Jeremy issues invitations. "Here" was Boston, and she would love to have said simply and lightly: "Sorry. Not a hope." She would love to have been the kind of woman who could say that with casual regret and then shrug and hang up.

Instead she held onto the receiver like a drowning woman clutching at a life-line. They were pulling her to safety now: Jeremy's voice, the background sounds of a city.

But is it really Jeremy I crave? she asked herself. Or is it just the vibrant echo of youth? And the lure of a city, *any* city, any real metropolis, gritty and boisterous: tidal waves of unknown people, of anonymity, of excitement; the huge ebb and flow of life lived avidly. Any crust would do, any reminder, any testament to that other lost self. (Once I soared, once my career was marked "fast track," once a small world turned on my opinions. Once Jeremy, reckless with desire, brought lilacs…. And then David, his star rising, obliterated everything else, threw a shimmer over the future. His and mine. Our glittering life together.)

Oh how young and arrogant and intoxicated with my own life I was, thought Juliet, dizzy with loss. Before this. The plummeting. This wingless limping around the cage of a small college town musty with propriety and smugness and myopia.

"Hello?" Jeremy said. "Hello? Juliet, are you still there?"

Don't go, she pleaded mutely, waiting for her voice to return from the golden muddle of the past. Don't leave me stranded here.

"Juliet?"

"Yes. Sorry." She could barely hear herself speak. "Bad connection."

"Can I see you before you go?"

The question flowed into her like Benzedrine. His eyes, as always, would give back that mislaid image of a woman lively with confidence, professionally significant, dazzling. She would be able to feed on the illusion that that other Juliet still existed since he could have no inkling of the slow seepage, the loss of vital fluids, that occurred in small provincial places.

"Juliet, is something – ?"

"No, it's just…I'm thinking…. Boston is impossible. The time, the children…it's truly impossible." Her voice pitched about like a kite caught in the cables that linked them, veered erratically away from intensity, alighted on the flippantly suggestive. "But somewhere in between? Montreal? Can you get to Montreal?"

Silence. As cold as the Canadian Shield that stretched endlessly northwards away from her. Jeremy was not in the habit of making large incautious gestures.

In her mind she rehearsed saying: Just kidding.

In her mind she said airily: I'll call you in thirteen months or so, when I get back.

She pictured herself hanging up and walking away. Shrugging. She pictured it so vividly she thought perhaps she had already done it.

"Montreal," he said. "What day?"

Panic.

How did I think I could arrange...? At such short notice! What on earth shall I...?

"I have to be there," she invented shakily, "next Wednesday. The McGill library. I need to look up a few references."

"Wednesday? Yes, that's possible. Next Wednesday then."

In Montreal their drinks were garnished with the light that fell like a blessing on Place Jacques Cartier.

"I don't know why it is," she said, noticing that the distance between their hands was diminishing slightly, "why I always feel this ridiculous compulsion to let you know my current whereabouts. At least roughly. It makes me nervous if you don't. As though some essential reference point had vanished."

"I know." He gestured with his hand and it came to rest a little closer to the center of the table. "We've preserved this image of perfection, the unblemished view of the lover." He used the word sardonically, deprecatingly, in a generic way. "We never contaminate it with reality."

"Such a relentless debunker of mysteries!"

She wondered whether he was married again or was merely living with the woman who had answered her first long-distance call. She did not wish to intrude on his arrangements, however temporary. She had hung up and called him again at his office.

Now they watched an old flower seller heft huge wooden tubs of begonias across the cobblestones, massing magentas and corals in front of his trestle tables.

"I know a few people teaching at McGill. Dropped in on them while I was waiting for you. They're looking for someone in my field." Jeremy leaned back and examined the light through his wine. "It's a marvellous city. I could live here."

"Yes. So could I. In fact I toy with the idea constantly." Then she felt embarrassed, as though she had made a proposition, and added quickly: "But any city would do. My sustaining escape fantasy. Any place big enough to offer me a position I'm not seriously overqualified for. Any place big enough for me to go to a concert without seeing my dentist and my gynecologist and my kids' schoolteachers and the candlestick maker."

"Is it really so awful?"

"Oh well, you know, on and off. I survive. After a fashion."

"When I picture you there," he said, "I think of a Roman candle on an ice floe. I would imagine you take the town by storm."

"It's not a place that approves of storms. Storms don't have the proper sense of decorum."

"There must be compensations. Clean air, no traffic jams?"

"Give me a gritty subway and freedom any time."

"Then why, for god's sake, *India?*"

"Well, because India.... Are you going to tell me you've never dreamed of the fabled East? Marco Polo, Vasco da Gama. Surely everyone, I thought everyone...." But she was embarrassed to admit to the jejune lure of travelers' antique and brocaded tales – of tigers, elephants, sandalwood and ivory, the whole exotic paraphernalia. "I thought you'd envy me."

"You must be crazy. Even your thought processes will turn rancid. *My* idea of a year's escape is an apartment in Paris with some Left Bank ferment and the libraries of the Sorbonne close by. Or, failing that, a London flat close to the British Museum with ale and politics in the local pub. But to move from sub-arctic isolation to equatorial isolation – I can't see the point of that."

"Isolation! In a country of over five hundred million? With that kind of crowding, anything could happen. Anything! That's what grabs me – after a near fatal absence of risk for the last twelve years."

"Poor caged bird who's forgotten how to fly. Done in by a surfeit of security."

"Not funny. You don't know what it's like, living in a place that's lethally safe."

Their hands had gradually moved so that their fingertips touched, an unnerving sensation.

"Well," he said. "If it's risk-taking you want, here we are. Alone in Montreal."

He laced his fingers through hers and it was like the pull of a current swirling her back to her own element, her own life that had slithered away from her. But then her heart snagged on something else, the hook of children, of those innocent sleeping faces damp against their pillows. (She would stand in their rooms at night and think helplessly: I would die for them. I would even go on living here in Winston, Ontario, for them.) And then there was David, she was caught on that hook too, she would never get him out of her flesh.

Jeremy lifted her hand to his mouth and ran his tongue across her fingertips.

Shall we? his eyes asked with an unwavering intensity.

No! hers replied, alarmed, hypnotized. Think of the chaos! That wasn't what I meant. (Was it?)

"Enjoy India!" he said lightly, withdrawing his hand.

"Think of me with jasmine in my hair."

"I'll think of you wilting from heat and humidity and covered with mosquito bites," he said unobligingly.

"You are cruel."

"No." He looked directly at her. "You are cruel."

There was some clouding – irritation? hurt? – in his eyes, but she could not – or was afraid to – read it. I have never known what he wants, she thought. Or what he really thinks of me.

"I wish you knew what you wanted," he said.

She was startled, and blurted without thinking: "I want to maintain my balancing act."

The hazardous, arduous balancing act of someone born on the cusp between eras. A mutant form on the Tree of Woman. She had evolved wings her mother never had, but not the free flight patterns of her younger sister, Annie.

Jeremy raised a sardonic eyebrow. "The illusion of risk," he said. "That's all you want, the *illusion* of risk."

Stung, she flared at him: "That's not true!" Oh, but maybe it was. Independence smoldered like sulfur in her gut, but domestic commitment was in her genes, heavy as lead. "Some things are too valuable to risk losing. It's pathetically simple, what I want. I wish we would move back to a city."

"We." He said it without inflection, as though a point had at last been clarified in some interminable negotiation. "And if you plural should continue for another decade to vegetate in Winston, what do you singular intend to do?"

"Another decade?" she echoed weakly. It seemed to her that a terminal diagnosis had been made. She would not look at his eyes. "I suppose," her voice faltered, "I suppose I'll try to keep juggling."

"Juggling what? Your virtue and your sanity? Or your male pawns, your nice little chessboard toys?"

She stared at him, fascinated by new revelations. And he, alarmed at his own indiscretion, blundered further into rage. "What is he, some sort of rabid contemplative? Is he *anchored* to the place? What the hell is the matter with him…?"

But he had to stop. It was against their rules, a violent breach of etiquette.

And she could not bear to have David attacked.

"It isn't like that. You don't understand."

"No. I don't understand." Irritably he signaled the waitress, impatient to be rid of the tedium of Juliet's ambivalence. "But your lack of honesty disgusts me. It's something you've acquired in Winston. You're ashamed of loving that safe little bourgeois cage so you keep up a pretence of wanting to get out."

"God, you're brutal! Is simple friendship such a costly thing for you to give?"

"Simple friendship." He laughed mirthlessly. "Let's not be disingenuous. If you wanted to leave Winston, you'd leave.

And whatever it is we've had between us all these years, let's not pretend that simple friendship is the right word for it."

"It's *my* word for it."

"As I've just pointed out, your provincial little town is a hot-bed of hypocrisy."

"If it's hypocrisy we're speaking of, why pretend you give a damn where I spend the rest of my life? You – the original free-wheeler. A life littered with discarded women." This was unpardonably against the rules, she thought; it was beyond the forgivable. "Oh god, I didn't mean... but damn it, I'm going to miss you, actually miss you...." A tremor had crept into her voice and she crushed it beneath the heel of her will as though it were a poisonous spider. "And you won't even remember I've left this continent." (If I begin to cry, she told herself furiously, I will never forgive myself.) "But I expect I can be spartan about it."

"Oh I don't doubt it. If it should cross your mind to send a postcard, I'll pin it over my desk. I daresay I'll recall where you are every time it catches my eye."

"Oh I daresay. A hunting trophy among many. Forlorn notes from women I have known."

"Juliet, Juliet!" He gestured in mock despair and laughed. "You should be burned at a stake." He leaned across the table suddenly and kissed her on the lips. "Now get the hell out of my life and I hope you rot in India."

3

Silken girls were carrying sherbet to Moghul emperors across glowing expanses of tapestry. Krishna and Radha, vibrant batik figures, dallied in a tangled embrace that was aesthetically exquisite if physically improbable. On a swing of carved ivory, they sat demurely as satiated lovers. And Juliet, browser amidst the fabulous jetsam of maharajahs and nawabs, thought: My life is a surprise to me.

David moved across the room and stood behind her. He touched her long hair lightly and rested his hand on the nape of her neck. It might have meant: You are Radha to me. He was excited by the ivory carving, artistically and sexually. He knew its history, would want to explain its iconography and significance. He would point out contrasts with that painting on the far wall where Radha, on another swing, breathed solitary love sighs. And she would listen partly out of habit, partly because his intellectual energy was a source of wonder to her.

Marriage has given me a staggering amount of esoteric information, she thought wryly.

University people, Mr. Motilal decided, whispering to his kohl-eyed assistant to bring mango juice. There were four kinds of Westerners: tourists, diplomats, hippies, and university people. He saw his position as that of an appraisal expert; the correct designation of Westerners was as important to success as the ability to know authentic antiques from fakes.

Not many Westerners found their way this far south, so close to the equator, but those who did were usually big spenders passing through on the way to Kovalam. They would flit in and out, spending only a few hours in Trivandrum but several weeks sequestered in the Kovalam Palace Hotel. Mr. Motilal kept his rooms air-conditioned. It was an irresistible lure and ensured lengthy browsing.

He reluctantly decided that these people, with two children in tow, were not Kovalam people. They would not be able to afford the ivory swing. But as they were clearly connected with the university, he would emphasize the small bronzes, relating them to incidents in the *Mahabharata* and the *Ramayana*. This would be a fruitful approach.

The assistant brought mango juice in small glasses on a silver tray and with deft experience offered it to the children first.

"Oh no, please, you must not," begged Juliet hastily. But it was too late. Jonathan and Miranda were already drinking with delight.

"But yes, indeed, it is our pleasure," murmured Mr. Motilal with a bow.

Chairs were brought.

"Please," insisted Mr. Motilal. "You must sit and rest. It is so hot. Even for us it is hot outside, though so cool and pleasant in here."

Juliet sighed. They were used to this sort of performance and dreaded it. It had been a mistake to linger at the ivory swing. The only way to cut short an otherwise interminable ritual was to buy something quickly. Unfortunately almost everything, being genuine antique artwork and priced for foreign collectors, was well beyond their range.

But it would not be possible now – or at least, it would be highly unpleasant – to leave without buying.

"Such fine bronzes," Mr. Motilal was saying. "Many people are buying. In the magazines, the art critics are saying – "

"Oh look!" Miranda broke into the soft patter of sales talk, pointing to a delicate sandalwood figurine.

"That is Lord Krishna," beamed Mr. Motilal. "He is dancing on the lotus flower and playing his flute."

But all of them thought: It is Prabhakaran.

"We will buy it," Juliet told Mr. Motilal. "It is very beautiful."

"Most beautiful, most beautiful," he agreed.

David lamented in a whisper: "I wish we could afford the ivory swing."

Juliet looked at it again, saw the daze in Radha's eyes as she swayed forever between poles, unable to stop, unable to get off. She glanced back at the batik where Radha was tangled with her consort, helplessly as ivy around a trellis. And Krishna, feeling the restive tremor in her limbs, would be thinking fondly of how she clung to him, how she needed him.

Mr. Motilal offered the flute player, boxed and wrapped.

"I'll leave you then," David said, as the outside heat swallowed them whole, "to tape those Brahmin priests I've been meeting with. Some fascinating oral variants."

He kissed the children, brushed Juliet's cheek with his lips. "You'll manage?"

"I'll manage."

He left with his tape recorder and she walked towards the market place with the children.

∽

"One dozen hens' eggs," she ordered in her carefully rehearsed Malayalam.

The egg man laughed because she could not master one of the several *l*'s, the one that had to be mysteriously rolled at the back of the mouth rather like a Scottish *r*.

He sat cross-legged on a small wooden platform under an awning of coconut thatch. In front of him were two huge baskets. The eggs in one were about the size Juliet thought of as regular or medium. Those in the other basket were tiny, like large pigeon eggs. The old man made a cone with a sheet of newspaper, gently placed a dozen eggs in it, and tied it ingeniously with thin twine. He chose the tiny eggs but Juliet now knew better than to ask for the others. They were ducks' eggs, porous and likely to be impregnated with whatever impurities were on the ground where they had been laid. She had learned this from the doctor who treated them after they had eaten the wrong eggs. She tried not to think of all the other unknown depredations that were perhaps being made daily on their health.

"Six rupees," said the egg man.

"Last week it was five."

The egg man raised his eyes to heaven in a gesture of melancholy resignation.

"Life is difficult," he sighed. "Like midday ground mists after monsoon rain, prices go only upwards."

A young Indian woman of striking beauty was standing beside Juliet. She now said something to the egg man. The words were too rapid for Juliet to unravel, but the woman turned and spoke to her in unexpectedly good English.

"He is being shameful. Most wicked. He is doing it because you are a foreigner. The real price is four rupees. You must not pay him more than four. Also," she added, "you must have a servant. The marketing is too difficult for you. Even Indian ladies are not doing it. It is a skill of the marketing servants. Then you will not be cheated."

She smiled and moved away. Juliet was conscious of her gorgeous sari of Benares silk, of her lavish jewelry. A small stir of excitement, of stares and whispers, moved with the woman like an attendant breeze. Such splendor was rare at Palayam Market.

The egg man waited impassively. For Juliet and the children he had become a sort of friend, one of the fixed points in the slow equatorial week. He no longer stared at them rudely, he did not molest them by touching their fair hair and faces, he simply sold them eggs and made small conversation. They were deeply grateful for such fragments of normal interaction. It was well worth two rupees extra. Yet Juliet would lose standing and respect in the market if she showed herself stupid, unable to bargain. In the next little bower, the merchant of rice and *gram* stood watching and listening.

On the other hand, what were two rupees to a Westerner? It seemed only right to pay a little more. She did not wish to appear ungenerous. Nor too patronizing. These were complex and swift inner calculations.

"Each week I will pay you five rupees and fifty *paise*," she said. "You must not ask for more."

The egg man and the rice merchant smiled. The solution pleased them.

But then the eggs were lost. To an accompanying cacophony of megaphones, a gust of demonstrators erupted into the market and in the scuffle Juliet and the children were knocked back against the stalls. Juliet tripped in the open gutter that ran along the storefronts, sinking to the ankles in vegetable slops and excrement of various human and animal kinds, pitching the delicate cone of eggs to the ground. She stepped out gingerly, leaving her sandals in the slime. A new pair could be bought for a few rupees from one of the cobblers in the market.

It was not a particularly significant or alarming incident, demonstrations of one kind or another being an almost daily event. She understood that the buffeting was an accidental side skirmish, that the main rout was heading up Mahatma Gandhi Road towards the tourist hotel and the Air India offices. Scores of red banners bearing a sickle crossed with a stalk of rice (instead of a hammer) fluttered over the marching chanting heads. There were other banners printed in Malayalam script, the swirls and scrolls of which were impenetrable to Juliet who had learned what she knew of the language by ear.

"What do the signs say?" Juliet asked the egg man.

He gazed at heaven and shrugged. He could not read.

"I don't suppose it's anything to worry about," she told the children.

One of the side-tracked demonstrators who had been catapulted into the narrow market entrance was brushing the dust from Miranda. He was stroking her cheeks gently in a wondering way. On such occasions Miranda, actually acutely embarrassed, would smile back with a sort of translucent shyness that was probably mesmerizing. Juliet had learned that to wander around South India with children was like wearing a magic amulet of protection. A woman alone faced endless difficulties but the presence of children was safer than chanting a *mantra*.

"It's all right. No harm done," Juliet told the marcher. "Except for the eggs," she added forlornly.

She offered another five rupees and fifty *paise* to the egg man.

"Is the woman trying to cheat you?" the marcher asked sharply, turning from Miranda.

He used a coarse Malayalam word for woman, and Juliet flinched.

"She is not cheating me," the egg man said simply.

"Why do you insult me?"

"Your children are beautiful as young nutmeg plants," the marcher said. "They have never cried for rice."

"That is true," she acknowledged nervously. "But nor have the children of the Nairs or the Brahmins."

"It is so. But you people, you want...what is it you are saying? You want to put the whole world inside your own pockets."

"We people?"

"The imperialists."

"Oh! That's not how I see myself."

"Nevertheless you are one of them. And when the forest

burns, the sweet sandalwood falls also with the ancient jack tree that has already rotted."

"Exactly. That is the trouble with forest fires. Doesn't it bother you, this indiscriminate destruction?"

He did not like to have his image turned around. He spat on the ground.

"Are we in danger then?" she asked.

"Who can say?"

She felt, at that moment, more angry than frightened.

"I am hoping perhaps you are not," he added gruffly, moving away to rejoin the demonstration.

"Have your children ever cried for rice?" Juliet asked the egg man.

"In the bad years they have cried, and some have died," he said. "But there have been good monsoons for many years, praise be to Lord Narayana."

"Do you believe that the Marxists can find rice for everyone when the monsoon fails?"

"If it is the will of Lord Narayana," he said, gazing across the market awnings at the towering *gopuram* of Shree Padmanabhaswamy temple.

They left him and haggled with the drivers at the auto-rickshaw stand, who vied with one another to win the western family as passengers for their frail little motorized vehicles.

Then the city was behind them, centuries dropping away by the second. Lurching along the ruts of the bullock carts, they were back in village time, changeless.

4

Juliet scrabbled at the entrails of a chicken and dreamed of home. The trees are turning red and gold, she thought; the air crisp. And whose body is Jeremy touching under a fall of leaves? Jeremy had begun to tear adrift from the past again and to float up into her dreams. Wistful lonely dreams. Last night she had been tangled in the vines beside the nutmeg field when she suddenly saw him walking towards her. She called out to him to pull her free. But just as their hands were about to touch he vanished.

She tugged at the long glaucous ropes of intestines and set them aside for burial. She would have to do it herself. If she gave them to Prabhakaran he would place them at the foot of one of the coconut trees close to the house and cover them with dead palm branches. Then the night would be monstrous with the savage snarls and death struggles of the scavenger dogs.

There were five unlaid eggs inside the chicken, in various stages of formation. The largest was a regular-sized yolk veined with a fine tracery of blood. The smallest was like a soft yellow marble.

If I had stayed behind, she thought, and let David come here alone, I could be in an apartment in Montreal. There would be an office to go to, with book-lined walls and a stereo playing softly. Later the children would be outside riding their bicycles and we could have steak for supper. (O steak! Such thoughts were inadvisable.) Then I could call a sitter and go wherever I wanted. Or perhaps I would call Jeremy. Hello again, my past, I would say. I'm back already. Are you married at the moment, or otherwise engaged, or between arrangements?

No. I would not call Jeremy.

She liked to keep Jeremy in the small space between dream and reality. She did not like to see him too often, daily life being an abrasive affair.

She went to the door and called up to the children.

"Come and see the baby eggs!"

Jonathan and Miranda were on the roof, a sort of elevated patio under a lacy canopy of palms whose shade was ineffectual. The red tiles steamed and broiled in the sun. Up there the children played long and secretive games, their imaginations flowering like rare jungle orchids. What would happen when they returned to public school and baseball and music lessons? If they ever returned. It was difficult to conceive of such a complicated project as departure, requiring planning and coordination and various kinds of vehicles that actually worked and had schedules and honored timetables. She had a vision of ancient buses and obsolete twin-engined airplanes sinking into the mud beside the abandoned tractor in the rice paddy. We will all subside into the monsoonal swamp, she thought, and lotus flowers will grow over us in indifferent benediction.

I didn't have to come, she reminded herself. I could leave any time.

"You don't have to come," David had offered.

"You said that twelve years ago, about Winston," she accused. "Anyway this time I want to go. You don't think I'm going to turn down a prospect of excitement?"

"Did I say that about Winston? Not quite like that surely." His brow was creased in earnest recollection. "I just never thought you'd come. I was afraid to ask you, I was afraid even to mention I'd been offered the position."

"And then you said: 'Just for a year.' If I didn't like it, we'd leave."

"Fortunately," he said, lifting a strand of hair from her eyes, "you found you could live here, and then the children came and – "

"David, I hate this place, you know I hate this place."

"So you keep saying. But I see your eyes when you walk on the lake in winter and when you read to the children at night and when you're coaxing lilacs and poppies out of May."

She sighed in a kind of despair. "You only keep one kind of evidence." But it was like trying to convince a gentle *abbé* at Reims Cathedral that the Virgin on the west porch – so serene, so folded into beatitude – had a heart of pocked and garishly painted plaster.

"Hardly anyone else can grow poppies here," David said. "It's amazing. I love their brashness."

(You see, the *abbé* at Reims might say with furtive pride, we have gargoyles too. Over here on the left, in our panel of the Last Judgment.)

It's impossible, she thought. It's really impossible. Why don't I have the sense to break loose? This is the obvious logical year to do it. Gradually. Easily. Almost unnoticeably. No one asking awkward questions. A legitimate year apart. Her imagination leaped towards Montreal like a snow goose returning to summer. Why was she fighting it? Why the panic? The act of severing was such hard work. Like trying to separate the roots of two plants that have become pot-bound in the same container.

"I don't want you to live anywhere against your will," he said, pulling her gently to himself and stroking her cheek with his hand.

You would think, she told herself sardonically, that the body would decently settle down after twelve years of marriage and two children, that it would learn decorum and mellowness, that it would not feel this animal leap of desire for a man it had slept beside for an epoch. *For at your age the hey-day in the blood is tame*.... Alas, poor ignorant Hamlet.

"Against my will!" She laughed. "You put a hex on my will. Every single damn day of my life, my will does gymnastics for you."

Sometimes she thought of Mary Magdalene with her wayward flaming hair sitting at the feet of Christ, her head resting on his goodness. The sounds of a party reach her, the sounds of bawdy revelry and political ferment, the whispered daring of the Zealots and the gypsy whirl of harlots at the tavern down the street. Beneath her penitent's robe her foot begins to keep time, tapping with the urge to dance; her thoughts quiver with the delicious danger of subversion. I have to go, she thinks. Just for an hour. I have to escape. And she turns to tell him. Really, she explains, we're quite unsuited. I'm not at all worthy of you, I'd like a little invigorating dip in the errant and imperfect.

I would never prevent you, say his huge brown eyes – his compassionate all-forgiving eyes. You must do as you think best.

And of course she cannot move. She is bound by a silken leash to a kind of gentleness more rare and beautiful than a unicorn.

"I can't seem to do anything about Winston," Juliet said. "I go on and on living here against my will. It's a life-sentence probably. But I know I want to go to India. I would like us to camp in the middle of a bazaar."

"It won't be like that," he said apprehensively. "Not where we'll be. It's very isolated, and I'll have to be away on field work a lot."

"Perhaps you're right, then. More isolation I can do without. I'll get an apartment in Montreal."

"But then," he said quickly, "we could probably do a lot of the traveling together. And just think of the children, what an experience like that – "

"Yes. I ought to be thinking of the children."

If she was contemplating splitting the children's world in

two, if she was really about to smash things up like the unregenerate bitch she was then this was the best time, the kindest way.

"There are risks for the children," he concluded. "Loneliness. And disease. That's a major anxiety. Perhaps, after all, it would be better...I'd be much freer...to get the research done, I mean."

"You would rather go alone then?"

Alone, he thought fearfully. Suppose when she went to Montreal (on parole as she put it) it was not just the city she lusted after? Suppose she saw someone...? He looked down the rest of his years as down a cheerless cave tunneling into dark nothingness. Yet there were people willing to add warmth and little tapestries of comfort. (Susan, for instance, would be waiting for him, lying in wait, though he must not think of that. It was shameful the way he could not always predict when she would cavort across his thoughts like a will-o'-the-wisp.)

"You would really rather stay? In Montreal?" he asked.

"I can't decide." She was afraid of loss. Afraid of the irreversible.

"As you wish." He was carefully neutral, he would never coerce.

He had always thought of himself as someone who would stay married to one woman for life. Especially when she had once crackled into his field of vision vibrantly as a lick of sunlight through a turning prism. He had not anticipated this slow fading, the light dwindling like a dream of waking.

India presented itself as Time Out. A space – empty, and yet busy with difference. If she were going to leave him he would have time to prepare. He could simply lose himself in work, produce a book within the year. He saw its covers edged with black, as on a bereavement card.

"I suppose I would get used to being alone," he conceded.

She tasted the permanent absence of David as something sharp and sudden and bitter.

"But really," she said urgently, "I think I *should* go. The children...it's not right they should miss out on such a –"

"I agree," he said, folding her into his arms. "I couldn't bear it if you didn't come."

The children were hurtling down the cement stairway from the roof.

"Ugh!" cried Jonathan. "Mommy! That stuff stinks!"

Her hands and arms were raddled with sticky remnants of intestine and flecked with wisps of feather and fluff from the plucking.

"Where are the baby eggs?" Miranda asked.

"Here."

Jonathan looked troubled.

"This largest one was almost ready to be a baby chick," he said somberly. "I can tell by the blood in it. It's been killed before it even had a chance to be born."

"Oh Jonathan, please! Things are complicated enough."

She gathered up the maze of intestines, towards which a phalanx of ants was already swarming across the polished stone bench, and set out on the path through the coconut trees to the rice paddy. The light underbrush growing on both sides of the track sprawled across its edges. She fought to keep her fear of snakes under control, ramming it down in her mind to a tight little knot of alertness, her eyes darting back and forth across the ground. This was probably why she did not notice the young woman coming towards her.

"Again we are meeting," said a voice as lilting and strange as Prabhakaran's flute.

Juliet was startled. It might have been Radha waiting secretly in the forest for her divine lover Krishna, so sudden and mysterious and beautiful was the apparition. The woman smiled and Juliet recognized her. It was the woman she had met in the market earlier in the day, the woman who had spoken about the price of eggs.

"Forgive me." Juliet was embarrassed by the pungent loops

trailing from her hands. "I am just going to bury these."

"You must not do this work. You must have servants."

"Oh no, really. I do have a boy, in fact.... It's just that....
Why were you at Palayam Market? Do you not have a servant
yourself?"

"Oh yes. I have a servant. Once I had many servants. I do
not myself buy in the market."

"But you knew the prices."

"A good mistress always inquires of her servant the cost. It
is necessary for the sound running of the household."

"Then why were you in the market place?"

"It is a special day for me. An auspicious day."

"Who are you? Why have I never seen you before today?"

"For many weeks I have not left my house. But now I shall
be walking again in public."

As she spoke she kept glancing along the path as though
either expecting or dreading company.

"But I thought...." Juliet murmured. "This is not a public
path. I mean I don't understand. Did you know that these are
the estates of Shivaraman Nair? I thought only – "

"He is my kinsman. I also live on these estates."

"Oh!"

The woman was like a gazelle, light as air, beautiful as lotus
flowers. Though her voice was soft and melodious, there was
a sense of urgency about her, a kind of nervousness poised for
defense or flight. Her silk sari fluttered like restive wings.
There was gold at her wrists and ankles, a spectacular diamond
and emerald ring on one finger, a nose jewel and earrings. It
occurred to Juliet that she had never before seen a high-caste
woman walking alone. In fact she had rarely seen one in public
at all. They never seemed to leave their houses except as passengers in their black Ambassador cars, chauffeured by their
husbands or the driver servant. Certainly she had never seen
one at Palayam Market before.

"Who are you?" she asked again.

"I am Yashoda."

"And I am Juliet."

"I know. My kinfolk have spoken about your family. You must please visit me."

"Thank you. I would love to. Where is your house?"

"Over there." She pointed behind her to the forested area beyond the rice paddy.

"I will certainly come. And you must visit us too."

"That is more difficult," she said sadly. "Now I am going. This meeting with you is auspicious. Twice is most auspicious. Thank you."

"Wait! Why is it auspicious? What do you mean?"

"Today is my birthday. I have consulted a very skilled astrologer to cast my horoscope. He told me that on this day I should take courage and appear again in public. He said I would meet a person of destiny who would bring me a great gift. I thank you for this."

"Oh, I don't think *I* could be...wait...!"

But she made *namaskaram* and was gone like a blown petal along the path.

Juliet buried her scraps in the warm mud beside the rice paddy. Amused and disturbed. Wondering.

Everything was so unreal. People appeared and disappeared swiftly and insubstantially as illusions. No letters came. No radio, no news, no proof of anything existing beyond the fluttering horizon of coconut palms. The rice grew into dreams, the paddy mud silted up memory.

She had a panicky sensation of free-falling through oblivion, a sudden radical doubt about her own continuity. She rubbed her muddy and gut-flecked hands in the grass and watched the ants, like undulations of brown velvet, mysteriously appear. For perhaps a full minute she kept quite still, her wrists and fingers brocaded with disciplined activity, brushed with a sensation feathery as the flickering of eyelashes. Then the ants were gone. Vanished. Her hands picked clean as bleached bones.

Thank god that Annie was coming soon, a brisk inrush of

evidence that everything beyond the paddy had not utterly extinguished itself in the secret way of ants.

And I will write to Jeremy, she thought urgently. Bring him out of the dreamspace. Weave a spell with tales of sandalwood and peacocks, lure him to reply. A letter would be something to hold, a talisman.

But would a letter ever reach him? And would he bother to reply? And would a reply ever find the unnamed road among the backwaters of Kerala, backwater of the world?

More practical perhaps to cable Annie. Simply: When? Please hurry.

Annie had called long-distance when plans were still shape-shifting.

"What have you decided?" she asked.

"I'm going."

"Well thank goodness. You'd be crazy not to. And I would have been furious."

"*You* furious? Why? What's it got to do with you?"

"In the first place, husbands and wives shouldn't be apart for so long. Too risky. In the second place I'm thinking of dropping out of law school for a while and bumming around Asia. Naturally I've been hoping for a free billet in South India."

"'Husbands and wives shouldn't be apart'! What kind of reactionary talk is that for an academic woman of this decade? And which lover are you up to now? I've lost count!"

"As a matter of sad fact, I'm between lovers. That's not the point. You are my link with stability and the middle class. What else is an older sister for? You and David are my living proof that perfection and permanence are attainable."

"Oh David is perfect, of course. I just add milk every morning for instant happy marriage."

"He's damn well very close to perfect. You can take my word for it, based on extensive and disappointing experience. I'm serious though. If you and David ever split up it would really unhinge me. Please keep that in mind when you're making any major decisions."

"You're a great comfort to me, Annie."

"Oh well. Ever your admiring sister. Listen, I can't afford to prolong this call. I'm so glad you'll be in the south. I already have friends I can stay with in Delhi and Pondicherry. I'll send a postcard when I'm coming. I won't be any bother. Have sleeping bag, will arrive. Love to David and the kids."

I will write to both of them, Juliet decided. To Annie and to Jeremy. I need to catch hold of my own life before it slithers into the underbrush.

She would visit the woman who lived in the forest beyond the paddy. She asked herself uncertainly: She *was* real, wasn't she?

5

Back at the house Miranda was scraping out the flesh of a coconut and Jonathan was shaking rice across the mesh pannier the way fossickers sift river silt for gold. Patiently he picked out grit and pebbles and dead insects.

Juliet made the curry paste, grinding leaves and berries and shredded coconut between the stone roller and stone slab. Over the fire the chicken was bubbling fragrantly in coconut milk and spices when Jonathan called: "Someone coming! Shivaraman Nair and some other men."

They peered out through the grille. Four men were visible in the distance, their crisp white *dhotis* and shirts flashing against the early evening shadows as they followed the winding path through the coconut trees. They all carried black umbrellas and the effect was rather comic; like a small congregation of somewhat portly penguins coming to the door.

"*Namaskaram.*" Juliet bowed slightly over her hands.

"Hello, hello, Mrs. David Juliet!" boomed Shivaraman Nair. "Where is Professor David?"

With him were his son, Anand, and two men she did not know.

"He is not home. He was visiting some Brahmin priests in Tampanoor. And after that back to the university, I think."

"Good, good. University is very good," beamed Shivaraman Nair. "Professor David," he explained to his companions proudly, "is great scholar. He is studying history of the Nairs of Kerala. From his deep knowledge he is writing a book in which he will speak of my family and my estates. Students in western universities will be hearing of us. Another time you will meet my important guest."

He turned to Juliet. Evidently she was a sorry substitute for Professor David. Not worth an introduction.

"I am wanting my kinsmen to see this beautiful house," he said. "They are visiting from Alathur in Palghat district and I am showing them inside. We will not be disturbing you. Please to continue your normal activity of this time."

"I am cooking in the kitchen so it is convenient for you," she said with quiet sarcasm.

"Yes, yes. Correct, correct," laughed Shivaraman Nair, untouched. "In the West," he explained to his companions, "they are not having any servants. Mrs. David Juliet is western woman."

They shook their heads in disapproving wonder that such things should be. "*Ayyo, ayyo,*" they said. Alas!

The men removed their sandals and left them at the doorstep.

Seething inwardly, Juliet returned to the kitchen. She could hear them touring the bedrooms, Shivaraman Nair giving a running commentary in loud and rapid Malayalam. She could hear them pick up objects – the children's books, David's tape recorder, Miranda's violin – and exclaim over them. She could hear the small portable typewriter being tentatively tapped.

They are so arrogant, she raged silently.

The house was Shivaraman Nair's toy. He had designed it himself and eventually it would be part of his daughter Jati's dowry, but in the meantime it was a profitable source of income as a rental property for Westerners. Previously a French dance troupe had lived there for a month while studying *Kathakali*, the classical Keralan dance form. A Russian cultural delegation had been resident for several weeks. A German botanist had stayed for a year. And now the professor's family. As Shivaraman Nair himself had told them: "I am very cosmopolitan man. I am knowing people from all over the world." He had also traveled as far as Bombay and Delhi.

The house (which was beautiful as a fantasy and had in fact been used as a set by an Indian movie company for a heavily romantic tale of tragic love) was his jewel. His pride of possession, his pleasure in sharing his masterpiece, was untroubled by any awareness of the sensitivities of tenants. The house is his stage, Juliet thought. The theater of his importance. And we are his prize puppets.

She heard the scrape of wicker chairs on the latticed porch. The men were settling in for siesta and discussion. Anand appeared in the kitchen doorway.

"My father says we will take tea now," he said.

They speak to me as though I were a servant, Juliet fumed inwardly. She repressed the urge to say something cutting. She bowed her head in assent, not trusting herself to speak. Was this, she suddenly wondered, why South Indian women always went about with lowered face and averted eyes?

She took a tray with teapot, cups, cream, and sugar to the front porch. It was not the correct Indian way. Tea was always served with the scalded milk and lashings of sugar already added. A sweet and sickly syrup of tea. Penance for those, like Juliet, who preferred to take their beverages without any sweetness at all.

Shivaraman Nair frowned.

"My wife must be teaching you our ways of the tea," he said.

"When you are visiting in our house," Juliet said evenly, "it is interesting, is it not, to learn *our* customs? Everyone may add as much milk and sugar as he wishes." She would at least preserve this chimera of independence.

"But this is not your house, Mrs. David Juliet," he said, immediately perceiving the flaw in her argument. "This is my house."

"And this is my tea."

There was a momentary hush. Then Shivaraman Nair

laughed with the good humor of an entrepreneur who has a marketable object of rare curiosity on his hands.

"This is the way of western women," he chuckled, worldly wise.

"*Ayyo, ayyo*," sighed his companions, shaking their heads forlornly.

Out of sheer irritation Juliet decided to pour a cup of tea for herself also. The cup rattled slightly against the saucer in her nervousness at the enormity of her action, but as calmly as possible she pulled up one of the vacant wicker chairs and joined the circle.

There was a stunned silence. A stillness. It was too much for the gentlemen from Palghat, who did not have the cosmopolitan advantage of those who lived in the capital, and who were in no way prepared for the outrageous ways of western women. With much muttering and shuffling, they rose and placed their cups on the table. They put on their sandals. Shivaraman Nair joined them hastily, without looking at Juliet. All three moved away from the door. They did not make *namaskaram*. Shivaraman Nair was talking volubly and quietly, explaining. Anand stood uncertainly in the doorway, shuffling his sandals, not yet moving away, clearly a little apologetic.

Juliet felt close to tears, and could not escape the sense of having committed some awful blasphemy even as she felt the wild injustice of their reaction.

"You are not understanding our customs," Anand explained. "And my uncles are not understanding that you do not understand. It is not correct for a woman to eat with men. This is against the ancient laws. Women must only bring food to men, and serve them. I know it is different in your country, but my uncles do not know this."

Juliet said nothing.

"My father and I are not angry with you," he said, "because we know that you are not understanding. Please continue to come to me for help with learning our language."

He made *namaskaram*.

Juliet also bowed her flushed cheeks over her trembling hands.

They were both standing in the doorway and so they both saw what happened on the path.

Yashoda was returning from her walk, stepping lightly and quickly. It was obvious that she had just come from the public road and was moving through the coconut grove towards the rice paddy. She paused for a moment like a frightened deer when she saw the little knot of men in front of the house. Then she lowered her eyes and resumed her quick walk.

Shivaraman Nair called out something sharp and harsh, a command. Yashoda began to run in a breathless tripping way. One of the Nair uncles from Palghat spat forcefully onto the ground. He had been playing agitatedly with a stone and now, in a sudden access of rage or outrage, he tossed it after the fleeing Yashoda as a landlord throws a stone at scavenger dogs to keep them away from the cows.

The stone must have struck her because she uttered a little cry. Her assailant screamed something after her, rhythmic words sounding like an incantation, a curse.

"My god, what is happening?" Juliet asked.

"This is the result when a woman does not follow the requirements of her *dharma*," Anand said. "That woman was married to my father's cousin. Three months ago her husband died. It is forbidden to a widow that she be seen in public for one year after the death of her husband. It is most especially inauspicious that she is wearing jewelry at this time."

Shivaraman Nair and the Palghat uncles began to walk away through the coconut grove. Anand still lingered.

"It is wrong of my uncles to be cruel," he said apologetically. "Their ways are still very orthodox. But it is also wrong," he added sadly, "for my cousin to disobey ancient laws. She is too modern. Her father has taken great risks with western travel and western education and western tutors and this is the result. She does not have the proper respect for our laws."

6

David placed a flower between her breasts.

"I am too angry and upset," she said.

"Little spitfire!" he teased, covering her body with a flight of kisses, soft and tantalizing as doves. "You must have crashed down on them like coconuts at harvest time. They were battered. Overwhelmed."

"They were bloody well barbaric!"

"Poor old men, what chance did they have? Their world is crumbling. Attacked on all fronts at once by two beautiful and bewitching *yakshis*." He stroked her inner thigh.

Juliet sat up, disengaging. "What is a *yakshi*?"

"A spirit, usually demonic, who takes the form of a woman of surpassing beauty to lure men to damnation," he explained, pulling her back into his arms. "She lies in wait to seduce the *sunyasin* meditating in the forest. He can only remain pure by killing her in spite of her extraordinary beauty. That is how the holy men rise above their brute senses. The rest of us yield in simple passion and are lost."

She smiled, and felt her body rising from the ashes of its rigid outrage like a phoenix, turning soft and moist and eager.

"Still," she insisted, unwilling to relinquish her right to be angry, "it doesn't seem possible that this climate gave the *Kama Sutra* to the world. It's too hot and damp. Another body feels like a penance. And of course the electricity has to be off as usual."

"I definitely prefer making love to you by the glow of an oil lamp. You look golden as Radha."

"I was referring to the ceiling fan. Which isn't turning."

"Let me distract you. There…. Are you still uncomfortable?"

"Well…" she murmured, turning to him.

And came like the monsoon after a long dry season. A jubilant storm.

Later she said in the darkness: "I forgot to tell you. Her name is Yashoda."

"An interesting name."

"Why?"

"Yashoda was the foster mother of Krishna, according to the legends. She had a lot of trouble with him when he was a child. Had to tie him up to her great stone mortar to keep him out of mischief."

I would miss his pedantry terribly, she thought fondly, deliberately tangling her legs with his so that she could feel his damp thigh against her crotch – still hot and swollen and ready to come again.

"Some people, however," he said, moving against her, "just can't be kept out of mischief."

"Meaning Krishna, of course."

"Of course. He was one of those people who can make the earth move too. He crawled off, dragging that mortar behind him and uprooted two trees."

Why should it be impossible to convince him to leave Winston? she thought.

"Hey," he said reproachfully. "What's wrong? What happened to the uprooting of trees and the earth moving?"

"Ahhh," she said, responding to his rhythmic insistence. "Ahh, ahh…."

"Oh god," he laughed. "You're gorgeous when you're like this."

"Promise me we won't go back to Winston."

"And have you pining for Lake Ontario ever after?"

We'll stay forever, if necessary, he told himself. Her discontents will fade like a photograph left out in the Indian sun.

They drifted into sleep, damp with sex and monsoonal heat.

Juliet dreamed she was drowning in the rice paddy. The warm mud was sucking her down, down, down. Yashoda floated alongside, pale as a reflection. Don't fight, Yashoda said. It's useless to fight. She was eating lotus petals.

I can't just drown! I won't! Juliet gasped, struggling, the mud at her throat.

But every time she reached for the levee to pull herself out, the Palghat uncles threw stones at her.

Jeremy! she called, seeing him suddenly and inexplicably. Jeremy! Help!

He was too absorbed in watching the antics of the Palghat uncles to hear her. He thought they were playing a game, senile children skipping pebbles across paddy water.

Jeremy! she shrieked, drowning.

But he turned and walked away, seeing nothing.

David! she screamed, waking, clutching at him.

But he slept on, dreaming perhaps of a woman pure as ivory, swinging through a world of innocent delight.

7

The Indian civil service and the Indian climate, Juliet thought, were engaged in a conspiracy to induce as many people as possible to opt for a life of contemplative withdrawal. It was the only way to cope. She tried pressing her fingertips together and inwardly reciting a *mantra*, the most calming she could think of: *subways, airports, intersections; subways, airports, intersections.*

She was sitting in the Trivandrum office of Air India. The room was crowded, the fan was not turning, the ferment of body odors was more pungent than curry, and the clerk at the desk – the sole clerk assigned to this roomful of inquiries – might have been engaged in the tranquil and delicate art of calligraphy. His movements were languid and precise, he leafed lovingly through schedules and timetables, he bestowed upon them his earnest attention, dignifying a select few with a rubber stamp. In passive deference, a man stood on the other side of the desk awaiting enlightenment. Could he, he had wished to know, get a flight to Delhi via Bangalore, instead of via Madras?

The clerk had looked at him with mournful scholarly eyes. The look had implied: Many books, possibly the Vedas themselves, will have to be consulted.

Hurricanes! Juliet screamed silently, invoking motion. *Dancers. Ants.* One had to ward off the lassitude that lay across India like a shroud, one had to protect oneself from the sinister voraciousness of transcendental tranquility. *Hurricanes, dancers, ants. Hurricanes, dancers, ants.* She beamed the incantation at the clerk's forehead but he continued with the delicate brush-strokes of his calling, impervious.

Three hours! she thought. I have been sitting here for three hours! I will truly go mad.

She was glad she had left the children to play at the house with Prabhakaran. (If only they would remember not to fish with bare hands in that polluted paddy water!) She turned over and over like worry-beads the post office card that had been delivered the preceding day. "Package from Canada. Please collect from Air India office."

Two hours ago, the limits of her small western patience already reached, she had gone to the desk, had butted in between the current supplicant and his approaching beatitude, and had demanded politely: "I wonder if you could just tell me if I am waiting in the correct place for a parcel pick-up?"

With the sweet slow grace of a swimmer, the clerk had raised his head and contemplated her.

Is it possible, Juliet had wondered, that we are all actually under water and I alone don't realize it?

"When your name is being called," the clerk had said reproachfully, "you may be coming to the desk and your questions are being answered, isn't it?"

Should I throw a tantrum? she wondered, surveying the quietly watching roomful of eyes. Why do they stare so incessantly, so rudely? As though I were a fish in a tank.

She had succumbed to the oppressive inaction and had sat down again, pleating the post office card between angry fingers. In the chair opposite, a gentleman in late middle age was looking at her with the kind of fixity he might give to assessing the ripeness of his jackfruit. Outraged, she stared back at him, determined to shame him into lowering his eyes.

But he gazed steadfastly on, untouched and unself-conscious.

❧

Mr. Matthew Thomas, who sat opposite Juliet, owed his name and faith, as well as his lands, to those ancestors of lowly caste whose eyes had seen the salvation of the Lord as offered by Saint Thomas the Apostle. And by later waves of Portuguese Jesuits, Dutch Protestants, and British missionaries.

Now, heir of both East and West, he sat quietly in one of the chairs at the crowded Air India office, waiting for his turn. It was necessary to make inquiries on behalf of a cousin of his wife's, and although his wife had died ten years ago, these family obligations continued. The cousin, whose son was to be sent overseas for a brief period of foreign education, lived in the village of Parassala and could not get down to Trivandrum now that the rice harvest was imminent. Mr. Matthew Thomas did not mind. He had much to think about on the subject of sons and daughters and foreign travel, and he was glad of this opportunity for quiet contemplation away from the noisy happiness of his son's house.

It is true that he had been waiting since 9:00 that morning and it was now 3:30 in the afternoon. It is also true that things would have been more pleasant if the ceiling fan were turning, for it was that steamy season when the monsoon is petering out, and the air hangs as still and hot and heavy as a mosquito net over a sickbed. But the fan had limped to a halt over an hour ago, stricken by the almost daily power failure, and one simply accepted such little inconveniences.

Besides, Mr. Thomas could look from the comfortable vantage point of today back towards yesterday, which had also been spent at the Air India office, but since he had arrived too late to find a chair it had been necessary to stand all day. At the end of the day, someone had told him that he was supposed to sign his name in the book at the desk and that he would be called when his turn came. Wiser now, he had arrived early in the morning, signed his name, and found a chair. He was confident that his turn would come today, and until it did he could sit and think in comfort.

The problem which demanded attention, and which Mr.

Thomas turned over and over in his mind, peacefully and appraisingly as he might examine one of his coconuts, concerned both his married daughter in Burlington, Vermont, and the western woman waiting in the chair across from him.

Burlingtonvermont. Burlingtonvermont. What a strange word it was. This was how his son-in-law had pronounced it. His daughter had explained in a letter that it was like saying Trivandrum, Kerala. But who would ever say Trivandrum, Kerala? Why would they say it? He had been deeply startled yesterday morning to hear the word suddenly spoken aloud, just when he was thinking of his daughter. Burlingtonvermont. Some American businessman had said it to the clerk at the counter, and there had been shouting and gesticulation in that peculiar manner of Westerners, and then the man had left in a taxi. And today there was a woman, pale as snow, who might have floated in from Burlingtonvermont itself.

This is a strange and wonderful thing, he had thought. And now he understood why these two days of waiting had been ordained. Some auspicious purpose would surely be revealed.

He thought of Kumari, his youngest and favorite child. Kumari, who on her wedding day, shyly radiant, had looked so like her dead mother that Mr. Matthew Thomas had had to turn away to hide his tears. What did she do in Burlingtonvermont? He tried to picture her now that she was in her confinement, her silk sari swelling slightly over his grandchild. A terrible thought suddenly presented itself to him. If she had no servants, who was marketing for her at this time when she should not leave the house? Surely she herself was not.... No. His mind turned from the idea, yet the bothersome riddles accumulated.

She was in her third month now, so he knew from the four childbearings of his own wife that she would be craving for sweet mango pickle. He had written to say he would send a package of this delicacy. *Dear Daddy*, she had written back, *please do not send the sweet pickle. I have no need of anything. I am perfectly happy.*

How could this be? It was true that her parents-in-law lived only five kilometers distant in the same city, and her brother-in-law and his wife also lived close by, and of course they would do her marketing and bring her the foods she craved. Of course, they were her true family now that she was married. Even so, when a woman was in the family way, it was a time when she might return to the house of her father, when she would want to eat the delicacies of the house of her birth.

He could not complain of the marriage. He was very happy with the marriages of all four of his children. They had all made alliances with Christian families of high caste. He had been able to provide handsome dowries for his daughters, and the wives of his sons had brought both wealth and beauty with them. God had been good.

But it was four years since he had seen Kumari. The week after her wedding her husband and his family had returned to America, where they had been living for many years. Only to arrange the marriages of their sons had they come back to Kerala. The arrangements had been made through the mail. Mr. Thomas had been content because the family was distantly related on his wife's side and he had known them many years ago, before they had left for America. So they had come, the wedding had taken place, and they had gone.

For four years Mr. Matthew Thomas had waited with increasing anxiety. What is a father to think when his daughter does not bear a child in all this time? Now, as God was merciful, a child was coming. Yet she had written: *Dear Daddy, please do not send the sweet pickle. I am perfectly happy.*

It had been the same when he had expressed his shock at her not having servants. *Dear Daddy,* she had written, *you do not understand. Here we are not needing servants. The machines are doing everything. Your daughter and your son-in-law are very happy.* Of course this was very reassuring, if only he could really believe it. He worried about the snow and the cold. How was it possible to live with such cold? He worried about the food. The food in America is terrible, some businessmen at the Secretariat had told him. It is having no flavor. In America, they are not using any chili peppers. And yet, even at such a time as this, she did not want the sweet pickle. Could it mean that she had changed, that she had become like a western woman?

He looked steadily and intently at the tourist woman. Certainly, he thought, my daughter will be one of the most beautiful women in America. White women were so unattractive. It was not just their wheat-colored hair, which did indeed look strange, but they seemed to have no understanding of the proper methods of beauty. They let their hair fly as dry and fluffy as rice chaff at threshing time instead of combing it with coconut oil so that it hung wet and glossy.

The woman was wearing a sari. Certainly that was better than the other western women he had sometimes seen at the tourist hotel, although in fact one rarely saw Westerners in Trivandrum. The ones he had seen usually wore trousers like a man. It was amazing that American men allowed their women to appear so ugly. True, he had heard it said that women in the north of India wore trousers, but Mr. Thomas did not believe it. An Indian woman would not do such a thing. Once he had seen a white woman in a short dress, of the kind worn by little girls, with half her legs brazenly showing. He had turned away in embarrassment.

Mr. Thomas was pleased that the woman who might be from Burlingtonvermont was wearing a sari. Still, it did not look right with pale skin and pale hair. It is the best she can do, he concluded to himself. It is simply not possible for them to look beautiful, no matter what they do.

Then his name was called and he went to the counter.

∽

Juliet thought: I will not tolerate this any longer, I will not. Yet if I simply give up and leave, how will I ever receive the parcel from home? Could I face this again on a different day? Never! But I cannot, I simply cannot sit here any longer. I will count to ten and then I will stand on this chair and scream.

On her count of eight, the door to an inner sanctum opened at one side of the room and a civil servant, by the mere hauteur of his eyebrows clearly superior to the desk clerk, surveyed the room for a moment and then withdrew, closing his door again. With the speed of impulse and exasperation, Juliet crossed the floor, knocked, and entered without waiting for a response.

The superior being was startled.

"Excuse me," Juliet said. "But I have been waiting over three hours for an opportunity to ask a very simple question. I know you'll be embarrassed by this inefficiency. I know you'll want to do something about it immediately."

She held the post office card out to him.

"This is not the correct place," he said, making no move to take it. "You must be waiting for the clerk at the desk in the other room."

"I'm afraid I will not be waiting one more insufferable minute for the clerk in the other room." Juliet spoke very quietly, looked the man squarely in the eyes, and fabricated with deadly intent: "My husband has powerful friends in the government, and there is going to be much trouble for somebody because of this delay."

A pallor, like the blanching of cashew nuts left out in the sun, passed across the man's face.

"There has been some mistake, dear lady. We are being most distressful, most distressful. You are having our fullest attention." He took the card from her and snapped his fingers so that a servant girl appeared from behind a screen. "Please be bringing mango juice!" he ordered her. He examined the card carefully. "I am giving this my most immediate attention. Most immediate!"

Then he left the room and Juliet sipped iced juice.

Ten minutes. Fifteen minutes. Here we go again, she thought.

And then he reappeared, the quintessence of regret. "I am

making very thorough investigations, very thorough, I assure you. There is absolutely no parcel for you at Air India office, Mrs. Professor. But I am making a racket, I promise you. Jolly bad show! I am telephoning the post office and discussing. It is their silly fault, all their fault. It is all a mistake. There was no parcel, no, absolutely never. They are assuring me. Jolly bad show, all this waiting. I am begging you to forgive."

Juliet stood as in a dream. Am I awake? Will peacocks swoop from the desk drawers?

She had to struggle against some demon of hysterical laughter that cavorted deep in her throat. "I am forgiving you," she spluttered. "I am absolutely forgiving you. Isn't it?"

∽

Matthew Thomas stood patiently at the counter. It seemed that his request was a complicated one. It involved searches and gesticulations and a certain amount of argumentation. This was the way of things. More delays were promised.

Mr. Matthew Thomas was not in the habit of letting life's little inconveniences upset him, but when he concluded his affairs with the desk clerk and left the Air India office at last, he was just in time to see the tourist woman leaving in a taxi.

She is leaving for Burlingtonvermont, he thought. He felt bereft, as though a miracle had come floating by like a wind-blown petal and he had failed to catch hold of it. He was not quite able to repress the thought that it had been an unkind day.

8

Along the rutted village roads that wound from the Nair estate to the beach, dark-eyed children massed to watch a passing wonder.

"*Sahibs! Sahibs!*" they chanted, running alongside, bare feet percussive on the red earth. Inside the lurching auto-rick Juliet and the children huddled close, hands raised to ward off the shower of pelted blossoms and stones.

Perhaps, Juliet thought, I am considered to have the Evil Eye. I must be simultaneously appeased and driven off.

"We should have brought Prabhakaran," she gasped. To mediate.

It was a relief to emerge, like a chrysalis spreading sudden wings, from the child-crusted palm-canyoned roads into the white glare of the beach. Sand, coarse, terra-cotta in color, embraced their sandaled feet like gritty fire. Directly overhead the sun slithered and smoked through a haze of water-heavy air.

Yet, strangely, what Juliet thought of as she slung her sandals over one shoulder and waded into the blood-warm surf, was Lake Ontario frozen. It was the remembered exultation, the same sense of awe at the margin of a vast body of water whose far shore cannot be seen. The Balboa syndrome, she supposed – whether silent on a peak above the Pacific, or alien between the coconut palms and the broiling Indian Ocean, or poised precariously between January and February on a wafer of ice beneath the bleak Canadian sky.

"Do you remember," she asked the children, "walking out on the frozen lake? How it seems to go on forever and ever, as though we might reach the edge of the world?"

They looked at her curiously, not seeing a connection, and splashed themselves with water that leaped back from their clothes towards the sun in instant vaporous tongues. She wanted them to savor the mysterious incongruities of their lives.

"Don't you remember how excited you were when you realized you were walking on water?"

They nodded vaguely, the surf frothing between their toes.

"Look!" she said, picking up the frayed husk of a coconut and tossing it as far as she could out over the waves. "It will wander through all the oceans of the world and one day someone on a ship from Montreal, sailing out of the St. Lawrence estuary, will see it floating between the fishing boats."

But the coconut came bobbing shoreward on the next wave and the children swam to meet it, competitive, awash in the present moment. Juliet sat on the sand beside their discarded cotton clothes and sandals, thinking of snowsuits and mukluks. And of that first of many winter odysseys in the small town beside Lake Ontario.

"It must be the oxygen!" David had shouted.

She knew what he meant although she couldn't really hear the words. The wind barreling all the way from Lake Superior took words and whirled them in flakes of sound as far as Nova Scotia. She knew he meant the taut hum of ecstasy, the sense of being caught up in elemental and exalted matters remote from the dwindling town where dull people crawled between morning and night.

She laughed and put her thickly mittened hand clumsily into his and called back, sending a futile missile of language into the blither of snow: "Let's keep going to the edge of the world!"

And the children, Miranda scarcely able to walk yet, reeled about like padded balls buffeted by an unseen playmate. Only their eyes were visible, clownish behind ski-masks, huge with wonder and the stimulant of cold. Breathless, they brushed icicles from their lashes and hurled their bodies into the wind and rolled in the snow, making angels with muffled arms.

Sometimes they scooped away at the drifts until they had laid bare a black window into the lake's secrets: air bubbles caught like diamonds, and small fish shocked into silver stillness, their deaths preserved like jewels until the thaw.

Ah, Juliet had thought, drunk on insights and oxygen, there are ways to cheat change and decay.

And they had hugged each other and danced and known they were not like other families, but set apart, blessed. Fumbling with the impediment of winter clothing, Juliet and David had kissed and their kisses had frozen on their lips, the shimmering salted rime of an epiphany.

Yes.

Epiphany.

And she ran across the hot sand towards her children and began to dance at the foaming edge of the Indian Ocean.

Mr. Matthew Thomas was so astonished by the sight that he forgot to look under the thatched cabin of the fishing boat drawn up on the sand beside him. At first he thought it was the Burlingtonvermont woman from the Air India office. It was so difficult to tell one Westerner from another. They all looked alike, especially the women. But then he realized that the two children frolicking at the edge of the waves belonged to her, so he was sure it was someone different. How extraordinary. Twice in one week! It must be because he was thinking so often of Kumari. Perhaps God sent these messengers. It was auspicious that she was with children. It must surely mean that Kumari would have a safe birthing.

The woman looked like a sprite from the sea with wind and salt spray whipping her long golden hair about her face. Little waves frothed and foamed about her bare ankles, wetting the edges of her cotton skirt, which wrapped itself damply about her thighs in a way that was disturbing to him. She seemed to be dancing in and out of the shallows as were her two children. It was certainly an extraordinary way for a grown woman to behave. Behind her a small crowd of Indian children followed at a slight distance, mimicking her with much merriment, but she seemed unaware of them. Or else chose to ignore them. He felt embarrassed for her.

Could it be the same for Kumari, he wondered with sudden pain. He had a vision of his daughter walking through the snows of Burlingtonvermont in her sari with a mocking group of American children chanting strange things after her. What was it like to walk through snow? Kumari had written that it was soft and powdery. Like sand, he supposed. Like sand that inexplicably froze the feet.

The woman and her two children and their retinue of pranksters had moved on along the beach, so he continued to look among the long snake boats for the family of Ouseph. The fisher people spent their entire lives on the beach. They did not even leave it to market their own fish, since this was the task of another sub-caste of the fishing community. Any of the scant wants that the sea and shoreline did not provide – such as rice, cooking pots, cloth – they bartered from the men and women who sold their fish. They went out to sea by day, and by night slept under coconut thatch awnings hung over their simple boats which were drawn up high on the sand.

Since they were of the lowest castes it would not have been fitting for them to visit Mr. Thomas at his house, even if they were ever to leave the beach, nor would it be proper for him to eat with them. But as they were of his faith, he was concerned whenever word reached him that a family was in particular distress. On this occasion he was bringing both food and money to Ouseph and his wife and young children. Ouseph himself had been ill for some time and their eldest son, who was still only a boy, had been taking out the boat each day because the livelihood of the family depended on the daily catch. A week ago the boat had not returned at evening and then a few days later had been washed ashore empty. Mr. Thomas went to offer what little comfort he could.

After a time he found them leaning against the simple lashed logs of their boat, gazing out to sea. Mariya, the wife, was weeping silently. The children were nowhere to be seen, probably capering along the beach in the wake of the day's wonder. Ouseph stared at him unseeing. He offered his gifts simply and sat a little way apart in silent sympathy. What could be done about the will of God? His ways were inscrutable.

When he felt that a suitable length of time had elapsed he bowed to the sorrowing couple and withdrew. He walked southwards along the beach watching the ocean rolling all the way down the blue distances to where Cape Comorin stood sentinel against the non-Indian world.

The Lord giveth and the Lord taketh away, he thought. From this sea had come Christ's own apostle, St. Thomas, with salvation. Missionaries from Europe had used boats as pulpits, preaching to the fisher people. And daily the ocean took back their converts to the bosom of God himself.

Then again he saw the vision coming to him from the sea, fair and strange as the Blessed Virgin.

"Hello," she said, smiling. She had a vague sense of having seen him somewhere before, but could think of no context.

He had not expected to be addressed and could think of nothing to say. He simply stared at her.

She bit her lip and looked away and he felt a rush of dismay and sympathy.

It is hard for them in a strange land, he thought. This is the way it would be for Kumari.

"Is it lonely?" he asked without thinking. "Away from your native country?"

"Yes." She was surprised. "Sometimes it is very lonely."

She looked directly into his eyes, her own wide and blue-green like the sea.

It was disconcerting to be looked at by a woman in that way. Improper. He lowered his own eyes nervously. Did Kumari gaze at other men in that way now?

The fisher children swarmed like flies, pressing against her, touching her, chanting. Mr. Thomas clapped his hands sharply and shouted an order. Immediately the children fell silent and backed away, scampering off to their boats.

"Thank you," said the woman in evident relief.

They began to walk along the beach together, her two children darting in and out of the water like dragonflies, laughing and calling to each other. He was relieved that the woman herself was now walking sedately beside him. He did not know what he would do if she began to dance again. Perhaps she had only been doing it because she thought no one but the children could see her.

He said: "I am having a daughter in America."

"Really?"

He looked at her sharply. Of course really. Was she accusing him of lying?

"She is living in Burlingtonvermont."

"Ah. Vermont is very beautiful. If you visit her, you must go in the fall when the leaves change color."

What astonishing things the woman said! If he were visiting his daughter!

"What is your daughter's name?"

"Kumari. And I myself am being Mr. Matthew Thomas, who is now humbly requesting the honor of knowing your name."

"It's Juliet," she said, unable to match his quaint and charming verbal flourishes.

"I am very happy to be meeting you, Mrs. Juliet."

They walked on in silence. But it seemed a friendly companionable silence.

Mr. Thomas marveled. Who would have dreamed that he would be walking and talking like a kinsman with someone who knew of Burlingtonvermont. It was quite astonishing how simple it was to talk to a western woman.

"My daughter Kumari is going to have a baby," he said.

"Ah. Your first grandchild?"

"No, no. I am having already seven grandchildren. But this will be my first American grandchild."

She smiled. "Then you will be visiting them."

He looked at her with amazement. "How could I do that?"

"It is so expensive," she said contritely. "Perhaps it will be easier for her to visit you. If her husband is on an American salary."

"It is not that," he said. "I am having sufficient money."

It was simply that he had never thought of it, and now he wondered why.

"You don't wish to visit them?"

"I do not know," he said uncertainly.

It was such a novel idea. He could not grasp it properly. His mind did not know how to hold it. It shivered about like quicksilver, tantalizing.

"And why," he thought to ask, "are you living in this country? Your husband is doing something with the government?"

"No. With the university. He is writing a book."

She looked at the sun falling into the sea, slow and smoldering, like a spent cannonball.

"I must go."

"Where are you living?"

"At Krishnapuram. On the estates of Shivaraman Nair."

"I will send an invitation. There are many things I am wishing to ask you about Burlingtonvermont. If you will graciously come to my house one day, perhaps we could speak of these things."

"With pleasure."

He regretted that he had given way to irritation at the Air India office. One needed only a little patience for auspicious purposes to reveal themselves.

9

The sound of the flute came keening into her sleep like a jeweled arrow. It had a bass accompaniment, a peculiar low throbbing sound that reverberated in the walls of the house. Her first thought was: it is the trumpeting of elephants.

She peered out through the ground mists and coconut trees. A gilded figure was tripping and dancing through the palms – Prabhakaran, clothed in sunrise and the music of boyhood abandon. Around and behind him six cows, moving soft and slow as velvet, gave their low vibrating responses to his melody. Exquisite as a page in an illuminated manuscript, she thought. The cowherd boy with his flute.

He was carrying the little vessel of milk in the crook of his arm, pressed against his body, to free both hands for the instrument. He is sure to spill some, she thought, watching him skip between the cattle with the exuberance of morning. She wondered why he was bringing the cows. They usually remained tethered in the courtyard behind Shivaraman Nair's house. It was Prabhakaran's task to feed them each day with the hay left after the rice threshing.

There was a pause in his fluting. A woman had appeared from the direction of the rice paddy, walking quickly and lightly. She had pulled the upper part of her sari over her head like a veil.

It must be Yashoda, Juliet thought. She had not seen Yashoda since the day of the stoning though she had twice tried to visit her. The first time, Jati, daughter of Shivaraman Nair, had come from the house to meet her.

"My cousin is ill," she had said. "She is not able to receive any visitors."

A few days later, Juliet had again entered the little forest beyond the rice paddy. The house had been deserted except for an elderly maidservant who told her that the mistress had gone to stay with her husband's family.

The woman now stopped to speak with Prabhakaran. After several minutes of conversation, Juliet saw the boy offer her the pot of milk. She held it high and tilted, a few inches from her lips to avoid pollution, and drank a little of the white stream which poured from it. She gave the vessel back to Prabhakaran and patted his head in an affectionate motherly way and stroked his face. Juliet saw the gleaming flash of the boy's smile. She was puzzled because she was certain it was highly irregular for a high-caste woman to accept food from a low-caste servant, an act which would be considered a form of ritual pollution.

A moment later the woman hurried away through the trees and Prabhakaran came on towards the house with cows and milk and flute.

"Milk," he smiled as he handed the vessel to Juliet.

"*Pahl*," she replied. "*Ubagaram*. Was that Yashoda you met on the path?"

He looked troubled and did not answer.

"I am not going to tell Shivaraman Nair."

He smiled gratefully.

"Yashoda," he assented.

She took the milk to the kitchen and emptied it into her cooking pot. He had already followed her and begun sweeping around her feet. With a flicker of annoyance she thought: He is like a shadow.

"Why did you bring the cows?"

He answered at length and with enthusiasm, but she could

understand very little of his dialect. She went to the door. The cows were wandering around the house, cropping the grass. She supposed he wanted them to have fresh greens as a change from threshing-hay. Or perhaps he merely wanted their company. He spent so much time with them each day, feeding them, murmuring to them, fondling them, that they must have seemed like siblings to him.

David and the children woke. They dressed. They had breakfast. While they dressed Prabhakaran swept the bathroom. While they washed he swept the bedroom. He wandered into private moments by mistake, but he was never embarrassed. He was not used to his presence having significance to anyone.

While they ate he swept around and between them and crawled under the table to sweep away crumbs. The palm-branch switches tickled their bare feet. When the children read or did their school work, he would stand silently watching for hours, distracting them, slowly twitching his broom to flick dust from the window bars – those ubiquitous rungs which guard all the openings in India, keeping beggars at bay, wooing infant breezes through their spaces as cobwebs lure flies.

They became used to Prabhakaran's presence, but not in the way one is supposed to become used to servants. There were times when Juliet's impulse was to treat him as she treated her own children in their maddening moments, to bestow a quick hug and say: Prabhakaran, I love you but you are driving me crazy! Just go outside and leave me alone for a while.

But India had made them hyperconscious of body movements and human touch as highly ritualized cultural phenomena.

Once she had asked Anand how to say: Please do not sweep in the house while the children are doing their school work.

For a start, Anand had explained, there was no equivalent for *please*. It all depended on the form of the verb. One verbal ending intimated a polite request. This would be used in conversation with equals. It would be quite improper to use this construction when speaking to a servant. The other verb form signified an order. Juliet could not bring herself to be peremptory with him, so Prabhakaran seemed always to be present.

Juliet was disoriented. On those occasions when he blundered into intimate moments, she no longer felt shock or outrage but a brooding unease. Individual privacy, she thought, is as western as television. We are unable to divest ourselves of the need for it. We are addicted to the luxury of choosing when we will be unobserved.

Perhaps one absorbed the pressures or spaces of population density at birth, by osmosis, in the air, in mother's milk.

Servants do not make life simpler, she saw. They complicate. They encroach and invade and disrupt. Unless of course one could manage to ignore them completely, treat them as nonpersons. That was a skill handed down through the high castes for centuries. Common to people of wealth and privilege all over the world, she supposed.

Once, on a day of steaming monsoon heat, with the sweat glistening all over his body, Prabhakaran had crumpled over his coconut-switch broom in the middle of the floor. He was still coiled up in the fetal position required by his method of sweeping. Juliet was in an anguish of remorse. She lifted him onto a wicker chair, turned on the ceiling fan, and wiped his face with a damp cloth. He leapt into consciousness.

"*Venda! Venda!*" he cried in alarm, grabbing his broom and sweeping a frantic renewal of energy. "*Venda!*" You must not!

"Don't be stupid," she said crossly. "Sit! Rest!"

But he had only swept more furiously, muttering, "*Venda, venda!*"

The cows were still cropping grass by the front door and lowing in at the windows. David left for the day and Juliet sent the children and Prabhakaran to the rice paddy while she did the laundry.

It was heavy work, crouching over the low sink, scrubbing

and pounding in cold water, a daily wrestling match with sheets and towels and clothing that could never be freed of the stink of excessively humid air. As futile a task as Lady Macbeth's hand washing.

With a vessel full and heavy on her hip, she climbed to the roof and hung the washing over a coir rope strung between bamboo poles. There were no pegs and the rope stained the clothes but it was the best she could do. She ran out of space so she climbed down again and draped the rest of the sheets over the branches of a low mango tree in the back courtyard.

Then she gathered all the sandals not being worn that day and took them up to the roof to bake on the tile under the sun. If she neglected to do this, green mold would sprout from the leather and the shoes would look like living things, bewitched forest creatures.

The three children came running back from the rice paddy with scummy water and aquatic life in their cupped hands to show Juliet their treasures.

"Drop it! Scrub your hands!" she said, exasperated. "How many times must I tell you that water is polluted! The sewer water from all the houses drains into the paddy. It is chock full of god knows what diseases."

Jonathan and Miranda exchanged a resigned look and settled in to their correspondence lessons and Prabhakaran dusted the window bars. Or stood looking over Jonathan's shoulder, dazzled by the speed at which he filled a page with hieroglyphs, until Jonathan gave him a pencil and showed him how to write.

"House. This is a *house*. H-o-u-s-e*."

"*Vitu, vitu*," Prabhakaran said, as he laboriously made an *H*. But he could not demonstrate how to write *vitu* in Malayalam script. Much giggling and whispering.

And Juliet, abstracted teacher, smiled on them and tried to write letters.

Dear Jeremy, she wrote. *You were right. I am pining for books and* snow and most of all for rationality. It isn't quite the lively adventure I was hoping for. I have been absorbed into the growth cycle, smothered by vines. I seem to be headed for imminent harvest and decay.

She tore up the letter.

Dear Annie, she wrote. *Upon reflection, I think your coming is an excellent idea. I definitely need adult company. (David is so busy, away at the university, touring the villages, etc.) I seem to be slipping inside the children somehow. We are never apart, all the old rhythms shattered. I am losing all sense of separateness.*

I look like – I am – a drudge, growing mold and changing shape like the shoes. Really, nonentity is contagious here. Even the massive trees are swallowed up by creepers.

I sometimes fear I will disappear just like that. Yesterday there was a large dead toad on the bathroom floor. From nowhere, battalions of ants appeared. It was all over in about an hour. No vestige of that huge squashed creature, not a single stray ant in sight. Do you see what I mean? No wonder that extreme forms of meditation and withdrawal flourish here. The days are drugged, memory is one more mirage. Are you really coming or did I dream it? Yours faintly, Juliet.

Dear David, she wrote. *Is there any point to this? I thought of India as a place of risk and dazzle, a place where I could feel at home for once and still be with you. It's more like a coma.*

You seem dazed with heat and research and have forgotten I hoped for elephants and bazaars. Memory, like everything else, is so tiring here. (Not that you've ever remembered my complaints of deprivation. You believe in Original Goodness, you believe contentment runs in everyone's veins, you remember only epiphanies, you are not an impartial score-keeper.)

I'm not blaming you but I need to get away, away from all this domestic lassitude, here or in Winston, what's the difference? I need a rest, I need some peace, I need the frenzied hub of a city.

I'm not blaming you, it's entirely my own fault. I should never have come, I should have gone to Winston, you were absolutely right about that twelve years ago, that day on the subway. Remember?

Anyway, I quit. I concede defeat. I am unregenerately urban, I pine for those places that inspire editorial laments in newspapers: the derelict overcrowded arteries of sprawling cities that heave untidily with history and event and garbage strikes and miraculous chance encounters.

I will grieve for you of course, I will grieve for the shattered unity of the four of us, just as unremittingly as I now grieve for metropolitan ferment. I'll write every day, I'll send telegrams, I'll entice you to Montreal. But just the same, I swear I'll go. I'm really going to leave. Yours regretfully....

She put Annie's letter into an envelope and tore up the one to David. She thought of Mary Magdalene shutting her ears to the tavern music. She thought of Radha hopelessly knotted into Krishna, going nowhere on her ivory swing, forever vacillating between untenable poles. She thought of that long-gone day on the Toronto subway, that day of momentous choice....

It was the rush-hour embrace and collision of bodies on the Yonge Street line, the hour of armpits and strap-hanging and suffocation. Loving it, Juliet let the sway of the carriage press her against David's body, wondering wickedly: Is it possible to disconcert him physically? Or is he pure as a choirboy, impervious?

Several months before they had met by chance in a gallery of fine arts. Juliet had been pacing from room to room, unseeing, because it was a day following one of those nights when Jeremy had not returned to the apartment, not even for breakfast. Not that this was something she had any right to be upset about. It was not a question of infidelity. They were not – as Jeremy put it – trying for permanence. They were merely celebrants of the present moment, they were open and free, and these things (these absences for which no one was accountable) were of no consequence. Except that in their wake Juliet suffered from something like vertigo, some sickening loss of balance, something anachronistic and primitive and shameful that one would no more admit to than announce a belief in the Flat Earth Society.

On her sixth circuit of the gallery – filling in the abyss of a lunch hour with movement so that she would not call Jeremy at his office – she saw that the absorbed young man in the Indus Valley Artefacts room was still standing as though in a trance before one of the glass cases. The man himself, she thought, was certainly the room's most interesting *objet d'art*. Rodin's *Thinker* standing up, perhaps. No. A far more striking blend of the ascetic and the sensual, something from the Quattrocento in Florence: St. John in the wilderness, stuffing himself with wild honey; or St. Sebastian waiting passionately for the arrows as for lovers.

It's his stillness that attracts, she thought, tilting her head to one side in appraisal. And his eyes: intense as lasers, liquid as dark honey. Yes, she had seen his kind on the walls of the Uffizi: all those *Portraits of a Young Man*, by Gozzoli and Fra Lippi.

He must have sensed her scrutiny because he turned, embarrassed, and murmured apologetically: "I'm sorry. I'm blocking your view. Selfish of me."

"No, please! Not at all."

But she was curious to know what had held him in such absorption. It was a bronze figurine of a dancing girl, less than six inches high, her body gaunt as spring twigs, her breasts like not-yet-ripened crab apples.

"What is so special about her?" Juliet asked. "I mean, she's graceful, but a trifle anorexic, don't you think?"

The man who had floated down from an Uffizi canvas winced.

"She was cast in bronze early in the second millennium B.C.," he said reverently "Close to four thousand years between the artist and us, and here we stand inches away from her I call that" he searched for a word – "a sacrament of history "

She raised her eyebrows in wry amazement. Is he real? she wondered.

"Look at her face," he said.

She looked and hazarded: "It's sort of Negroid. Flanged

nostrils and lips. And she certainly doesn't approve of being stared at."

"Pre-Dravidian. And after her there was nothing for fifteen hundred years. Think of it. Not a single artefact for all that time! And then suddenly a carnal explosion at Mathura and Sanchi – all those bountiful breasts and buttocks that crowd the stupas and temples. It's a different iconography entirely. This one's so exquisitely non-voluptuous. She was probably a sacred prostitute."

"Really?" Juliet looked at the miniature, at the naked boyish figure, with fresh interest.

"Yes. We deduce it from the bracelets and their ritual arrangement. And the stylized pose."

The dancer's matchstick left arm was sheathed from shoulder to wrist in bangles. An armor against what? Suddenly the awe of the gentle pedant beside her settled on Juliet like a mist of light. She was drawn into the magic.

Who was the woman, the actual flesh-and-blood woman, who four thousand years ago had tossed her head back with that look of disdain? For what priests or lesser men did she dance, clad in nothing but bracelets? And what was she thinking when she jutted out her pelvis like that, its cleft visible and taunting? Did she despise the watching male eyes? Did she dream of enticement or of smashing, with her jewel-mailed arm and her fist clenched like a boxing glove?

Well? demanded the haughty eyes. Do you think you're any smarter after four thousand years? Have you figured out a better solution?

As Juliet formulated her answer she realized that the Quattrocento man was moving on. It was like an eclipse.

"Oh please don't go," she said impetuously, catching hold of his arm. "I feel as though you've peeled cataracts off my eyes."

He was decidedly embarrassed, exposed, stripped now of the protective instructional role. She saw that he was not as young as she had first thought, that he was a number of years older than she, and that a network of fine lines radiated out from the black and mesmerizing eyes.

"I was going to the concert," he said awkwardly.

"Oh."

"Of course, you could come." He seemed appalled that he might have been impolite. "It's free, you know. Every lunch hour, in the third-floor music room."

In the music room a group of students played on shawms and crumhorns and viols. Music of the fourteenth and fifteenth centuries.

"It's beautiful," she whispered. "Though I don't know what to listen for. I know nothing about it." Tempting him to offer instruction. And he did. Over coffee afterwards. Over dinner that night. Over lunch the next day. His name was David, he said. She thought: I knew it would be a saint's name.

She did not tell Jeremy about him. Why should she? Their rules did not require it. And how could she explain him? It was like finding a unicorn in a city park. He beckoned her into a world hung with intricate glowing tapestries and haunted by the melody of extinct instruments.

One day he called her at her apartment and Jeremy answered the phone.

"For you," Jeremy said neutrally.

David spoke in a rush of confusion. "I'm sorry...I didn't think...I had no idea.... Please forgive me." He hung up.

She called him back. "What did you want to ask me?"

"It's nothing. I had tickets for a concert.... But it really doesn't matter."

"Where should I meet you?"

"Are you sure?" He seemed both nervous and reproachful.

And later, after the concert, he said stiffly: "It was presumptuous of me. I don't wish to interfere in your private life."

"You're not interfering. I live with a guy on and off, that's all. His name's Jeremy. We don't police each other."

"I see. Are you in love with him?"

"He's an exciting person," she said. "Brilliant, I think. Politics and ferment, that's his thing. Mine too, I guess. I mean, I'm doing my doctorate in history but paying my way as a researcher for a politician. Housing statistics, watch-dogging government spending, speech-writing, that sort of thing. Gathering material for a book as I go. I love it."

Amazed, as though a long telephone conversation had turned out to be a wrong number, David said: "But the art gallery? The concerts? I simply assumed you were –"

"I'm a hybrid. Or maybe just a dilettante. As an undergraduate I had a terrible time choosing between history and political science and literature and art history. I had to toss a coin, more or less."

"I see. Then of course you have a lot in common with...with this man."

"He stretches my mind. Gives me wings."

"And you are...it seems you are in love with him?"

"That's a state of being he considers anachronistic."

"But are *you* in love?"

"It's amazing!" she said. "You can say the word without the least trace of embarrassment. The way the rest of us say sex, or fuck, or something."

"You haven't answered my question."

"I don't know how to answer it. I suppose, if love is measured by the degree of pain I feel when I know he's with someone else, then yes, I suppose I'm in love with him."

"I see." David rested his elbows on the table and rubbed his eyes jerkily with his fingers. "I think it would be better if we didn't see each other again."

"But why ever not? I love being with you."

He looked at her sadly as though she were the bronze dancer in the glass case, as though an immense mystery of time and cultures separated them.

"When the code on the Indus Valley tablets is deciphered," he said, "I might be able to explain. I've enjoyed knowing you."

She could not believe he would walk out of her life. She leaned towards him, flinging a net of seduction. What would it be like to make love to David? She and Jeremy made love like animals in heat. But with David, she thought, it would be like Tristan and Isolde, splendid, languid passion against a backdrop of Celtic music – harps and viols and haunting wooden flutes.

"David," she murmured, her eyes bright, "do you think I wouldn't make love to you because of Jeremy?"

She might have struck him across the face.

He said sadly: "I think we live in different worlds and speak different languages, Juliet. In another age I would have been a scholar priest, I suppose."

And he did walk out of her life. When she called, he was never home, or else didn't answer.

So, she thought, shrugging. One more loss to absorb, I'm an expert. And the sunless weeks passed – weeks without unicorns or sacraments of history or viols, although she went regularly to museums and concerts and galleries from which he perversely stayed away. Until the day she saw him again on the subway....

"David!" she called with gauche abandon, pelting down the platform. "David, I've missed you terribly."

He could not disguise his agitation or delight and she felt triumphant.

"Couldn't we have dinner together?" she pleaded. "Please."

"How can I refuse?"

And on the lurching subway car she rocked against him, wanton as Mary Magdalene with her harlot's heart, hoping to scorch his body.

From above he said into her ear: "The subway is unbearable at this time of day. Like a circle in Dante's hell."

"Oh no! I love it! You never know whom you'll meet. And look at the faces. I wish I could paint."

"I hate it," he said. "The ugliness, the pushing and shoving.... I love small towns and green and open spaces."

"Oh well then," she said blithely, secure in her power, "we're incompatible. I couldn't live without a subway."

But he looked so stricken that she said quickly: "I don't necessarily mean that literally. I do like ferment, though."

"Actually," he said, "I'm leaving next month. I've been offered an assistant professorship at a small university."

"You're leaving?!" Even in the harsh artificial light of the subway there was a sense of rain clouds massing, of the sun shrouding itself. "Oh, I suppose congratulations are in order. Where are you going?"

"It won't interest you."

"What a statement! I've been desolate for lectures on art history and for crumhorns and shawms, and you tell me I won't be interested in the fact that you're leaving!"

"It's the middle of nowhere. It doesn't have a subway or even a museum. It's exactly the kind of place you couldn't stand."

"Where is it?"

"Winston, Ontario."

"I've never heard of it."

"Exactly."

"How do you know I couldn't live there?"

"Are you interested in trying?"

"Are you asking me?"

"Would you marry me?"

"Oh!" she said, dancing on the toes of other passengers, flinging her arms around him. "Yes, I would!"

Later he said: "It's crazy, you know. You'll hate it. And then you'll hate me."

"Impossible!" But feeling the first chill of small-town disorientation, she asked uneasily: "If I do hate it, do we have to stay there forever?"

"Of course not. Let's give it a trial year. Or you could even stay here for a year and then I could come back...."

But the thought made both of them nervous.

"I have some loose ends to tie up," she said.

Neither of them mentioned Jeremy.

But Jeremy himself was incredulous. "You're moving out just like that?"

"You always said that was the way it should be. No rules, no shackles."

"Yes, but I didn't think...I assumed we were both sufficiently civilized.... Well anyway," he shrugged, "at least I am. Your half of the bed will be waiting when you want to move back in."

"We're leaving town. We're getting married."

"Married!" She might have announced she was having her feet bound. Or being measured for a chastity belt.

"Why should you care, Jeremy? In the past month you've stayed out more nights than you've stayed in."

They stood staring at each other. Jeremy looked like an animal wounded but belligerent. His pride is hurt, she thought. He did not mean for the rules to be played both ways.

He had his hands on his hips, his feet apart. An urban buccaneer.

If the city were to be bombed, she thought suddenly, and we were all survivors crawling out of the rubble, Jeremy would grab a megaphone and stand just like that on top of a pile of smashed history.

We'll rebuild here! he would shout. Right here! Let's get organized, everyone pitching in. I'll start off getting rid of this debris....

And David would be sifting through shards with the care of a jeweler.

Look! he would whisper with excitement. (And the news would pass from mouth to mouth like rumors, like music.) The basement of the old art gallery, it's survived! Look! Paintings and tapestries and bronze figurines. Come and sit, everyone, and admire and give thanks. It is a sacrament....

And where, Juliet thought urgently, do I really want to be? On a dais with a megaphone, directing history? Or dreaming in the grotto of art?

And the real trouble was: she wanted both, she had always wanted both.

"Is that what all this is about?" Jeremy asked finally. "My staying out for a handful of meaningless nights?"

"No." (Absolutely not! Surely not?) "It's about" – she took a deep breath and flung the words at him like a convent girl swearing at a nun – "it's about my falling in love with David."

"David. That guy who phoned?"

She nodded.

He spread his hands in a gesture of incredulity then placed them on her shoulders.

"Well," he said. "What can I say? I hope you've made a sensible choice." He brushed her forehead with his lips. "Be happy, Juliet."

Over the years she had come to realize there was no such thing as the right or wrong choice. Only a road taken and a road not taken.

What was truly amazing, however, a never failing source of astonishment, was where the road taken led. Who could have dreamed it would lead to India, to a house in a coconut grove from which she would write letters back to her past? To a house and courtyard swept daily with a tuft of palm leaves? To a place where she would pound out laundry in a manner used by women since the time of the gaunt bronze dancer of the second millennium B.C.

She went out to the courtyard. If the sheets and towels were left to broil in the sun ten minutes too long they became as rigid and body-punishing as a *fakir*'s bed of nails.

One of the cows was contentedly munching its way through the bedding.

"Oh no!" she cried, exasperated, seizing a stick and running into the courtyard. "Stop it! Stop it!"

The three children came running, and Prabhakaran, a look of horror on his face, flung his arms around the cow, crooning and scolding in Malayalam.

Her raised weapon stilled itself in mid-air.

"Naughty cow! Naughty cow!" he said. "O bad little one! O

sweet little trickster! O naughty darling!"

The cow continued to devour the sheet with calm indifference. Jonathan and Miranda began to laugh.

"It's all right, Prabhakaran," Juliet said. "I won't hurt it."

She thought ruefully: Cow molester! Even my sins are becoming unrecognizable.

10

It was not just the rank smell of curried breath and sweating bodies that caused David to sway with nausea in the lurching university bus. He was too tall for Indian buses and every time the driver careened through a pothole his head would bang harshly against the metal roof. He was rammed so tightly into the men's section that he could not even free an arm to protect his head. He had tried, merely calling forth a grunt of discomfort from the student against whose ribs his arm was trapped.

But he was used to this by now and would scarcely have noticed it if he had not slept so badly, if the ghost of a fear, like an ugly black furry creature, had not scuttled into the corners of his night.

She had called out in her sleep again. Possibly someone's name. Possibly a name he had not heard for twelve years, but had never forgotten. Jeremy. But of course he could be imagining it. It was absurd to think after all this time...but then how could he be certain? Sometimes a small shadow – a fleeting thing like the grayness thrown by a wisp of cloud – passed over the long miracle of his happiness.

Yet he had only to summon up the sight of her reading to the children or feel the flamboyant orchid of her body opening to his, to know that all was well.

But yet again there were those moments when she seemed to retreat from him, when her abstracted eyes roamed through some unfocused middle distance, suggesting secrets. And what did he really know of the deceptions of which human beings were capable? What had he known, what had he ever dreamed possible, of his own capacity to deceive? Once he would never have believed that there had been lurking within himself, within the clear pool of his own life, a wild amphibian thing, predatory and libidinous. One night it had astonished him, rushing forth like a pterodactyl (something primeval, something he had believed extinct) swooping out of some uncharted swamp within him, blinded by the searchlight of a casual young explorer.

It had seemed to him, after that, that he should never presume to comprehend intention or cause and effect or the inflections of another's thought. His own motivations baffled him sufficiently. So what could he expect to know of Juliet who was simply the most intimate of strangers? And what did he know of himself? Of how he would defend himself against past ghosts or future losses?

In any case, perhaps it hadn't been a name she called out. Just gibberish. For weeks now she had been tossing and moaning at night. Lying in bed with her was like trying to sleep on a small boat whose jib has flapped loose from the bowsprit.

It's the heat, he thought. And the isolation.

"What are your nightmares about?" he had asked once.

And she had looked startled. "I don't have nightmares."

She claimed to remember nothing. She did not seem to know he had held her, whispering comfort while she shuddered and cried out, feeling the sheets become drenched with sweat.

Isolation and lethargy. Perhaps she feared losing her place in the world, slipping from civilization without a trace. It was a fear that smoked around him like fog each evening when he re-entered the coconut grove. The toothless old women who sat under the trees would look up from the braiding of palm leaves, peering at him through the evening mists, and he would think: The same ones, surely, watched the ancient passing of Mahabali, the great king. Time is but a wink of their weathered eyelids. And he would feel relieved that in the morning he would be meeting with university colleagues who had visited London and Toronto and New York.

India had probably been a mistake. Not the adventure she yearned for. No paradisal retreat. More like a narcotic. I couldn't live without subways, she had said long ago. And he had always been amazed that she had chosen him. He had always known it was a miracle. He liked to think he had taught her a tranquility which was new to her and valuable, but it was always possible that he had taken her statements of discontent too lightly. It was hard to know. She did everything, even speaking, so extravagantly.

Last night he had held her tenderly, sheltering her with his arms from the marauders of her sleep, when she called for help.

Not to him.

Is it happening then, he had wondered, turning away, staring into the past. Did she see him in Montreal, that man from the past? (*I live with a guy on and off.*) Was it the sort of thing that was never concluded? Had he, David, been holding her against her will all these years? Should he begin to prepare himself for change?

He had let Susan twirl in his mind like a lucky charm at a carnival, trying to infect himself with her circus gaiety.

Like that astonishing time, the night of the pterodactyl. He had been working late in his office, reference books spread around him, the room littered with drafts of a paper he was writing. It was after midnight and even other night-owl colleagues had gone home. He was alone in the building.

Late spring rain was pattering against his window. And then some hail. Hail? He turned, and for a mad moment thought he saw a ghostly face pressing against the pane. But his was a second-floor window. He turned back to his desk and began stacking books. Definitely time to go home to sleep.

The tapping on the glass became more urgent. To jolt himself back to reality he crossed the room and opened the window. It was the old sash kind, with an aluminum storm-screen combination more recently installed in the outer frame. And there, nose pressed against the screen so that it ballooned inwards to touch the inner glass, was Susan.

"Good God!" he said, sliding the screen open.

She was clinging to the fairly substantial branches of ivy that had been smothering the building for a hundred years, and now came clambering into the room.

"I've been working late on my term paper," she said. "I was just passing by and saw your light on so I thought I might as well hand it in now."

"Good God," he said again, helplessly, retreating to his desk and sitting down.

She was dark and dazzling as a gypsy, her wet black hair slicked around her cheeks and neck, light breaking in the raindrops on her lashes, her damp jeans steaming, her blouse soaking wet and hugging her like an advertisement for breasts.

All this for me? he thought humbly, ecstatically, fearfully. For a forty-year-old associate professor with not enough publications and hair receding at the temples and a wife who sometimes retreats into a private labyrinth for which I have no map?

Oh careful, careful, he warned himself. Students are off limits. Besides, it was scarcely credible.... Was it a joke, a dare, something for discussion and laughter in the student pubs? Poor old fool, speechless with excitement, could hardly get his pants off for trembling, came in two minutes, poor deprived sod.

"Well," he said dryly – the urbane professor, with an arch eyebrow to acknowledge the droller aspects of life – "your dedication will be taken into account, Miss – ah – Miss Fraser, but the paper will have to be graded on its own merits, of course."

"Yes. Oh, of course. Oh you didn't think I was trying to...oh dear...."

The high-flying kite of her impetuous self-confidence

pitched and floundered in uncertain winds. She looked irresistibly vulnerable.

"You don't even remember my first name, do you?" she asked plaintively.

"Oh yes, I do. Indeed I do." Too quickly. A rush of words, almost slurred. Steady, steady. Back up.

He cleared his throat and said, without inflection: "Susan." But there was a slight unevenness to his voice and he had to cough.

"You've practically destroyed this term for me. I've hardly managed to get anything done." Her voice quick and breathless as birds in flight. "It's your eyes. Your huge sad brooding eyes. Every night I fantasize about making them smile."

"I don't believe you," he said, amazed, wanting to believe her, afraid of behaving like an idiot.

"I'm terribly wet and uncomfortable," she said, shivering noticeably. "You don't mind if I just dry off, do you? Before you throw me back into the night, I mean?"

She peeled off her blouse and it was much too late for caution.

So what if it is just a circus act, he thought, as she swung her gypsy feet toward the ceiling. What if they do make fun of me later. He plunged into exhilaration like a stunt man from a trapeze and he did not even care if there was no safety net.

But afterwards he had been appalled by this new knowledge of himself. I am frivolous and self-indulgent, he thought. I am morally unreliable, blown about by the merest whim of desire.

Every night for months, with Juliet in his arms, he had yearned for absolution. He had longed to say: I have something to confess. I have behaved shoddily and dishonestly. Forgive me.

And it was not the fear of losing her or the fear of her outrage that prevented him. It was the fear that she would not acknowledge the enormity of his wrongdoing. The fear that she would open her eyes wide in wry surprise and say: "David!

You *are* human like the rest of us. What a relief."

Lying beside Juliet in the South Indian night, David had decided: If she wants to fly back to turmoil and subways, if it is someone flawed and faithless she wants, maybe I should confess about Susan. Maybe I would seem more exciting.

He had watched the last translucent red chunk fall from the mosquito coil and settle into ash. He got up to light another one, but not before he had slapped his arm twice and flicked the bloody little corpses into the dark. He imagined the mosquitoes hovering in cloud-like battalions around the house, sending in scouts every two minutes: Okay, men, the coil is out! We have sixty seconds to attack before they light another one!

He had fallen asleep watching the smoke spiraling up from the glowing tip, and dreamed of Juliet.

He dreamed that he had come home in the early evening to an empty house. He felt alarmed, sensing tragedy, and ran through the trees towards the rice paddy. To his immense relief, there was his wife standing among the areca palms surrounded by children, their own included. She seemed to be handing out ice-cream cones.

Jonathan and Miranda came towards him, blissful, licking rapturously, a tantalizing flavor he could not place.

"It's jasmine," they told him. "Jasmine ice-cream. It's fantastic. Mommy makes it."

"Juliet!" he called, and she turned towards him, scattering sweets and flowers, jasmine streamers trailing from her hair.

He held out his arms and she came running, in slow motion like the woman in a television commercial, eager and beautiful as first love. He braced himself to scoop her up, their hands touched.

And she jerked herself away.

"Oh!" she said. "The sun was in my eyes. I thought you were someone else."

In a fanfare of red dust, the bus slammed to a halt at the university, crashing David's head against the ceiling. The passengers spilled out like lava, steamy and unstoppable, men first. Except for David. As always, from force of habit, he stood back for the women to alight before him. As always they responded by giggling nervously into their hands, eyes lowered. It occurred to David: Perhaps they think my intentions are lecherous. He waited for the last of them to file past him in a rustle of saris and streaming coconut-oil-soaked hair. Then he got off the bus, a courteous clown, unable to change his habits, an object of bewilderment and mirth.

It was to be another of those days, the library inexplicably closed to research. One more arcane festival. Or perhaps the librarian had mysteriously absented himself again – a family wedding or birth or death in some outlying village, no doubt – the prerogatives of his rank inviolable, no substitutes permitted at the library desk.

With weary resignation, David waited for the bus going back into the city.

Wasted hours and days.

And wasted years? No, he would never believe that. Luminous years, no matter what lay ahead. Once she had run to him, reckless, in the subway at rush hour. Once she had danced into his days. He could not expect to cast her in bronze and keep her in a glass case forever.

11

Between baskets of mangoes and trailing loops of jasmine it moved like a small conical volcano, its slopes fluid and black as scree, eruptions of astonishment leaping outwards from its mysterious core. Stares and jabberings spread like lava from its side, lapping the far edges of the evening market.

No one had ever seen a woman move so anonymously, so shapelessly, through the Chalai Bazaar. Never in living memory had the enveloping Muslim garment been seen in Trivandrum. No one had believed that women were still kept in *purdah* anywhere outside the remote mountain fastnesses of Jammu and Kashmir or the most secret backstreets of Old Delhi.

She must be a Pakistani. Who could guess what still went on in Pakistan, a nation of religious fanatics whose god was never a child?

Ayyo, ayyo, murmured the voices that surrounded the walking tent as flies cluster and buzz around sweet *jallebis*. Alas! How that Muslim god must fear women! A god who had never played the flute, never danced, never sighed for Radha in the forest. A god who covered women with sacks, like walking dung hills. *Ayyo, ayyo!*

When the veiled woman directed the tiny rectangle of muslin – window of her eyes – at the watchers, they stepped back, spitting betel juice to ward off inauspicious occurrences.

She was the wife of a Pakistani diplomat visiting the Secretariat, the rumors claimed. No, countered others; she was the daughter of a wealthy rug merchant of Srinagar. He wished for an educated daughter who had seen the world but who had been kept pure, aloof from temptation.

There was a persistent suggestion that she was, without doubt, the delectable concubine of a Himalayan chieftain, a former petty prince whose fabulous lands and palaces stretched up into the snowy spaces above the Gulmarg and overlooked the pleasure gardens of Shalimar.

And how was it that such a prince with his pomp and retinue was visiting Trivandrum undetected, save for this one clue of his swathed and mummified mistress? Doubtless, opined certain pundits, he was being courted in secret by the Russians in the House of Soviet Culture behind Tampanoor Junction, being tempted, in that building of austere grayness, with limousines and fantastic weaponry in return for a certain ease of passage down from Tashkent into Kashmir.

Such was the sophisticated discussion Juliet overheard between a young pharmacist and a young doctor who stood in their white shirts and white *dhotis* at the entrance of their booths. In the bazaar the medical professions took their commercial chances along with the flower sellers and grain merchants and peddlers of dried cow-dung cakes, vying for attention and customers. The young doctor was doing well: he was handsome; the plaque on his booth listed many obscure and scholarly letters after his name; large capitals indicated HOMEOPATHIC MEDICINE (based, that is to say, on ancient and trustworthy *ayurvedic* principles rather than on alien western science); and a final trump line proclaimed him an EXPERT SEXOLOGIST, promising, through the ingestion of herbal potions, pleasurable cures for all erotic difficulties and disturbances (for men only, of course, though this was not stated, it being universally known that the sexuality of woman is inexhaustible and rapacious).

The prince's concubine floated on, in her fluid tented way,

past the gentlemen of medical profession and political opinion towards where Juliet, with her children and Prabhakaran, was buying *brinjal* and *kumpalanna*. The children stared in silent awe, as apprehensive as the *peons* who shuffled aside from her coming. There was something eerily inhuman, demonic almost, about that faceless column of fabric.

The figure came alongside Juliet where she stood beneath the flare of coconut-oil torches at the vegetable stall. A hand the color of *café-au-lait* emerged from the black folds and began feeling and prodding the purple *brinjal* just as Juliet was doing. Two women engaged in an ancient domestic skill, assessing the ripeness of eggplants. The fragrant smoke of the vendor's sandalwood sticks curled around them.

Juliet watched the hand moving close to hers, exploring the swelling hillocks and dimpled amethyst valleys of *brinjal*, following, it almost seemed, her own hand like a shadow.

A sudden flaring tongue of torchlight lit up a ringed finger with quick gemfire. Juliet stared at the ring, a crusted circle of emeralds and diamonds, in confusion. Surely she had seen it before?

At the same time the ringed hand closed over hers in a compelling and pleading grip. From the recesses of black cloth a muffled voice whispered urgently: "Juliet! Please do not show surprise. Please continue in your buying, only listen to me! Help me, please!"

Juliet stared at the *brinjal*.

Yashoda's voice had been smoky with anxiety, her hand trembled. The seller of vegetables was watching the two hands clasped over his produce.

"*Shari*," Juliet said, extricating the eggplant and her hand, offering the purple fruit. "This is good *brinjal*. You may have it. I will find another."

Yashoda bowed towards her and whispered quickly: "Please hide me! If I am discovered there will be much trouble for me."

Juliet murmured back: "We have a taxi waiting. If you could pretend to faint, I will get you out of here."

With a soft moan and some poignant fluttering of hands, Yashoda crumpled gracefully.

It was effective melodrama. The crowds babbled in a paroxysm of excitement and rumor, but parted to allow movement to the waiting taxi. The young doctor pushed eagerly and importantly forward but at Juliet's insistence consented to carry the limp, blanketed bundle into the car. He did so with solicitous awe.

Juliet was grateful for the safe cavern of the ramshackle vehicle, reassured by the reliability of the known driver. He was one of the two young men whose base was Shasta Junction near the Nair estate, men who lived and slept at the Junction in their rusty taxis, who were known to all in that district.

As soon as they were inside and the doors shut, the market hush gave way to mob bravado. Boys by the score swarmed over the hood and roof, peering through the windshield with flattened noses, craning to gawk upside-down through the sides. Giggling like hysterical schoolgirls, their betel-stained teeth flashing, a mêlée of men leaned in through the windows, stroking the children's faces, running their fingers down Juliet's hair with exclamations of wonder. No one, however, attempted to touch Yashoda. There was something too potently inauspicious about her shrouded huddled blackness.

Juliet held herself rigid and impassive to the mauling. This had happened so often and yet she never became inured to it. Instead, a sense of embarrassment about her own body would engulf her. An obscure shame about her fair hair and skin. She felt like a zoo animal, or a fish in its tank blinking out at the myriad eyes of the curious.

"Start the car!" she ordered the driver. "Start moving!"

And gradually bodies fell away as moths who have flown too close fall back from a lamp.

Juliet slumped back in relief.

"Yashoda, *where* did you get that thing, and what were you trying to do?"

"Talk softly," begged Yashoda. "Even the taxi driver must not know. If word should reach Shivaraman Nair...."

The children blinked in astonishment and Prabhakaran gasped, a hand over his mouth.

"Hush, Prabhakaran! Please, you must never speak of this."

"Never, never!" he promised.

"Yashoda, *why*...?"

"For disguise. It is the only way I can move in public without being recognized, without disgrace. But I did not stop to think how strange...I was not expecting such tumult, such staring."

"I could have warned you about that," Juliet said grimly. "How do you come to have one of those things, those body sacks?"

"From Srinagar. I have been there once with my father on a business trip. Oh Juliet, I am so unhappy, even my father cannot help me. I will die of loneliness."

"I tried to visit you twice."

"Yes, yes. I was sent away to my husband's family in Palghat. They are very strict and conservative. Shivaraman Nair told them that I am bringing disgrace on the family. I was forbidden to leave my hut. All my jewelry was taken. Only by bribing a servant with the golden waist chain hidden under my sari was I able to send a message to my father in Cochin. He rescued me and I had some days, such happy days, in my father's house again, but he has called Shivaraman Nair and they had long discussions. My father offered money and I was permitted to return."

"Why did you have to return? Why not stay with your father?"

"Ah," she sighed. "If only it were possible. Cochin is so much freer than Trivandrum. It makes me sad, Juliet, that you are living in this city instead of Madras or Cochin, and you are thinking all India is like this. It is difficult to explain our South Indian ways. But now I am frightened. How can I enter the estate? If I am seen in this garment it will soon be known about the bazaar. To be seen in public is bad, to disgrace myself as a

Muslim is much worse. If I remove this now, it will be known that I have left the estate. I will be sent to Palghat. Shivaraman Nair told my father one more chance only."

"How did you leave the estate? When did you put that thing on?"

"I put it on in the forest. This afternoon I walked many kilometers through the far side of the forest beyond my house, the far side of the estate, until I came to the Kottayam Road. I gave a silver nose-ring to a bullock driver and he brought me into the city on his cart." She paused, thinking back. "It was very exciting. You cannot realize, Juliet, when I am so lonely and bored, how exciting it was. But I did not think enough about the return, I was too eager for the adventure of leaving my prison. I did not think about how long it would take. I cannot walk back through the forest at night."

"I can't see any problem. Who will see you in the dark? Just keep low and out of sight as we drive past the Nair house. You can take that off inside our house and walk home."

"Ahh, you do not know how far talking is going here. The taxi driver will tell all his passengers, all the men in the toddy houses at Shasta Junction. Shivaraman Nair will hear. He will ask you: Where is the strange Muslim woman who visited you but did not leave? It will be found out."

"Then I will introduce you as we pass the house. My Muslim friend from the far North."

"No, no, no! It will be seen that this friend does not leave your house again. Oh it is impossible. I have been so stupid. I will be sent to Palghat."

"No. Wait. I have an idea. Say nothing at all."

The taxi slowed at the gates of the Nair estate. Shivaraman Nair was visible in the glow of the oil flare, sitting on his porch enjoying the cool of evening, missing nothing. He moved with lordly graciousness to greet the taxi while the driver opened the iron gates. He frowned sternly at Prabhakaran. He did not approve of servants riding in taxis. They should be sent on the bus or on foot.

"*Namaskaram.* I have brought a friend who is the daughter of a Pakistani merchant," Juliet invented glibly. "We met when she was traveling in the West with her father. They are visiting very briefly. They leave tonight on the plane for Karachi."

"Most welcome, most welcome," said Shivaraman Nair excitedly. "So many peoples from all over the world are visiting my beautiful house. This is the first time we are having a Pakistani lady. Most welcome."

The robed figure inclined its head courteously.

The taxi proceeded through the coconut grove. At the entrance to their house, Juliet told the driver to wait. In a short time he would be required to take the Muslim lady to the airport. Juliet would pay him now, in advance, for the waiting and the whole trip.

Some time later the veiled lady entered the car silently and was driven to the airport. She quailed a little before the rush of public interest as she alighted, but made her way to the ladies' lavatory and locked herself into one of the booths.

What a wild goose chase, Juliet thought, gingerly placing her feet on the two cement footprints above the black and fearful-smelling hole of the latrine. How long will I have to stay in here before the room empties of the curious, before I can emerge as a Westerner, creating my own different current of excitement? And the speculation will go on forever. Where did the strange swaddled woman go? Why was she never seen again? Eventually Shivaraman Nair will hear of it. But perhaps by the time he asks me about it I can laugh it off as the chatter of airport servants and taxi drivers. Mere rumor.

In the meantime, she thought with pleasure, I feel alive again. Like a kid on an adventure.

She bent over and turned on the little tap that projected from the wall six inches above the floor. This and a small plastic pitcher beneath it were the only aids to hygiene. She filled the pitcher and let its water sluice around the slightly concave floor of the booth. It was not a very effective device, as the stench and the crusting of flies over excremental remnants testified. Juliet let the tap run noisily while she removed the voluminous tent and stuffed it into her carry bag.

She waited, listening for silence, hoping at least for a different set of people in the outside room. And then, mercifully, the power failed. In the darkness and confusion she emerged and moved quickly out to the taxi stand, taking care to look for a driver who was unknown at Shasta Junction.

∽

She should have warned me, David thought, turning from the face that glowed in the lamplight. Juliet had not, somehow, prepared him adequately for Yashoda. He had not anticipated such eyes, such blood-stirring vulnerability, such exquisite fluidity of movement. He could not entirely blame Shivaraman Nair for locking her away. The male fear of a *yakshi*, of bewitchment. Like Radha on her ivory swing, the woman would float through dreams forever.

She shimmered in silks and jewels, incandescent in her defiance. It must have been sweet revenge, he thought, to have been dressed like that under her black tent.

"My father would have permitted it," she was saying. "He did not want to send me back to Trivandrum, but he had no choice. My mother died many years ago, my younger brother has married, and now my sister-in-law is the mistress of my father's house. It is her right. She did not want me to live there."

She smiled sadly at David with lambent helplessness and he held his breath.

Juliet, returning from the airport, entered their sudden stillness, saw the thread of connection between their eyes, galvanic as invisible blue fire Even David? She was surprised by a fleeting stab of jealousy

But, after all, another woman had already come between them: India, the earth mother herself, the great voluptuous slow-moving slattern, opening up her secrets and excitements to David. Ignoring Juliet.

She felt cheated. Yashoda had been *her* adventure. Even that had been stolen.

"My father is very wealthy," Yashoda was saying, "and he entertains many foreign visitors because of his spice-exporting business. He is very progressive – he even allows wine to be served to his guests. Before my marriage I was mistress of the house, ordering the household supplies and managing the servants and entertaining the important guests. I have met ladies from London and New York. They have such exciting lives! Also my father travels to these cities and once, when I was younger, he took me with him to London."

She sighed. "That is why it is so difficult for me to live like this. Now when I return to my father's house, I am only the widowed daughter. My brother's wife is the mistress. It would not be auspicious for me to be the hostess of these banquets, although my father permits me to sit at table with the guests." She paused. "My sister-in-law was angry about this. Her kinsmen, who share with my father in the business, were also angry. They said I would cause misfortune and loss of money. Already they were angry with him about the wine. My father laughs at them, but it is difficult to go against the family."

"But why did you come back here? Surely it would be better to live a restricted life in your father's house than here?"

"No. Because of my sister-in-law. There is no longer any privacy or freedom in that house. At least in my small place in the forest I am my own mistress. Except..." she sighed again, balancing debits, "in Cochin I can go walking in the market and here I cannot."

"Why doesn't your father send you to London or New York for a while, since he has contacts there?"

"Oh, for a western woman that is so simple. For us, impossible. A woman can only live with kinfolk. There must be a husband, or a father, or an uncle, or her husband's kin to shelter her. There is no other way."

"But Trivandrum of all places. Surely you have relatives in other more cosmopolitan cities?"

"That is the saddest part for me. In Madras and Bombay it is no longer necessary for a widow to be secluded. I wrote to my uncle, Mummy's brother, in Madras. He was very fond of me, but his wife has said no. Widows bring bad luck."

"Perhaps," David said thoughtfully, "perhaps if I went to visit your father in Cochin – I do have to make a trip up there at some time – perhaps he would let you come back with us when we leave. For a visit. If you were to be living with a family he knows – "

"Yes, yes, it is possible. This is what I have dreamed, but it seemed only a dream. That is why – when my astrologer said I would meet a person of destiny – that is why, Juliet, when I met you on that day, I thought you would find some way to rescue me. And today you did. But the greatness of my astrologer is now truly revealed. Oh Professor David!" She leaned slightly towards him, breathing enchantment. "You are having very powerful magic. You are making life very beautiful."

12

Prabhakaran came to the house with a note. It read:

Professor David and Mrs. David Juliet.
   We are pleased to be wanting you to take the midday meal with us. At noon precisely. Bring also the children. Shivaraman Nair.

Which verb endings would he have used if he were writing in Malayalam? Juliet wondered. Surely he cannot already have heard of the strange disappearance of the Muslim woman at the airport?

At noon precisely they presented themselves. Shivaraman Nair and Anand were sitting under the shady vines on the front veranda. Mrs. Shivaraman Nair came to the door. *Namaskaram*, everyone murmured, inclining the head.

"We are being very happy to have you in our house, Mrs. David Juliet."

"Thank you, Mrs. Shivaraman Nair. I am most honored."

Juliet had made a futile attempt to overcome the lengthy formality of names. Originally they had all called her Mrs. Professor David.

"My name is Juliet," she had said. "Please call me that. What is *your* name?"

"I am Mrs. Shivaraman Nair."

And thereafter she had been called Mrs. David Juliet.

They left their sandals on the doorstep and entered the house. It was sumptuously furnished in teak and ivory, and underfoot were thick Kashmiri carpets and cool spaces of polished stone and marble. In the hallway a magnificent brass peacock lamp, about five feet high, its seven wicks charred from the morning's *puja*, was festooned with a garland of scarlet flowers. In front of the lamp was a small image of Vishnu and in front of that a bowl of rice and fruits had been placed as an offering. Sticks of sandalwood were burning slowly in brass censers and the whole house smelled heavily fragrant.

David and Jonathan were invited to join the men in the front room while Juliet and Miranda were ushered through to the women's living room at the back. A number of women, whom Juliet supposed were relatives, were already there. Was it a festival day? Or some family celebration? Or a family council to consider the problem of Yashoda? Mrs. Shivaraman Nair did not perform any introductions or give any explanations, but smiled benignly and disappeared in the direction of the kitchen.

None of the women acknowledged the presence of the new arrivals. Perhaps I am expected to initiate conversation, Juliet thought. She said: "*Namaskaram*. I am happy to meet you. I am Juliet and this is my daughter Miranda."

The women turned to look at her but said nothing. They did not register any surprise or interest. They went on sipping their tea. Occasionally they spoke to one another but mostly they were silent.

Fifteen minutes elapsed. The women sat silently sipping. Miranda looked imploringly at Juliet and rolled her eyes expressively. Juliet could feel a maddening itch on the soles of her feet. She wanted desperately to stand up and walk about.

Then Mrs. Shivaraman Nair reappeared with Jati, who was carrying a tray. They offered their guests tea and joined the circle. Jati sat near Juliet who sipped the sickeningly sweet beverage without pleasure.

"Would you like to see my college magazine?" Jati asked.

"Yes indeed." Juliet was profoundly grateful for the prospect of conversation.

Jati fetched a glossy booklet that bore an insignia of a lamp, a cross, and a Latin motto. *Annual Magazine of All Saints College for Women* read the title, in English.

"You go to a Catholic college?" Juliet asked in amazement.

"It is taught by the Sisters. It is an English Medium College," said Jati proudly. "It is forbidden to speak Malayalam."

Juliet knew that the rubric "medium" referred not to educational level or quality, but to mode of communication.

"But I am surprised that a Hindu family would send a daughter to a Christian school. Don't the Sisters instruct you in the Catholic religion?"

"No, no!" Jati was puzzled by the idea. "There are not being many Christian students at this college. They are not affording. It is for the daughters of the Nair families. The Sisters are teaching the best English. English is required to make a good marriage."

"Are the Sisters European?"

"No, no," she said, surprised. "They are Malayali ladies."

Juliet leafed through the magazine. It was so like what she remembered of her own high school yearbook in nature and quality of content that she had a strange sensation of time-traveling. There were little poems about snowflakes – from people who had never seen snow! There were the usual jokes on Shakespearean lines: *An ill-favoured thing, sir, but mine own* (handing your school report to your father) and *There's a divinity that shapes our ends, rough hew them though we may* (Lakshmi's daring short haircut obtained on her visit to Bombay is growing out again).

"Don't the students ever write poems about peacocks or the temple flower sellers or the monsoons?" Juliet asked.

Jati looked disdainful.

"At our college, we are studying *English* literature."

"Did Yashoda go to a college like this?" Juliet risked asking.

"My cousin," Jati said stiffly, "was educated in Cochin. Her father has paid for some western tutors. She has not been taught by Malayali ladies. She is...very...*modern*."

Clearly a derogatory word.

It became increasingly difficult to sustain conversation. They lapsed back into the silent sipping of tea. The minutes crawled on. Miranda was a monument of passive agony. From time to time, Juliet would make brave little forays into speech, valiant breaches in the ramparts of silence. Her words would settle quietly into the carpet, a brief phrase or monosyllable the only response, the battle lost. She wondered for what conceivable reason it had been necessary to come *at noon precisely*. She would not have believed it possible that a group of people gathered for a social purpose could sit together for so long without speaking. She wanted to scream.

And then suddenly, through the window into the courtyard, she saw a woman – the echo of a woman – leaning over the household well like a trail of unshaded jasmine bruised colorless by the heat.

Yashoda! Juliet thought with a leap of furtive excitement and dismay. Then they must know. About the market. She is being punished. They have made her one of the courtyard widows, reduced her to that sorority of obsolescence, left out in the sun like spoiled fruit to be blanched and dried.

"Excuse me." Juliet stood suddenly, scattering the decorum of the Nair women every which way like skittles, and ran into the ferocious embrace of the noonday heat.

"Yashoda!" There was only dust and haze between them, then only the well. On the surface of the water their reflections touched, head to head, like *yakshis* conferring or *chakora* birds butting self-destructively.

Yashoda looked somehow...denuded. No jewelry, the peacock brilliance of her silk saris exchanged for the drab cotton of a widow. She was like a person whose light has been extinguished. Like a stripped Christmas tree thrown beside a snowy sidewalk for collection.

"How did they find out?"

"They know nothing. They suspect only. There was such talk at the market. And also at the airport."

"I won't let them do this! It frightens me. It threatens me. It threatens *me!*" Juliet said.

Their reflections collided and merged.

"It is nothing, a warning only," Yashoda said. "In two days, three days, this will be over. I will be back in my house."

"Mrs. David Juliet! My mother is bringing fresh tea. You are not wanting it to be cold, isn't it?" Jati stood in the doorway of the house, watchful as a cat.

Yashoda and Juliet bowed to each other in formal farewell, making *namaskaram* over the household drinking supply. Their fluid heads and hands merged again, their breath rippled the water, circling them with furrows.

"Three days," Yashoda whispered. "Four at the most. Will you come to my house this week? Will Professor David come?"

"I'm sure he will," Juliet murmured, and then returned to the eternity of the silent tea ceremony.

Miranda, having been abandoned for ten minutes, looked at her mother in silent reproach. The Nair women sipped as though nothing had happened.

After what seemed an interminable passage of time – it was well over an hour – Mrs. Shivaraman Nair returned to the kitchen and a few minutes later came to summon Juliet and Miranda to the dining room. Juliet saw to her surprise and pleasure that they were to sit at the table with the men. She understood the magnitude of this concession and tears of gratitude came to her eyes.

She inclined her head to Shivaraman Nair. "I am honored."

He laughed heartily.

She had noticed that he greeted everything she said with laughter, as though she were an amusing child or a clever toy.

"I am understanding the customs of western people," he said.

First they were all invited to wash their right hands at the enamel basin with its chrome faucets, a prominent item of dining-room furniture. Then they sat around an immense polished teak table. The female relatives remained in the other room. Perhaps now they will at least talk to one another, Juliet thought.

Mrs. Shivaraman Nair and Jati did not sit at the table, but served them throughout the meal, hovering like nervous, if ponderous, butterflies. All the Shivaraman Nairs were substantial testaments to prosperity. It seemed to be a mark of caste. One flaunted one's lavish eating habits as one's wife and daughters flaunted jewelry.

A huge plaintain leaf, from the banana palm, lay on the table in front of each person. Mrs. Shivaraman Nair heaped a small mountain of rice onto the broad end of each frond, then Jati ladled out various curries in little mounds along the leaf, the hottest and spiciest at the tip of the green "plate," proceeding through a diminuendo of palate fires to the cooling curds at the other end. One ate with the fingers of the right hand, making a "mush" of rice and curry.

From time to time Mrs. Shivaraman Nair would take something from the refrigerator, the most imposing item of furniture in the room, its teak-paneled recess a distinguished foil to chrome and white enamel. Each time she would ostentatiously unlock it with a key from the immense bunch that jangled at her waist. Then she would remove some item or other and relock the door. It was gratifying to draw the guests' attention to such a modern appliance.

Eating was a serious business. There was no conversation during this part of the meal, though the room was extremely noisy with the sounds of mastication and digestion, with thunderous belching and clearings of the throat. Jonathan and Miranda were red in the face from a suppressed urge to giggle. They dared not look at each other. Anand and his father bent rather low over their plantain leaves, their eyes on the food.

Eventually Shivaraman Nair became aware that his guests had ceased eating.

"But you are such poor eaters!" he boomed in astonishment.

The hosts' orgy of eating petered out with the third helping, and everyone turned to tea and talk.

"Tell me," David said, "what do you think of Raj Narain's behavior in London?"

The *Indian Express* had been giving lively accounts of the minister's arrival in the United Kingdom and of his tantrums at Heathrow Airport and at the Indian High Commission in London.

"That man is a peasant, a clown. He is very embarrassing," said Anand.

"He can't be stupid," Juliet countered, "to have defeated Mrs. Gandhi for her own seat."

"Ahh!" laughed Shivaraman Nair. "Your wife is understanding politics. Very remarkable! Very remarkable!"

Juliet was reminded of Samuel Johnson's comment about women preachers in the eighteenth century. She felt like a performing dog.

"For my son also I want this kind of wife," Shivaraman Nair expatiated with enthusiasm. "After my son is finishing his medical degree I am sending him to university in America. He will be needing very educated wife."

"For this my father will allow one thousand rupees less in the dowry," said Anand dryly, grinning at Juliet.

She smiled back. I like him, she thought.

"What do you think of Narain's statement," David pressed them, "that as long as there is English spoken in India the British Raj is still here?"

"He is wanting North India Raj!" said Shivaraman Nair angrily. "He is wanting Hindi Raj! Malayalis will never accept this! When he is saying *no English*, he is meaning no Malayalam, no Tamil, no Kannada, no Telugu, no South India! Only Hindi! English is necessary for all states to remain equal. We do not want imposition of Hindi! That man is stupid, but also dangerous for Malayalis."

"Is he as dangerous as Mrs. Gandhi?" asked David.

There was an awkward pause

"Janata Party has made much criticism of Mrs. Gandhi," said Shivaraman Nair stiffly. "But what have they done to show they are better? It is still the same people in the machinery of the governing, the same red tape, the same bribery, the same corruption. The system is just the same. Nothing has changed. It is the system prevails."

"Then you would like to see the return of Mrs. Gandhi?"

"Yes, yes. With Mrs. Gandhi things were working better. Morarji Desai says she was against the people. But now all across the country there are more attacks on Harijans than before."

"But surely, there is no chance of Mrs. Gandhi's regaining power?" David asked.

"Yes, yes, she will come back."

"Raj Narain says that the Janata has destroyed Indira as Lord Krishna annihilated the evil *Kaṃsa*," Juliet said.

"Oh ho!" laughed Shivaraman Nair. "He is stupid man. You are most knowledgeable about politics, Mrs. David Juliet! This is most remarkable!"

"But Mrs. Gandhi is a woman!" Juliet pointed out. "What I find puzzling is that all the books I read before I came to India said that the women of Kerala were very advanced and independent because Kerala was a matriarchy. They said that women here were freer than in North India. But I do not find this true at all. Your women are not independent. You do not permit them many freedoms." She was afraid to mention Yashoda. "And yet your inheritance laws have been traditionally matriarchal."

Anand explained. "Matriarchy," he said, "means *nephew* inherits, not son."

"That doesn't make sense!"

"But yes!" Anand was patient. "A man can never be certain beyond all doubt that he is the father of his wife's children. But his *sister's* son must carry the family blood even if the sister has been with many men."

Juliet laughed sourly. "So much for matriarchy."

13

In the mornings now, just at daybreak, they woke to a rhythmic drumming in the foundations of the house: the throbbing
of threshing flails. This was harvest month and even though
there was a problem with nightly rain – local opinion was
divided as to whether this was a prolonging of the first monsoon or a premature arrival of the second – the harvest was
nevertheless proceeding. But the rain was flattening the crop
and lessening the yield and making the threshing more difficult.

Twice a year the rice was harvested. Every sixty days the
coconuts yielded another cash crop. Even the most frequently
walked tracks between the trees and through the banana
clumps and around the lotus pond and the rice paddy seemed
always about to slither out of sight like snakes under dense
grass. It occurred to Juliet that everyone got up at dawn to
keep the jungle at bay, to pit the human passion for taming
and tending against all that raging growth. If we overslept one
morning, she thought, the clove vines might smother the
house. We would never cut our way out of the thicket.

Impenetrable, everything was impenetrable. Like the wall
of family surrounding Yashoda. A day after the dinner party
she had been spirited away. Or so it seemed. Only the old
maidservant was in the house in the forest and she was
unable – or afraid – to understand Juliet's Malayalam. Juliet

made tactful inquiries at the Nair house. Had Yashoda gone to visit relatives? The Nair family raised its eyebrows in bewildered innocence. What could Mrs. David Juliet mean? Their kinswoman continued to live quietly, as was proper, on the estate. Perhaps she had been walking in the forest when Mrs. David Juliet visited. Or perhaps, through shame, she had hidden herself.

Yet for two weeks now, no matter what time of day Juliet visited the house beyond the paddy, Yashoda was mysteriously absent. And the old maidservant, like a tropical sibyl, mouthed riddling responses to all questions; oracular Malayalam, impenetrable.

Perhaps Yashoda was simply *maya*, illusion? Perhaps she dandled in and out of reality on the pendulum of Juliet's imagination, a figment of need, a reflection in a well, a transposed identity on an ivory swing.

Crouching now over the low sink, pounding at the sheets, Juliet felt faint with heat and exertion, dizzy, trapped in the web of dankly green days.

Soak, rub, wring. I should capitulate and hire a servant. Scrub, twist, pound. I feel a hundred years old.

All her finger joints were swollen and in the mornings she had to massage her stiff and painful hands to life.

One of your problems, she told herself, is that you never know when you're beaten.

She slumped on the floor beside the sink and leaned her head against the polished stone bench.

And Jeremy came riding out of the West to cut his way through jungle walls and rescue her with a kiss from the drowsy tropics.

Once, long before David, they had spent a day together hiking through springtime woods, drifting apart to pick berries and lilacs. She had lost her footing on a muddy embankment, pitching downwards into a clump of wild raspberry canes. Her ankle had caught on something, a root, a stump fragment, she could not tell. She was strafed with scratches and her twisted ankle throbbed. With every move she made to extricate herself the thorns clutched at her clothing and tore her skin.

She called out to Jeremy and he called back, but their voices echoed weirdly in the still woods and it was some time before he pinpointed the direction of her cries and found her. By then blood was trickling down her cheeks and arms and legs. What she remembered most was the sudden whiteness of Jeremy's face and the reckless way he hauled and ripped at the endless looping raspberry runners.

They were both covered in scratches and flecked with beads of blood and they lay on the grass beside the raspberry canes and the lilacs. For a long time they had simply clung to each other.

The memory came back to her now sharp and clear as physical sensation, thrusting its way into her vision, between her thighs. She felt weak and swollen and filled with Jeremy. Then he had picked lilacs and covered her with them, on her belly, in her hair, between her legs. She remembered lying there sticky with their mingled juices and blood, smelling of fertility and springtime.

My god, she thought, disturbed, why is all this coming back to me now?

She stirred and sat up again. She brushed the scene like a bothersome cobweb from her eyes and carried the basket of wet laundry up to the roof.

Then she saw riding towards her, not Jeremy through the raspberry canes, but the mailman on his bicycle which bucked its way along the path between the coconut palms. He was a bizarre figure in his widely flared khaki "Bombay bloomers." He also wore a khaki shirt and knee-high khaki socks and a pith helmet, and seemed to have stepped out of a Somerset Maugham story or an old movie of the British Raj.

His visits were disappointingly rare, though momentous, and Juliet hurried downstairs to meet him. Such astonishing proof he brought that the world beyond Trivandrum continued to exist after all, just as though there were no rice harvest; that distant relatives continued to live by schedules and timetables; that remote banks and mortgage companies and other such institutions actually expected them to fill in forms by certain prescribed dates without understanding that they had stepped quite outside of time.

But the mailman had no airletters bearing foreign imprints. Only a postcard from Delhi, the Red Fort against a blue sky. And scrawled across the back:

Have sleeping bag, backpack, and Hindi dictionary. Can't tell for certain when I will reach you. Am hiking around, using bus and train, and stopping where whim and love affairs take me. Currently spending a few days with a gorgeous man named Dinesh who's a scriptwriter for the Indian movie industry. Friend of a friend. He studied film at Ryerson and I looked him up. He's a great Hindi teacher among many other talents of which I won't speak on a postcard. You may meet him when I come, who knows? Love, Annie.

How easy it must be to be Annie, Juliet thought. Untrammeled.

She felt suddenly that she wanted to leave India before her sister arrived, before she was consumed by a jealousy of Annie's freedom. But then thought: Perhaps she will jolt me back to life; perhaps she will refresh me with an awareness of the gains that balance the losses. Perhaps I will catch her off guard and glimpse the underside of freedom which is quite possibly not as dazzling as it seems from weary middle age. Perhaps I should look at her clinically, close up, before I do anything irrevocable.

14

David always left the house early, savoring the quiet green walk through the coconut trees before facing the shadeless heat of the road and the madness of the buses. He was startled one morning by the sudden appearance of Yashoda. Was she returning from a walk or had she been waiting for him? It was weeks since they had seen her.

"Professor David," she said softly, looking up at him through the folds of the sari that she had pulled across her face like a veil. "Will you permit me to speak with you a few minutes?"

Her sari was plain white, of fine cotton. She was without jewelry. There was nothing to detract from the exquisite perfection of her unadorned face.

"Please!" she begged, her dark eyes hugely dramatic above the white veil. "I have only you who can help me."

Oh lady, he breathed silently. Don't hand me so much power. I don't know what to do with it.

"What has happened?"

"As you see...they have taken all my silk saris and my jewels. Except for some that I keep hidden in a chest beneath the floor of my house. Always, since they sent me to Palghat, I have hidden gold in several places so that I can buy my freedom. Now circumstances are not looking auspicious again. I think they are knowing about my visit to the market, although nothing can be proved. But there is such harshness, and I am to go nowhere, nowhere. Professor David, I am going mad with boredom and loneliness."

She moved closer, like a supplicant, and instinctively he reached to comfort, a hand on her shoulder, the other lightly brushing her satiny cheek. A momentary gesture.

"What can I do?" he asked.

She clasped his hand. "You have such power, such authority with Shivaraman Nair. Could you not be my protector, my guardian, *now*, as you were suggesting it could be in your country? Could you not take me into the family? I could be – how do you call it? – the nanny for the children. I could go everywhere with you. I could be free. Oh, there would be a little scandal, but I would not care. There is nothing he could do to you."

David knew then how the hapless fly feels, cradled in the sticky caress of the web, embroiled in a net from which there would never be any escape.

"Yashoda," he said. Gently, firmly, professorially. With conviction and with cowardice, with integrity and with panic. "I am a guest of Shivaraman Nair. I am a scholar of this culture, someone who tries to be sensitive to it, to understand why its rules are different from ours. I cannot…it would be grossly improper for me to violate those rules."

"They are not *my* rules," she said tearfully.

"I know," he sighed. "But they are Shivaraman Nair's."

"Even my father disagrees with him."

"And it must be your father who helps you. I am an outsider. I cannot, I simply cannot abuse my host's – "

"Oh Professor David, you have lied to me Only you have sufficient power You said you would help me "

"I will, I will. Please don't look at me like that I will speak to Shivaraman Nair I will write to your father today "

"But this will be taking so long before anything changes, Professor David. And perhaps they will send me to Palghat again and I will have to do the work of a village widow Out in the courtyards, the sun will turn my skin to leather and my hands to chaff and I will become old and ugly."

"That would not be possible, Yashoda. You are the most exquisite…the most beautiful—"

"But it *is* true, it *is* true!" she insisted. "Have you not seen the women who sit in Shivaraman Nair's courtyard? The ones without color in their saris, with faces brown and cracked as dead palm leaves? Haven't you seen them?"

"Yes, I've seen them. But Yashoda, they are old women."

"Yes," she said bitterly. "Truly they are old women. They are Nair widows. One of them is twenty-six years old, and one is thirty, and the others are not yet forty. But I am young, young…!" She began to beat on his chest with her hands, drumming her way out of prison. "I want…before I shrivel up and become old…I want…I have never had…since my husband died…." Her energy petered out in a whimper and she whispered: "I want love, Professor David."

Oh no, he thought. Oh no. Don't complicate my life in this way. I have no skill at all in handling complications of this sort.

"Of course," he said awkwardly, holding her two hands between his, calming her. "It is understandable. You are missing your husband…."

"Our parents chose for us, Professor David. We did not meet before the betrothal. He was a shy man, not handsome."

Yakshi indeed, he thought, striving to stay free of her spell. Bewitching. Oh I could take you so easily for all the wrong reasons. Your vulnerability and mine. He knew now that it was within him, the capacity for heedless impulse. Because of Susan, he knew that he did not always know what he might do. It terrified him.

"I will write to your father, Yashoda. It is all I can do."

He leaned down and kissed her gently, chastely, on the forehead. When he turned to watch her drift away towards the paddy, he saw Juliet, obscured and dappled through overhanging palm branches, battling with the laundry on the roof of the house.

Did she see us? he wondered uneasily.

15

Is it solitude itself that causes strange fears? Juliet wondered. Or only the sense of lost powers? This nervousness I feel, this premonition of misfortune at the sight of Yashoda battering David's heart with her fists, is it simply the primitive fear of being eclipsed? Or is it a more violent sympathy for Yashoda? Is it our intimate and kindred knowledge of cages, of the trapped bird beating its futile wings?

She seemed to see a confusion of blood and brilliantly mangled feathers, an inevitable wounding, a bird of paradise plummeting endlessly past the stares of small Canadian towns and Indian villages alike. Flamboyance will not be tolerated, the impassive watchers said. We do not permit changes.

"It's always been done this way, dear," the woman on the telephone said to Juliet. There was only the gentlest hint of frost in her voice. "I don't think it would be very nice for a new young faculty wife to upset tradition, do you?"

Nice! Juliet thought with dismay. I have never wanted to be nice.

"It's the great occasion of the year," the woman continued. "When the alumnae return and the board of trustees gathers, we have tea and sandwiches in Winston Hall. And the young faculty wives have *always* poured tea. It's a great honor."

"Yes, I'm sure it is. I can fully appreciate…." Juliet struggled to be politely regretful. "It's just that there must be many others to whom it would mean more…. And I'm terribly busy, teaching part-time you see, and working on a book."

"A book! Oh my dear, how sweet. Such clever young wives we get these days. A children's story for the little one on the way?"

"No, actually it's a history of political campaign strategies I began when I was – "

"But you *must* take a rest, dear. All work and no play…. Now we're assembling in the lounge of Winston Hall at three and I've got you on the first shift. And one more thing, it's traditional to wear white gloves for the occasion. The silverware, you know."

"I regret that I must decline."

"My dear, it simply isn't done, to decline."

And at three o'clock, gloveless, Juliet held a baroquely silver teapot as though it were a weapon, pouring tea into Royal Albert cups and thinking scalding thoughts. She was wearing a black turtleneck sweater, a black velvet mini-skirt – the year was late in the sixties, a decade which had left Winston untouched – and black mesh stockings.

"After all," she had told David furiously, "it's a wake, isn't it? The end of my life as a normal intelligent woman!"

Among the pastel silks and gloved hands and coiffed hairdos, she looked like a witch's foundling. She tossed the long blonde mane of her hair like an unbroken colt who will never consent to be bridled.

"Oh my dear!" The telephone voice, stricken, materialized at Juliet's side and Juliet turned to offer combat with flashing eyes. She knew what the woman would look like, had already pictured her when they spoke on the phone – silver-blue hair lacquered into place, figure corseted in rectitude, vapid bourgeois eyes – but in fact she was frail and bird-like, vibrant; and aghast as a robin who has found her nest wantonly smashed.

Juliet thought of grandmothers and of gentle souls who mourn for the past.

Immediately contrite, she thought: I am just as judgmental and insensitive, just as dogmatic. What right do I have…?

"I am Mrs. MacDougall," the woman said, extending her hand in mournful reproof, "and I do reproach myself for not explaining adequately the formality of the…you poor child, you must be dying of embarrassment."

"No, oh no, not at all," Juliet said hastily. She set the teapot down and took Mrs. MacDougall's soft-gloved hand in her own. "It's entirely my fault. I'm sorry, truly I am. I didn't even stop to think you might be hurt. I just thought it better to establish that I'm not the tea-pouring type. I'm only a faculty wife by a kind of accident. I mean I don't think of myself that way at all."

Mrs. MacDougall put a slightly trembling hand to the cameo brooch at her throat. "There are some of us," she said softly, "who made brief brave stands a few centuries ago when we were young. And had to spend our lives learning to take defeat gracefully. My dear – Juliet, isn't it? – I believe I will like you, but I fear for you. I hope Winston will not be too unkind."

It seemed a quaint warning and Juliet never gave it a second thought. But there were many guests at the alumnae reunion who were less inclined to make allowances, and though Juliet was indifferent to their disapproval she was to learn, over the years, that a small town has subtle and sometimes vicious ways of not forgiving deviations from the norm.

Juliet imagined the Nair women pouring tea under the savage sun. I'm afraid, she thought she heard them murmuring to one another, that Yashoda is not being very nice about the proprieties. I'm afraid she is not fitting in.

She wanted to seize Yashoda and warn her: Don't fight. It's useless. You'll destroy yourself and I can't bear to watch.

"Mommy! You're hurting me!" Miranda's voice was full of alarm.

112

Juliet blinked, surfacing as from sleep. "Where are we?"

"Near the market, I think. It's hard to see." Jonathan, solicitous, touched her face. "Is your forehead all right?"

"My forehead?" She felt the swelling with her fingers and a spreading bruise gave back soft bleats of pain. "Jonathan, what happened?"

"You bumped it when the taxi stopped. Will they let us through, Mommy?"

Let us through?

She tried to focus, dazed, and saw that the taxi was stranded in a sea of demonstrators, red banners tossing above their heads, hundreds of faces pressed up against their frail lives like threats.

Dear God, she prayed urgently, cradling the children to herself, feeling the prickle of excitement and of fear.

"What do they want?" she asked the driver in Malayalam.

He turned, uneasy, and said something she did not understand. It was, she supposed, meant to be reassuring, but she watched helplessly, caught in the slow awful sway of a nightmare, while he opened his door and got out and abandoned them to the crowd. Can this possibly be happening, she wondered, or am I still hallucinating?

Faces clustered at the open door and she stared back at them, impassive, paralyzed.

She stared into a face she remembered – from where? From an almost forgotten accident by the egg man's stall – and said to it, as though repeating a catechism: "My children are beautiful as nutmeg plants, but the sweet sandalwood must also burn."

She might have struck the young man with a whip. He leaped onto the running board of the old car, grabbed a megaphone from another marcher, barked orders at the crowd which fell back like a tide receding. He threw himself behind the wheel and drove until the red banners were far behind them, until there was only the normal tumult of bullock drivers and thousands of pedestrians and buses and auto-ricks and cows.

Beside the canal that meandered from the market down to the temple, he stopped and turned to face his passengers.

"Thank you," Juliet said simply. "Oh thank you. Without you I wonder what might have...would anything bad have happened?"

"Who can say?"

He was watching her as though she were a map he was learning to read. "You remembered me," he said. "You remembered my words."

It seemed to astonish him, to suggest to him a hitherto inconceivable connection between them.

"One remembers insults," she said evenly. "And moments of danger."

Instantly she regretted it, seeing his lips tighten.

"This is not a good time for you to be in Kerala." He was harsh, flinging advice her way as he might throw crusts to a starving dog. "The clashes in Delhi – Mrs. Gandhi, Desai. And many of us are wanting neither. Go back where you are coming from, rich lady. To where no one is crying for food. I am being too busy finding rice for my family to keep on saving yours."

"You don't even know who we are," she cried, stung. "You don't know anything about us."

But he was gone.

In the oven of the driverless car they felt sick with heat and foreignness and dangers too closely brushed. The canal water and the mango trees beckoned.

By the rivers of Babylon we sat down and wept.... The psalm came to Juliet suddenly from childhood, an echo of a devout grandmother's recipe for solace. "The Psalms have never failed me, Juliet. An answer for every human sorrow." And there was further comfort in the warm muddy water of the canal as it bathed their ankles. *But how shall we sing in a strange land?*

"What will we do?" Jonathan asked.

"We'll sit here and rest. And think what to do."

And think what to do. We need help, we need com . need a friend.

But whom did she know in this city? She knew the egg man and the vegetable man and the woman who sold limes. There were a few dozen words she could exchange with them. She knew her landlord and his family with whom formalities must be kept. She knew a young widow who was forbidden to spend time with them, and an angry young man who appeared and disappeared in market-place commotions. And once at the beach she had met a courteous gentleman...yes, who had later sent a *peon* with a message to the Nair estate. They had been out when he came but had found the note.

With the energy of fresh optimism she rummaged in her canvas bag. Somewhere, somewhere, forgotten till now.... There it was, an address and a phone number. But how would she call in a city of no public telephones? A city where only a handful of wealthy landowners and merchants were fortunate enough.... "Mr. Motilal's emporium!" she exclaimed. "He cannot refuse me."

And indeed Mr. Motilal, purveyor of antiques, graciously consented.

And Mr. Matthew Thomas, friend of wanderers, caused difficulties to vanish like morning mists. "You must be staying right there in Mr. Motilal's emporium where there is air-conditioning, isn't it? And I am coming very swiftly. Most immediately."

It was not, of course, so very immediate. But eventually he picked them up in his car and took them to the Simla Coffee House, an unsuspected island of serenity behind the Secretariat.

"I am very grateful," Juliet said as the children sighed happily over mango-flavored ice-cream. "We were so shaken up. Is it really dangerous? Would the students attack us?"

"Huh!" With a wave of his hand, dismissing flies. "Kerala is always like this. It is nothing. Empty noise."

ng? No danger at all?"

evident.

, he thought of his daughter Kumari bewil-
nowstorms and the deadly unimaginable speeds
es on highways.

e said, "I'm so glad we met!" Impulsively she clasped
his hands and after a moment of shock at the impropriety,
after a nervous glance around him to see if they were observed,
he patted her arm in a fatherly way, willing solace upon his
distant daughter.

Wistfully he asked: "Will there be someone for Kumari...?
Someone to explain?"

Who can say? she thought, echoing the gruff young man
who had saved and then abandoned them. Who could say? All
over the world there were cruelties and thoughtlessness. And
also instinctive acts of kindness.

"Oh I hope...." She saw the plea in his eyes, the way he willed
her to promise happiness for his daughter. "I think...oh yes,
surely there will be someone like you for Kumari."

She had not realized what power she had to confer blessing.

16

Over the mosquito coils and oil lamps and the fug of curry and coconut oil, Juliet caught David's eye.

"I met two fascinating men today. Actually I had met each of them once before."

"Did we have to have fish *again?*" Jonathan whined.

"No. We could have had chicken but after today's little adventure I couldn't face playing daisy-chains with intestines."

"It's marvellous the way you attract men," David said. "No matter where in the world you are. They materialize like churchgoers at Easter and Christmas."

"Couldn't we have some really profane imagery once in a while? How about: 'Like mongrels around a bitch in heat'? Or at least some local coloration: 'Like temple urchins around a tourist'?"

He smiled at her, delighted.

(It's that look again, she sighed inwardly, treasuring it and chafing at it The *abbé* with his statue of the Magdalene anointing Christ's feet: A genuine fallen woman reclaimed! he thinks with racy reverence

"I want hamburger," Jonathan said.

"Hamburger " Miranda picked it up, a tearful plaint, old cravings and disorientations overwhelming her

"Why can't we?" Jonathan persisted.

"I've already told you why a thousand times. Because you

can be sure that any beef the Muslim merchants sell in the market has been found dead on a roadside somewhere. Of tough old age or disease. You think any of them wants to get mobbed for killing a cow? Put some more yoghurt on your fish."

"I'm sick of yoghurt, I'm sick of fish. I want some – "

"Remember the mango ice-cream?"

"Ice-cream!" Their eyes lit up. "Can we go again tomorrow?"

"Okay, that's a promise. Now eat – "

David raised his eyebrows in surprise. "Mango ice-cream?"

"I've been trying to tell you, if everyone would let me finish."

"Ah. The men you picked up."

"My! Your slang is getting quite risqué! Actually, one of them picked *me* up, more or less literally. And I suppose, in a manner of speaking, I made a pass at the other one. I did solicit his company. And there was an exciting moment when hundreds of men mobbed me."

"Could you transpose this into a quieter and more intelligible key?"

"Doesn't it bother you, men massing around me like mosquitoes over the paddy?"

"It's never bothered me. It flatters me. Gives me a sense of having outbid the rest of the world for a rare treasure at an art auction."

"How come nothing ever rattles you? Why can't you have the decency to be nasty once in a while? Or suspicious? Or jealous?"

You know nothing, he thought, of the anxiety you have stirred up since you called out to someone in your sleep. Of how a voice I heard once on the telephone twelve years ago has begun to haunt me. Yet it was base of him to doubt her.

He said quietly: "Because you remind me of a cherub in Chartres Cathedral. Or is it Notre Dame? Anyway, there's one with a wicked glint in its eye and a faintly lecherous smile, but there it soars over the choir screen, pure as a hymn."

No, she thought. You've got it the wrong way around. I have a misleadingly innocent face but a gypsy heart and wayward feet. Yet how could she convince him? And even Jeremy claimed: *the illusion of risk, that's all you want.* Was she tamer or purer than she liked to think?

"Funny you should mention hymns. I thought of the Psalms today. Our lives were in danger, you know. We could have been killed."

His eyes flicked towards her, wide with alarm, but wary, knowing her capacity for extravagance.

And immediately she regretted her instinct for melodrama, seeing an unnecessary fear somersault through the children's thoughts.

"I'm just joking. We had an adventure. Hundreds of men stopped our taxi to wave at us and we felt like royalty in a carriage, didn't we?"

"I didn't like them," Miranda said. "I was frightened."

"Well, even the Queen probably doesn't like it too much, you know. It's part of the job. And then fortunately one of the men said, 'Okay, gentlemen, thank you very much. They would like to leave now.' And he drove us to the canal. And then the other man, who was the Matthew Thomas I told you about, that man I met at the beach, he came and picked us up in his car and took us to the Simla Coffee House and bought us mango ice-cream. And we had a wonderful day, right?"

Oh yes, the children agreed. The mango ice-cream was wonderful. And could they really go again tomorrow?

"Would you mind," David said somberly, when the children were in bed, "telling me what really happened?"

"Just what I said. It was a Marxist demonstration, that's all. But not in the least dangerous. I have Matthew Thomas's word for it. The three splinter groups are constantly demonstrating against each other. They go on all the time. Quite harmless."

"That's probably true," he said slowly, pondering it. "The

119

really interesting thing is the way the caste structure has penetrated even the Maoist group. I've been analyzing some of their leaflets for Hindu symbolism and what's amazing – "

"Oh David, David!" She wound herself around his body, teasing him. "I'm sure you're going to tell me every tedious detail."

He grinned sheepishly.

"And are you going to tell me you weren't scared? With a mob surrounding you?"

"Of course I wasn't scared."

"The Psalms just came to you naturally, as part of the general exuberance of the occasion."

"Well. I may have been nervous for a few minutes, before I grasped the situation. But only on account of the children."

"You're such a magnificent liar," he said, kissing her.

17

In the scant shade of a banana palm which hung over the granary wall, Juliet sat cross-legged, watching the children, watching the threshing, fanning herself with Annie's postcard.

Slender Harijan women, delicately balancing vast bundles of fresh-cut rice on their heads, filed in from the paddy and dumped their loads onto the shiny earth of the granary – really a large courtyard with walls of sun-dried mud.

The women formed two lines facing one another across the spreading mountain of hay as though they were taking up positions for a minuet. The members of one line lifted their six-foot paddles high above and behind their heads in unison and crashed them down on the cut stalks. As they raised them again, the flails of the other line descended. Thwack-thwack-pause. Thwack-thwack-pause. Juliet found herself silently composing chants to the rhythm. Mon-soon time, mon-soon time. Tri-van-drum, Tri-van-drum. My *mantra*, she thought. I will drift helplessly into a transcendental stupor.

Contemplating the strong young bodies of the threshers, she thought: Blessed are those who are poor in Kerala. For their bodies are aesthetically superior to those of the overfed rich and they give great pleasure to the beholder.

She wandered out into the paddy where elderly women moved through the sucking mud with little hand sickles, painstakingly cutting stalk by stalk. Poverty and age had shriveled them; they were gaunt, their faces weathered as the rocks at Cape Comorin.

The threshers wore close-fitting midriff blouses with their brightly batiked *lungis*, but the reapers were bare-breasted, old enough to have been raised in the days when it was improper for low-caste women to wear an upper garment. Their trailing earlobes, once punctured by heavy dowry jewelry long since sold for food, swung to and fro like slack ropes.

Shivaraman Nair appeared suddenly from the granary gates, businesslike in his white shirt and *dhoti*, stark and aloof as a god among his gaudy underlings.

"Good morning, Mrs. David Juliet!" he thundered in boisterous good spirits. "Are you enjoying watching my rice harvest?"

"Very much," she replied, saluting him with hands together and inclined head. "The paddy is so beautiful with its ring of tall trees – like a green jewel that someone has dropped down between the coconut palms."

It was simplest to be slightly excessive in conversation with Shivaraman Nair.

"Yes, yes! Correct, correct!" he said, delighted. "That is exactly what my paddy is being. You are putting it very correctly, Mrs. David Juliet. You are appreciating Indian beauty. Oh, I am *so* wishing that you could see the movie which was made on my estate. All this paddy and my house – my house that you are living in – are looking so beautiful in the film. It is in color. Very excellently made. All over India they are showing this film, in Hindi cinemas and Tamil cinemas, with translation. Everyone is seeing my estates and loving. In this paddy the lovers are meeting and they are going over there into the little forest. But their love is forbidden and the family is punishing the girl. Then the young man kills himself from sorrow. Very beautiful. So sad and tragic."

"Is the movie based on a true story? Was there a tragic love affair here on your estates?"

He was taken off guard.

"No, no! You are not understanding, Mrs. David Juliet. Sadness is in poetry. Art is being tragic, only art. Life itself is not sad. These things are not happening in real life because the parents are choosing wisely. That is why our marriages in India are always very good. We are not having divorce in India. In the West your marriages are very bad because young people are choosing for themselves, isn't it? This is very foolish proceeding, very foolish. Young people cannot make such deep decisions wisely. It is very terrible, these thousands of divorces in the West. I am reading in the newspapers. Our way is much better. It can be seen in the marriages."

"Perhaps you are right," she said politely.

If she were to ask him: But are Indian marriages happier? they would not be any closer to understanding one another. They would disagree so totally on the interpretation of happiness and on whether it was in any way germane to marriage. He might well ask her: Do marriages in the West allow husband and wife to fulfill their *dharma* correctly?

"I hope that when your children are marrying, Mrs. David Juliet, you will be remembering the better ways you have learned in India, and you and Professor David will choose for your children."

"I hope that when my children are grown and considering marriage, Mr. Shivaraman Nair, they will remember what they know of families in India and in our own country. I hope this will help them to choose wisely for themselves."

"*Ayyo, ayyo!*" he said wonderingly, shaking his head and gesturing with his hands to indicate despair and amusement. "How would a father buy a husband for such a woman? How is Professor David living with this arguing? Such lack of respect for authority would have to be sweetened with a very large dowry, Mrs. David Juliet."

"But surely," she said demurely, "with your beautiful house as the bridal gift there would be no problem. Your son-in-law would be happy to marry a *yakshi* if he could live with her in that house."

"Yes, yes," he said delighted. "Very true, very true, Mrs. David Juliet! Again you are putting things very correctly!"

He clapped his hands with pleasure like a child who has watched the balloon man at the fair release all his strings at once.

"Now I must speak to these Harijan peoples," he said abruptly, having suddenly remembered that he was a prince of the land who had come to the paddy on business.

"I have heard that all the rain is affecting the harvest. Is this true?"

"Yes, yes. It is very bad, very bad. It is not natural between monsoons, all this rain. But when *dharma* is not followed, everyone is suffering. Truth is broken. Nothing is keeping in correct bounds, people or monsoons."

She was taken aback by the sudden darkness of his mood. And bewildered.

"How has *dharma* been broken?"

He did not answer but looked with hostility across at the forest beyond the paddy.

He means Yashoda, she realized uneasily. He must know about the market escapade. Did he see her with David the other morning? How long had they talked?

Shivaraman Nair clapped his hands sharply and called an order to one of his superintendents. The man in turn clapped his hands and relayed the order to the workers in the field, who began to assemble before the neatly stacked piles of cut rice on the levee.

The sun was high in the sky now, too savage for working under. Daily wages were to be meted out. Each worker received a small bundle of rice to carry home to her mud hut where she would thresh it and winnow it and cook it for her family. Obviously, Juliet thought, there is scant insurance against tomorrow's hunger.

Although the workers and Shivaraman Nair were within hearing distance of each other, all queries were addressed to the superintendent who relayed the messages back to Shivaraman Nair. There was something comical about it, and it was silly and inefficient, a throwback, perhaps unconscious, to the days when Untouchables could be cut down with a naked sword for coming within ninety-six paces of a Brahmin or forty paces of a Nair.

Shivaraman Nair was unaware of Juliet now, intent on dispensing wages and decisions which he doubtless felt to be just and equitable.

She made her way carefully along the serpentine levees towards the forest beyond the paddy.

18

The forest was different. Juliet stepped outside of time altogether, even out of Indian time which drowsed along slipshod and haphazard from dawn to sunset. The forest was dank and dark and secret. The sun itself, that blatant strutting tyrant of the paddy, could only peep through its chinks like a voyeur.

Of course this was where the lovers of Shivaraman Nair's movie would come, thought Juliet. Of course it was where all lovers would come. It was where Radha would wait for Krishna, perfumed and ornamented, pining on her bed of springy pond reeds, her kohl-lined eyes darting along the path, the little bells on the slender golden chain about her waist tinkling impatiently.

Juliet breathed in the damp pungent smell of vines and fungi, the fragrance of bushes which still flowered in bright splashes where the sun fingered them through gaps in the treetops. In front of her feet the decaying ground cover suddenly heaved and rustled. She froze and watched the undulation glide away under the trees. Snake!

She rallied herself: Yashoda walks here every day. She licked her dry lips and walked on again. At first she thought it must be her imagination but then she was sure she could hear laughter and splashing and now and then a few notes of a flute. She reached the edge of the clearing and stood hidden behind a screen of ferns, feeling like an intruder.

The house was small with large thatched eaves that kept it in shadow. It was of hand-made sun-dried brick, thickly white-washed, humble and traditional, not like the newer more splendid houses on the estate. It was in fact one of the original houses of the old Nair *tarawad*, that social and political unit of the extended family which, like the estate itself, had been broken up considerably over the last fifty years.

Beside the house was the obligatory well and beside that a small pond, or lake, actually the original family tank used for ritual bathing before *puja*. Yashoda was swimming in it, or playing, only her head and shoulders visible, and Prabhakaran was standing at the edge doing little frolicking dance steps, intermittently playing a few bars on his flute, but interrupting himself with peals of laughter. He seemed to be teasing her, chanting something, advancing to the water's edge, fluting, laughing, retreating. Every time he advanced, Yashoda would slap the surface of the water hard with both hands and splash him. She was laughing and scolding.

Juliet watched with amazement. She was certain that it was highly irregular for a Nair lady to flirt and play with a servant boy in this way. She could not translate what they were calling out to each other because they were speaking so rapidly in the shrieking high-pitched rhythms of excitement and merriment.

Then Yashoda lifted both arms high in order to splash Prabhakaran and Juliet's eyes widened as she saw Yashoda's breasts rise out of the water.

It was only for a moment.

Now the water lapped her shoulders again and her black hair floated around her like a dark lily pad.

Juliet looked about, puzzled, and finally saw the sari fluttering like a streamer from high in a mango tree.

He has stolen her clothes, she realized. Prabhakaran has climbed the tree and put her sari out of reach. That is what the teasing and scolding is about.

Juliet had often seen women bathing in India, at public wells, in village streams, in temple tanks, in the ocean. They always did so fully clothed, their wet saris wrapping their bodies like an extra skin. Yashoda must surely have come to take for granted the isolation of her daily existence. Yet she did not seem to be offended by Prabhakaran's presence. In fact she was clearly enjoying herself, flirtatious and excited as a schoolgirl.

Of course, Juliet reminded herself, Prabhakaran has seen *me* naked, and I was the only one disconcerted. Perhaps it meant nothing to Yashoda because he was just a servant. Or just a child. Perhaps for someone young and beautiful and sensual and condemned to widowhood, it was a safe sexual outlet.

She remembered their meeting on the path outside her house, one early morning when Prabhakaran had offered milk. There was certainly some bond of affection between them, that of an abandoned child and a young woman yearning for motherhood perhaps, or simply the kinship of two lost and lonely children. If society had already tossed Yashoda carelessly outside its barriers, perhaps the codes of class and caste no longer had any hold over her. A friend was a friend.

It seemed to Juliet, watching them, that they were two children, pure and undefiled, playing harmless games in a paradisal garden. She turned silently, like a guilty voyeur from a sacred scene, and made her way back through the forest, watching for snakes.

And with the dark swiftness of a snake the air ahead of her moved. Took shape, erect and swaying like a cobra. She felt the dizzying reverse jerk of her blood against the body's momentum.

But it was Shivaraman Nair, equally startled, entering from the paddy. Looming with threat. She slid into a different fear, an anxiety to protect.

"You frightened me! I thought you were a snake," she said, laughing a little, breathless.

He seemed more disoriented than she was. His eyes had not adjusted, she was still part of the shadows. And with the sun behind him like an excessively bright halo, he seemed to her simply a black portent, unreadable.

He recovered himself at last. "You have been visiting my kinswoman."

"Yes." She had to stall him. Lure him into conversation. "It is difficult for us...for me...for a western woman...to understand why.... It seems to us very unfair, this isolation."

He did not answer but nor did he make any attempt to continue on his way. He seemed as reluctant to move as she was. The long pause made her nervous.

"Your customs are so...puzzling to us. For example, this practice of confining young widows...." If he could just be tempted into lengthy explanation and defense.

But he was abrupt, irritated. "You are married, Mrs. David Juliet. You are also a mother, yes, you are being a good mother. Even though you are having wrong habits of lacking in respect for men, you are a virtuous woman. Yes, yes, that is my opinion. Therefore you are not understanding the ways of such a woman as my kinswoman."

"What do you mean?"

"A woman like that, so soon after the death of her husband, to show no respect. There is no goodness in her. Who can tell what such a one will do? You are not understanding that sort of woman, Mrs. David Juliet. Their thoughts wander after men, straying in all directions like the roots of the banyan tree. This rottenness will spread, everything will suffer."

How unjust, she raged, shaking with suppressed anger. How primitively male! And yet, and yet, scandal will inevitably cling to Yashoda. She is too beautiful for her own safety. David is mesmerized. Even I am under her spell. Even Shivaraman Nair?

And he would stride on towards the pond, his crass suspicions glibly confirmed. "Have you come to take her away again?" she asked, playing for time.

"No, no! No, no!" His vehemence bewildered her. "You are

quite wrong, Mrs. David Juliet. I was not visiting my kins-woman. Not at all. I am inspecting the timber of my forest."

"Oh."

Why such energy of denial?

A disturbing thought presented itself, but she brushed it aside as improbable. Surely it was only her febrile imagination.

He scared her then by a sudden roar of anger. She could not think what she had done, but she was not the object of his wrath. Her delaying tactic had been overly successful. Prab-hakaran was behind her on the path, snap-frozen, suspended in flight like a statue of winged Mercury.

Shivaraman Nair spoke volubly, raging as white water, spitting and foaming and unintelligible in Malayalam. Prab-hakaran trembled visibly, a dark blush spread across his face and seemed to cover his bare torso like a rash. Shivaraman Nair reached the climax of his crescendo of fury, clapped his hands sharply, and Prabhakaran came to life again, fleeing.

"Who can tell what that woman will do!" stormed Shiva-raman Nair. "Everything is breaking its bounds! With a *peon*! A *peon*! That boy is no good, Mrs. David Juliet. He is lazy. There must be more work for him. There must be no more taxis. He is a *peon*. Please be remembering!"

He turned and strode back towards the paddy, smashing ferns with his feet.

Barbarian! she fumed silently.

∽

When Prabhakaran came with the evening milk she took him aside.

"Has there been trouble for you? What did Shivaraman Nair say to you?"

The blush spread over his body again and he trembled. He would not speak.

"Did he say you were lazy?"

He nodded.

130

"That is not true, Prabhakaran. You are a hard worker, a good worker. To us it seems that you work much too hard. Is that all he said?"

He shook his head.

"What else?"

Silence.

"I cannot tell you," he said at last, miserably, tearful.

He is a child, a child, she thought with anguish. And he has been accused of adult misbehavior. He may not even understand. He has no one to talk to, no parent to offer refuge. She put her arm around his shoulders.

"Would you like to stay here tonight?"

"*Venda, venda,*" he replied nervously, backing away. Adult. Distanced. With responsibilities of his own. "I must stay near the cows."

Jonathan and Miranda were calling from the bedroom: Story time! Story time!

"Stay and hear a story before you go then."

And he smiled and became a child again, joining the huddled circle on Jonathan's bed, waiting for Jonathan's translations and subtitles, eyes widening at the adventures of those children who found a magic door in the back of a closet and slipped through it into a secret and fabulous world.

19

Time smoked around Juliet like the vapors that followed the rains. What day of the week was it? What month of the year? Only the hours had their seasons and identities: the dawn of Prabhakaran's arrival with milk; the morning's agony of scrubbing with swollen knuckles; the recess of lime drinks and lowing cows; the school work; the long slow dance with paddy rice and coconuts to prepare the evening meal; the coolness of the grove at dusk; story time; the damp sleep of exhaustion.

Then begin again, begin again, begin again.

And the paths that snaked between the coconut palms radiated out to the rest of the city like tongues licking at fragments of events, before curling back in upon themselves, folding their garnered morsels into the blurred cave of Juliet's heat-stunned memory. Down some of the paths Annie was coming towards her, forever in slow motion, never getting any closer. On others, braiding themselves around the market, the abrasive young student led chanting cohorts. Somewhere Mr. Matthew Thomas beckoned graciously, promising coolness and safety. And always Yashoda flitted back and forth between the trees like a woman on an ivory swing – translucent, a trick of the light, an artist's fantasy.

Was it real, that flash of silk under the areca fronds? There! Over there! Now darting, kingfisher blue, beside the paddy.

Or was it part of the dream? Of the soft-edged mirage of time passing?

The cows were real, that was certain. She had clothing with chewed-up sleeves to prove it. (There was always too much laundry for the coir rope on the roof, always something that had to be draped on the trees in the courtyard.) And Prabhakaran was real because the milk came each morning.

He had told her a strange story which was surely part of her dream. Though he had been insistent and voluble. Yashoda, he said, had asked him to bring her astrologer secretly to the house beyond the forest. Much money had been given and a horoscope had been cast.

It was difficult for Juliet – even with the mediation and translation of Jonathan and Miranda, who could communicate with Prabhakaran in that astonishing way of children – to piece together the prediction for which gold bracelets had been tendered.

It seemed that Yashoda had asked what would happen if she appeared in public again.

In spite of opposition, the astrologer had said, her future was looking most auspicious. There was a certain conjunction of stars in her sign, indicating both the coming of love and some great upheaval over which she would no doubt triumph. A fair woman and a messenger boy were indicated. (Myself and Prabhakaran, Juliet thought instinctively. And then, shaking the heat from her brain with irritable cynicism: How transparent those astrologers are. They don't even need to be unusually observant.)

An older man was also indicated, Prabhakaran reported. All these would be figures of power. (Is she weaving a net for David? Juliet wondered wryly. Or is it Shivaraman Nair?)

There was an area of darkness, a death – here Prabhakaran had shivered and spat, but Juliet thought: It is the death of her husband; it is already in the past; oh cunning astrologer!

At the appropriate time – and this, Prabhakaran said, had

been calculated for an additional fee – Yashoda should again venture out to the public road. Although her kinsman would be angry he would be unable to harm her on that particular day because of an auspicious meeting with one of the figures of power.

(Will she waylay David in the grove again? Juliet asked herself. Or will I be the one who is expected to perform miracles?)

But it was Annie who arrived on the day designated by the astrologer, Annie who burst like a trajectory of reality into the haze of Juliet's dreamtime. Jonathan and Miranda saw her from the rooftop where they were playing.

"It's Annie!" they shrieked, pelting down the stairs. "Annie's here!"

Juliet peered through the grove. How lightly Annie moves, she thought with envy. No baggage. No encumbrances. A new breed, by the luck of birth year.

Annie, who was disgustingly exuberant, scooped up the children and bear-hugged them, swirled Juliet into a dance of excessive high spirits. "Oh, isn't this country gorgeous? I never want to leave. You must be practically delirious with happiness living in the middle of these coconut trees."

Imagine, Juliet thought, at my age, tasting the vinegar of sibling rivalry. There I am: my younger self, my road not taken. How unfairly radiant. How immoderately certain that the world is a lucky charm dangling from her wrist.

"Yes," she said sardonically. "Delirium *is* a daily hazard."

"It's so...so pristine! No western ugliness or cultural clutter or inhibitions! So...*untrammeled*!"

Juliet thought: Surely I was never quite so embarrassingly glib about everything non-western and non-middle class? "Untrammeled! Perhaps you should take your blinkers off."

Annie's eyebrows pleated themselves in bewilderment. "Is something bothering you?"

"It's just that your euphoria is based on a degree of ignorance you should be ashamed of." Juliet had a barely conscious awareness of pitching about like a kite in storm winds, but careened blindly on. "It's slightly sickening."

Annie stared. "What on earth is the matter with you?"

Embarrassed, Juliet would, at this point, have shaken off the prickly-heat of irritability if Annie had not touched a certain nerve with a sister's deadly aim.

"The Winston dowager herself! God, you're stuffy sometimes. And a middle-aged bore."

Reeling, Juliet thought: Can it be horribly true? Am I smeared with Winston as with birdlime? Will I break out in white gloves?

"Look!" she countered angrily. "Within blowing distance of your hot air, there are serfs and a widow who may as well have her feet bound. Come and be introduced to reality."

"Maybe I'll just take the train right back to the *ashram* in Pondicherry."

"Oh perfect. Do that. Go live it up with a bunch of affluent western drifters getting high on meditation and self-indulgence and sex. That's more your style, Annie. I wouldn't want to confuse you with a few harsh truths."

"God, you're a mouthy bitch! And to think all my life I've lived in your shadow. To think I've envied you. To think I've wasted years feeling a failure because of you!"

"You've what?"

"Years of Mother saying: 'When are you going to settle down like Juliet?' 'When are you going to give us grandchildren?' 'When are you going to become *responsible* like Juliet?' 'When are you going to realize that you can combine commitment with career (with a *moderate* career, placed in the right perspective!) like Juliet?' When are you going to become goddam bloody perfect like Juliet?"

"Oh Annie! I never forgive anyone who makes me cry." She threw her arms around her sister. "I *am* a mouthy bitch. I'm out of my mind with heat and isolation. Don't you realize I've been jealous of you for years?"

"That's a laugh! Of what? Of my trail of busted relationships? Of my solitary chain-smoking nights?"

"But you've always been free as a bird. You walk away with a shrug and a laugh, you can't be touched. You're unhurtable." Like Jeremy. It was *still* a secret obsession: to find a chink in his armor. Not for revenge, not to cause chaos. Just to know if he had ever once tossed at night because of her.

Annie laughed. "We learn the skills for our own survival. I've *learned* to shrug and walk away with a smile. You think I'm going to wear my heart on my sleeve? I'm a walking armadillo, not a bird, but I'll keep up a damn good flying act just the same. I do have pride, I'm a hell of an actress. And I will admit I've cultivated the art of the present moment. If you've got no future, that's all there is. Seize and enjoy is my motto."

"Mommy!" Jonathan interposed urgently. "Have you and Annie finished fighting now?"

"You see?" Juliet gestured with her hands remorsefully. "The perfect mother, traumatizing her children with verbal violence. Feel free to tell their grandmother, if it'll make you feel better." And, turning to her children: "I'm a little frayed at the edges these days. Sorry. Did I upset you?"

Jonathan's face was flushed. "Someone is coming."

It was Yashoda.

"Okay, Annie. Brace yourself for a more jaundiced view of the erotic and pristine East. This is the widow with bound feet and chastity belt."

Yashoda approached Annie as though Annie were a manifestation of Lakshmi, goddess of good fortune. After introductions, she could not restrain herself.

"Oh Annie, you have come on a special day! You are auspicious. Your power is blazing as the sun when it falls into the ocean at Cape Comorin. You are bringing my freedom!"

Annie laughed, a little embarrassed. "Oh, that's me, all right. Scattering liberation as I go."

Auspicious people, Juliet thought sourly, seem to be a dime a dozen.

"Please," Yashoda begged. "You must all come to my house now. We will have tea."

"Wonderful," Annie enthused. "And I'll regale you with tales of high adventure and forbidden love in Delhi."

"I hope you'll make allowances for my sister, Yashoda. She likes to shock. Don't be offended."

"Oh I am not offended, no, no! For me it is very exciting listening to this talking."

Yashoda is like a prisoner on day parole, Juliet thought. Every little thing gives pleasure.

On the way to Yashoda's house the children, resident experts, gave a running commentary on the house, the lotus pond, the banana clump, the rice paddy. Only when they reached the forest did they fall silent. They had not been in it before. They moved along the track single file, Yashoda leading.

As they neared the clearing the sound of the flute reached them, pure and haunting. Prabhakaran was sitting at the edge of the pond, his feet idly dangling in the water, playing to the lotuses and the tall blue lilies that swayed with every breath of wind.

"How lovely!" whispered Annie. "He looks like Pan."

Like Blake's lamb, Juliet thought. Innocence before the Fall. *Did he who made the cobra make thee?*

"Like Krishna," Yashoda said.

"Prabhakaran! Prabhakaran!" the children called, and the image dissolved in laughter and splashing and chasing.

Inside the small house, Yashoda's maidservant brought tea. Annie gazed around raptly.

"How marvelous to live alone like this in the forest! It makes me think of Thoreau and of Yeats' isle of Innisfree. You know: *And I shall have some peace there, for peace comes dropping slow....* And the small cabin and the lake water lapping. Even Yeats didn't have lotuses though."

Juliet partly listened to fragments of conversation, Yashoda's voice drifting by like a dimly heard flute.

"Our fathers chose for us. I had met him only once before marriage. But I was content because he intended to go to the London School of Economics after graduation. And I wanted very much to go to London. After marriage we had affection for each other.

"Perhaps when Professor David and Juliet are returning to Canada....

"I am very much wanting to experience love." Yashoda's voice meandered dreamily on. "When I was studying for my B.A., I have read Shakespeare. My favorite was *Romeo and Juliet*. Also I loved very much *Wuthering Heights*. That is the sort of love I would like to experience."

As she talked she was idly playing with the gold chains around her neck. Her hand moved back and forth stroking her glowing coffee-colored skin, and now, daydreaming, her fingers strayed lower so that she was lightly brushing the upper part of her breasts that swelled above the low-cut sari blouse. It was a totally unself-conscious gesture, solitary, absorbed. There was something infinitely sad and yearning about it, and Juliet and Annie watched her, mesmerized, full of pity.

"Surely there is something we can do," Annie said.

"Oh I knew you would help me, Annie. If you will protect me, it is possible. Shivaraman Nair can do nothing to you. I do not want to be locked up! I love the noise of the market! I want to go there with you!"

"But Yashoda," Juliet said nervously. "Shouldn't we plan something more discreet? It would be very discourteous of us to offend Shivaraman Nair publicly – "

"Oh Juliet, for heaven's sake! Politeness can be just another form of cowardice. In fact, I see no reason why you and I shouldn't go on a trip together, Yashoda. Cape Comorin, why not?"

Yashoda clapped her hands with delight. But then, abruptly, she was frightened by this heady leap from daydream into possibility. The ebb and flow of her courage was tied to a perception of protective magic. "Ah, I cannot! Only *today* is auspicious. We must go today, or they will send me to Palghat."

Annie raised one eyebrow. "Yashoda, I have been on trains and buses all day. I'm exhausted. We'll be just as safe in a few days' time. There's nothing they can do to us."

Annie was so certain, so confident, so invulnerable. What harm could possibly penetrate her aura of safety? Yashoda remembered her astrologer's words: *A fair woman, a figure of power.* She took courage. She felt exhilarated.

"Oh Annie, Annie, thank you. This was a truly auspicious meeting."

Juliet was silent. She was full of awe for Yashoda's brave, if somewhat reckless, defiance of centuries of custom. And Annie's response was no different from her own initial reactions. But she felt washed by a vague sense of dread, a foreboding. The dark hostility of Shivaraman Nair had gradually been seeping deeper into her consciousness, spreading like a contusion. *When dharma is broken, everyone is suffering.*

In her mind's eye she saw it again: the bird of paradise mangled on the floor of its cage. Ridiculous, she told herself crossly.

Still, still, persisted the gnawing sense of unease in her gut, it is not that one believes in the custom itself. One is however aware of the power of the society that believes.

But Annie and Yashoda were talking animatedly, trading confidences and intimacies like old friends. Dinesh, the movie playboy in Delhi, was already married apparently, with a wife and children safely tucked into some Punjabi village, but was nevertheless so very available and dashing. Yashoda was listening wide-eyed.

Juliet watched them as from a great distance.

She felt very old, freighted with the knowledge of loss and the awareness of evil and the possibility of harm.

20

Juliet observed David's startled reaction that evening.

It must have been a shock, she could concede to herself, to come home at dusk and find without warning the three women, animated, like a corona around the oil lamp. And who could blame him for staring at Yashoda, as though at Galatea taking on flesh, perhaps, and then averting his eyes nervously and guiltily and refusing to look at her again?

She could not blame him. There was that other factor too – she understood it, she empathized. On which side of the line between dream and reality were they at any given moment? In the way he hugged Annie, in the way he held his children, in the way he put his hand tentatively against a wall and pressed it until his knuckles turned white – testing the solidity of things – in the way he kept not looking at Yashoda – as if saying: Is she really here this time? or in my mind? – she recognized an abiding malaise that she shared with him.

They were in the lotus land, the land of *sunyasin* and meditation, where old men lay on beds of nails; and ropes, so people said, uncoiled themselves upwards into air; where no one could keep track of what was temporal and what was eternal; where things which existed in the mind had more substance than the blurred mirage of the external world.

We drift in a waking sleep, Juliet thought.

That night, under the sluggish fan, David took Juliet with a wildness that was disturbing, almost frightening.

"I love you," he murmured. Convincing himself. Reciting a protective charm. Whispering a *mantra.*

When they made love it was as though they were trying to hold a lost civilization between their damp slippery bodies.

Afterwards she asked him: "Will Annie really carry out that mad scheme, do you think? Taking Yashoda with her on a trip? And should we assent?"

The questions seemed to anchor him for a moment in reality.

"Ahh," he said awkwardly. "They did discuss that, didn't they? I was only half following.... I missed the gist of things."

"Should we allow it?"

He looked at her blankly, and then rubbed his eyes, trying to summon misplaced critical faculties. He asked uncertainly: "Is it our concern?" Oh but it was, he knew. It was so much and so intensely and so primitively his concern that he was unable to say a word. Yashoda drifted through his mind like a *yakshi* on a swing, back and forth, mesmeric, a hypnotist's trick.

"We should discuss it in the morning," Juliet offered. "When we're not so drowsy."

But each morning put on its own fresh vagueness. Only Annie, when she moved, carried the faint echo of energy and decisiveness with her. Her denim jeans smelled faintly of cities and subways, her eyes were unclouded, not bothered as yet by monsoonal fogs. There were moments when she could even, briefly, jolt David and Juliet into debate and disagreement. And then she would skewer them on the rapier of her western certainties: Your judgment is impaired by heat and isolation. You are not being objective.

And perhaps she was right.

⌁

Annie and Yashoda went to Cape Comorin for a few days. They hiked through the back of the estate to the Kottayam Road so no one would see them leave. But it was inevitable that Yashoda's absence would be noted. It was only a matter of time.

I think this is a major mistake, David told himself. The sort of thing that makes the world accuse us of cultural arrogance. But if I had made a serious effort to prevent their going, Yashoda might have misinterpreted me, might have thought I'd changed my mind and wanted.... On the other hand she might have felt persecuted, all avenues of escape blocked.

In his heart of hearts he pondered a different, more elemental question. Why did she turn so quickly to someone else? He felt bereft. Jealous. And therefore distrusted all his motives and had done nothing.

And Juliet thought: Of course, Annie is right to pitch in on the rebel side. Women of the world unite, etcetera. I'm afraid of complications myself, and yet I'm glad of someone else's brash confidence. But she could not escape the conviction: We ought not to be interfering. We are on quicksand. Besides, it is selfish of Annie to flit off so carelessly when I need some time to myself, someone to help with the work and the children.

Her mind wandered to David's impending temple visit. The long awaited permission had come through, the temple astrologers had calculated the auspicious day and hour. It was to be a momentous occasion, a rare privilege, since the State of Kerala strictly prohibited non-Hindus from entering its shrines.

"Shivaraman Nair is coming," Jonathan called from the roof.

"I feel so improper with a belt around my *dhoti*," David said nervously. "Even if it can't be seen."

Juliet was busy with camera and light meter, taking readings in the doorway as Shivaraman Nair reached the house.

"*Namaskaram*," she said.

"*Namaskaram, namaskaram*. Mrs. David Juliet, *you* are not going to the temple. Absolutely not possible. It is only Professor David I am taking."

142

"I understand." She fumed silently: Your views on women have already been made quite explicit. "I only want to take a photograph of you and my husband in your *dhotis* before you leave."

"Very good, very good," he boomed, delighted. "Yes, yes, it is auspicious day, auspicious visit. There must be photograph. You will send me a copy, isn't it?"

"Certainly. Could you stand here, please?"

"Have you taken your bath as I prescribed it, Professor David?"

"Yes, I have done everything you told me."

"You are looking very fine, very fine, in a *dhoti*, Professor David."

"Actually," David faltered, "I haven't been able to wear it properly. You see..." lifting back the flap and revealing the illicit belt.

"Ahh! No, no, no! This is not the way. I will do it."

And Shivaraman Nair swiftly ripped off the offending western item, wrapped, pleated, tucked, stood back.

Juliet readied her camera. And Shivaraman Nair, who was perpetually smiling or storming or guffawing, immediately composed his face into a blank stare. He believed it to be the only suitable expression for something as permanent and momentous and auspicious as a photograph.

Alone again, Juliet thought when they had gone. The men march off to action. Annie and Yashoda are light-years away. And the children and I...the children and I....

She sighed wearily, forgetting how to be annoyed. Soon her ankles would spread roots, she would be knotted into the ravenous earth that sucked at the underside of trees, her hair would bloom extravagantly with jasmine. Perhaps she would smell like sandalwood. Like the sandalwood Krishna who played forever on his silent flute, ceaselessly consoling them for the ivory swing in whose stead he had been purchased.

She took the small carving from its dining-room niche, from the recess where a Nair family shrine would otherwise be, and thought longingly of the air-conditioning in Mr. Motilal's emporium. Radha would still be there, too costly for stray tourists, dizzy on her swing since the days of the Raj, but fanned by the soft breezes of twentieth-century technology.

Juliet scraped the fluting Krishna lightly with her fingernail and the sharp sandalwood fragrance rose thickly and suddenly, a stimulant, invigorating as a breath of city air. She pressed the statue against her cheek and inhaled its spicy essence as though it were a relic of the lost power to make decisions, as though it might impart energy.

Can't we *do* something? the children pleaded. Something different? The market or the bazaar or that ice-cream place where Mr. Matthew Thomas took us? You promised, you promised.

Yes, *do* something, that was the answer.

The market, yes....

∽

Only one death, Juliet saw with relief. That's something.

She was standing with her children and Prabhakaran at the mouth of Palayam Market, the air jagged with screaming. On Mahatma Gandhi Road a bus had plowed into a buffalo cart laden with grain. The blood of the cart driver made red tributaries in the waterfalls of rice that sluiced into the market. She hastily despatched the children to the flower seller's with some money. She did not want them to see the mashed body when the splintered cart was swept away.

They had watched the bus tipple and rock like a rowboat on the lip of a cataract. But it had stayed upright and the screaming faces pressed against the window bars were now surging out of the narrow rear door.

A young man was helping the frailer and more elderly people to disembark. He seemed to sense her scrutiny on the back of his neck. He turned and stared insolently back.

144

God, she thought, dismayed, wrenching her eyes away. I'm part of the climate. I stare as rudely as everyone stares at me.

"Come on!" she called to the children. "Let's visit the egg man." But the young man's face? It kept turning up like a market-place refrain.

"I see you are having a servant. These are the ways of imperialists. And of the friends of the Nairs."

It was their abrasive and impetuous rescuer, who had abandoned them in a taxi. Juliet was balancing a cone of eggs. She had a sense of *déjà vu*.

"Ahh, the Marxist." She eyed him coldly and directly. "Last time we talked you made me feel guilty and apologetic. Now I don't feel so accountable for all the suffering of South India. As it happens, I would think I disapprove of Nair arrogance and abuse of power as much as you do. And Prabhakaran here is like one of my children. More or less."

He bit his lips uncertainly, sheepishly.

"Western women," he said, "are most...most" – he searched for a word – "most...*unexpected*."

She felt obscurely flattered. Conciliatory.

"Would you like an ice-cream?" she asked.

"An ice-cream?"

"There is an amazing little place behind the Secretariat, you know, called the Simla Coffee House. They actually serve ice-cream and it's very good."

He hated to be patronized. He had some high-caste professors, western educated, who treated him like that. The token Untouchable, tame. She smelled of imperialism. He spat on the ground.

"Suit yourself," she shrugged. "I'm taking the children. Do you think Prabhakaran will die of capitalist poisoning if he eats ice-cream? Shivaraman Nair certainly wouldn't approve. You and he are in agreement on that point."

He stared at her, baffled.

She stared back.

"I will come," he said.

They fenced warily over small dishes of mango-flavored ice-cream.

"I'm Juliet. My children are Jonathan and Miranda. And Prabhakaran."

"My name is Prem."

She was preoccupied. What, she wanted to know without preamble, was the policy of Indian Marxists towards young widows? She told him about Yashoda.

"Does she suffer hunger?" he asked. "Does she have to work in the fields or carry rocks with bare hands to obtain food?"

"No," Juliet sighed.

"Does she have to sell her body in order to obtain shelter from the rains?"

"No."

"It is not a major problem then."

"It *is* a major problem. It's a matter of basic freedom. She is kept a prisoner. She is forbidden to wear jewelry...."

"Oh! It is a question of *jewelry!*" He spat on the floor.

"Forget the jewelry," she said angrily. "It's not a man's problem, is it? Whether he's rich or poor, Nair or Untouchable, nobody keeps him prisoner in that way. It's a question of basic rights and of freedom."

"It is a question of the boredom of a wealthy lady of leisure. It is a question of female vanity. It is a question of jewelry."

"If I chewed betel nut, Prem," Juliet told him wearily, "I would spit the red juice on the floor beside you."

And she stared moodily out of the window, noting the curling green line of trees that indicated the canal. Somewhere, just out of sight, it lapped the bank where Prem had abandoned her in a taxi. And beyond that it wound muddily south to the temple tank where David would be, with Shivaraman Nair and Anand and flocks of scholarly priests who would listen to David's opinions.

In the world of authority and exploration and freedom.

The world of men.

21

On the stone steps of the temple tank, old men and old women sunned themselves, their purified bodies and laundered garments sending up individual foggy convection currents. In the tank itself more bodies, hidden by the murky water from the waist down, washed their sole garments while taking their ritual baths. Streamers of cotton cloth from unraveled *dhotis* and *lungis* floated on the water, their wearers pounding and scrubbing them inch by inch. Then, in the privacy of the opaque tank water, they wrapped themselves again in the garments and came out onto the steps to dry in the sun.

"Do we need to bathe here also?" David asked.

"No, no!" Shivaraman Nair was offended. "This is for people not having family tanks or modern bathroom in house."

They continued past the tank, past the booths of the trinket sellers and flower sellers, towards the towering *gopuram* of the main east gates of Shree Padmanabhaswamy temple. *Shree Padmanabha:* He with the Lotus Navel. Vishnu.

Anand was waiting for them at the top of the steps. As they ascended towards him, two temple guards advanced and barred David's way with crossed axes of the curved and hooked medieval variety. Their eyes were hostile and the sharp silvered edges of their weapons looked deadly. Shivaraman Nair produced a document, a lengthy legal-looking affair entirely in Malayalam script except for David's signature. The guards, however, could not read, and much argument and gesticulation followed. Eventually the guards withdrew.

Sandals and shirts were removed and left at the gates. David, flanked by his two hosts, passed beneath the tumultuously carved figures that cavorted in tier upon tier of the *gopuram.*

His first impression was of endless space. From outside the high carved walls, the temple had appeared to be one immense sprawling mega-monument. But now they stood in a vast courtyard with the shrines themselves in a separate structure in the center of the yard. Light and spaciousness overwhelmed him as presences, part of the mystery, his eyes vaulting up above the pointing *gopuram* to the domed roof of the sky, the soaring carvings seeming to curve like Gothic struts towards their central ornamented boss, the sun, that blazing eye of Shiva himself.

Hundreds of voluptuous maidens, their full breasts uncovered, jeweled chains at their rounded hips, drapes parting around their thighs, watched David silently. Their stone hands proffered little oil lamps like gifts. Each maiden was a pillar supporting a sort of cloister that ran around the outer edge of the courtyard. It seemed to him – a trick, no doubt, of the blinding sunlight – that Juliet and Susan and Yashoda, endlessly multiplying themselves, were leaning towards him, offering delights. But as his eyes adjusted to the light he saw that they could not be western women, they were all Yashoda, who surrounded him like an aura. You cannot escape me, she whispered. I am everywhere.

"The statues are magnificent," he said to Shivaraman Nair, disciplining himself, asserting scholarly faculties. "It must be spectacular at night when all those oil lamps are lit."

"Yes, yes, very beautiful! But now we do not use oil lamps, except for special festivals. Now," his host gave a proud flourish of his hand, "we are having electricity for evening *pujas.*"

"Except also when the power is failing," added Anand, realist.

David grimaced. He would have retained the use of oil

lamps at all times. He felt the same disappointment that the sight of loudspeakers on the minarets of the mosque at Palayam had caused him. The *muezzin* call was a broadcast recording!

In some ways, he thought, I am more resistant to change than they are. Yet if they can run electric cables through these stone cloisters, why should they be surprised that a young widow rebels against ancient laws?

David would have liked to linger among the lamp-bearing maidens a little longer, but he followed his guides into the stone hallway that led to the central shrines. Coming out of the brilliant courtyard he found it difficult to see anything in the soft gloom for several minutes.

As his eyes adjusted to the twilight, he realized that he had become the central attraction for a flock of young assistant priests, all chattering with excitement over the rarity of the occasion, each anxious to be the authoritative guide to the temple's treasures and history. He also became aware that the hallway was a veritable gallery of superb life-size sculptures. His pulse quickened, the blood pounded in his veins, every synapse of his scholar's brain prickled with a current of excitement. He felt like Balboa on his peak in Darien. The first Westerner to see them, his entry permissible under the dubious rubric: "Hindu by professional research."

The sculptures were chiseled from a very dark granite, the forms massive yet graceful. He knew they had been done late by the standards of Indian temple art, mid-eighteenth century, but recognized them as infinitely superior to anything else he had seen in Kerala. And he felt they were the equal of many more ancient and more classical pieces he had seen in North India.

He was rudely buffeted out of his rapture. Arms seemed to be clutching from all directions, pushing, pulling. This way, this way, this way, voices were saying. He moved forward in bewilderment. The cloud of priests had closed in on him like a fog, obscuring vision. They had become impatient with his long stillness in front of the statues, he had not been listening to their accounts of famous miracles, they wanted to show him one of the temple marvels.

He was led to the musical pillars, a cluster of stone pipes of varying thicknesses, running from floor to ceiling like cave stalagmites. Someone gently manipulated his head so that his ear was pressed against the columns. Someone else beat the pillars at random with bare hands so that a series of haphazard notes, low and sustained, dinned in his ears. His hosts waited inquiringly for his opinion. There was a glaze of high anticipation on their faces, a sort of breathless waiting for the inevitable accolade. He felt like a captive before the Inquisition, so many expectant faces looming close and watchful in the darkness.

"It is very interesting," he said awkwardly. "Most remarkable."

"Ahhh!" There was a communal release of breath.

"Yes, yes!" affirmed a multitude of voices, proud and delighted. "Remarkable, most remarkable!"

And they insisted that he again have the pleasure of listening. And again. Over and over. He was frantic to escape from the humming in his ears and head.

A young priest, anxious to show other wonders, finally rescued him, pointing out carved scenes from the life of Krishna. His guide launched into an account of Jayadeva's *Gita Govinda* and of Lord Krishna's sport with the *gopis*, of the allegorical meaning of all those cowherd women leaving their husbands and children at the first sound of the flute. The women were, said the priest, a symbol of the soul's yearning after God, its readiness to abandon earthly concerns in the search for salvation, the desire for union with the Supreme Lord.

David was thoroughly familiar with the poetic and interpretive traditions being expounded, and his thoughts wandered naturally from the *gopis* to Yashoda. Beautiful reckless women. Risking everything to get what they wanted. Did Indian tradition after all sanction Yashoda's actions just as it had always forgiven the *gopis* for their tempestuous indiscretions?

No. He thought not. There was too big a gap between divine allegory and social practice.

Yet Indian poets and artists had always found Radha and the *gopis* irresistible. That vibrant spark of rebellion. The world well lost for love. For David also it was intoxicating. Juliet careening after him, heedless and totally unself-conscious through subway crowds. Susan climbing into his office window. Yashoda tilting her jeweled nose at convention, pummeling his caution with her fists and her need for love.

And if he were to give in? If he were to go one evening to her house beyond the forest – because of her deprivation, because he was only human – what man would blame him?

Perhaps he was not even capable of refusing. Vicarious risk-taking, he thought, that is what attracts me. I seem powerless to resist it. I am a connoisseur of daring women, of dangerous lives. They delight me as works of art delight me. I collect them.

A sudden insight: he had never pursued or pined for Juliet or Susan, never needed to. Miraculously, they had fallen into his life like meteors, offering themselves. And he had been amazed, disbelieving; had made token efforts of moral restraint; had accepted them (Yashoda too?) as quickly and easily as a museum accepts art endowments: as gifts, graces.

Perhaps, like comets, their presence in his life would be transitory. Within a day, within an hour, Yashoda might look elsewhere for love. How simple that would be, the removal of temptation. How desolating: like an eclipse of the sun; like the theft of an art treasure.

Perhaps even Juliet would leave his days as swiftly and nonchalantly as she had entered them, a brilliant migratory bird, plumed with splendor and regrets. And he would be powerless to do anything about it. As though he had had a premonition, as though the vibrations of the musical pillars had shaken loose intuitions and repressed realizations, he felt a chill. No doubt it was merely the subterranean breath of the temple vaults.

He leaned against the stone pandemonium of the *gopis* who cavorted about Krishna, and closed his eyes, evoking the green spring shoots of his marriage; Juliet at rush hour running towards him. But the subway branched perversely with areca palms and his wife was the jasmine-haired woman of his uneasy recent dream: *I thought you were someone else,* she said, turning away, floating on by.

In nights of equatorial drift and panic, she called to someone else in her sleep. Pinioned in a small town or in a dusty Indian village, loyal, she nevertheless sneaked away from her husband in dreams. And perhaps in thought? And perhaps in future intention?

A thousand tiny memories and innuendos of malaise assaulted him: just that morning, the leap of fire in her eyes when Shivaraman Nair had said: *You are not permitted, Mrs. David Juliet....* And then, when David had turned back to see her forlorn and solitary in the doorway, the burned-out look, the look of quiet ash as it falls grayly through a grate. He had seen it before, that look. Back in Winston sometimes: she would stand staring from the window of their house like a woman behind bars, like a woman absorbed in a dream of somewhere else, someone other. (But it was such a fleeting mood. Surely he was right to discount it.) And what of the occasional unexplained long-distance phone calls? (But he would never inquire. It would be base to be suspicious.)

Sometimes, when she went alone to Montreal – for library research on a flagging book – his thoughts took on a brief muddiness, reptilian. What did she do when she was alone? When she was free. Despising the thought, a malignant thing crawling from Pandora's box, he would ram it quickly below consciousness.

She would return with a glow that disturbed him, although it always faded quickly in Winston, transplanted, seemingly, from its natural earth. His anxiety would flare briefly.

My falcon, he would think. Wild and dangerously beautiful. I never expected to catch or tame her, but she bound herself to me willingly. One day she will not return to my wrist.

But then he would scoff at his own alarm, at his overly fertile imagination. I take metaphors too literally, he would think. I trace them like arabesques, I follow improbable trails convoluted as the acanthus borders of ancient manuscripts.

Nevertheless...nevertheless...she was someone who *could* leave him. Someone who could easily live alone. She was a self-generating giver-off of sparks. She had never been, never would be, dependent on him. He had never wanted her to be. And yet it was an alluring temptation, contemptible, but potent: to be needed desperately. As Yashoda would always need someone. Yashoda was vulnerability itself, stirred to rebellion only by her fear of the more absolute vulnerability of widowhood and solitary aging.

Perhaps he should simply seize the moment. (If he were to be abandoned, what could he do? What did he know of the wiles of hanging on?) Perhaps when Yashoda came to him again, the wings of her caged desire beating in panic, perhaps he should simply....

This is my fatal weakness, he thought. My Achilles' heel. In the core of my scholarly soul, I seem helplessly susceptible to a certain blend of vulnerability and rashness. I cannot predict what I will do, I cannot tell when the pterodactyl will swoop out from the fen of my libido.

It unnerved him, this possible loss of moral control, and with a sense of urgency he pulled objectivity and probity around himself like a knight girding on chain mail for impending jousts. He cast about for cerebral anchors, and was relieved that it was time for the midday *puja*. The flock of priests bore him forward to the great shrine of Vishnu.

The image was behind a screen, its doors as yet closed. About a hundred devotees began to gather for the ceremony.

Men, women, and children, families, mothers holding babies, Brahmins and Nairs, beggars and shopkeepers, students and field laborers.

Music began to echo through the cavernous vaults of the shrine room. Drums, gongs, conch shells, flutes. The temple seemed to throb with music, barbaric, splendid, primitive. David felt his blood pound to the rhythm of the drums, a wild exaltation overpowering him.

Vedic hymns and prayers were being intoned by the priests against the backdrop of the music. The sonorous chant of the Sanskrit *shlokas* mesmerized, the clouds of incense drifting around the devotees contributed to a heady sense of free-floating. The priests raised the fruit and flowers and *payasam* to be offered to the god as his midday meal. Faster and faster beat the drums. David soared to the heart of the mystery, his pulse hammering. As the music raced to an almost unbearable, almost orgasmic climax, there was a final roll of drums and the doors of the shrine were flung open. David bowed his head in the presence of a great wonder.

Analyze this euphoria, analyze, begged some faint scholarly memory, some trained faculty for criticism and skepticism. Later, later, he told it.

Physical sensation returned to him at the touch of the chief priest's thumbprint. David's forehead was smeared with sandalwood-paste in the ritual Vaishnavite marks. The devotees all held their cupped hands in front of them like communicants at an altar. The assistants to the chief priest placed a section of plantain leaf on each pair of hands. They carried baskets of the sacramental flowers and food that had been given to Lord Vishnu, and were now to be distributed to the faithful as *prasadam*, visible grace.

Shivaraman Nair turned and offered David a portion of his own *payasam*, the sweet and delicious sacred gruel. Neither seemed able to speak. They ate together, and David thought with amazement: We have grown fond of each other. He is a man of sensitivity and integrity. He will not harm Yashoda.

Outside Shivaraman Nair said: "There are one hundred thousand gods yet only One. We are in agreement, yes?"

David said carefully: "You do understand that I am not Hindu? That I study Hinduism as a scholar only?" He knew his academic interest bewildered them, he was never quite sure how they interpreted it. "But I will never forget the moment of *darshana* and the moment of sharing *payasam*."

Shivaraman Nair laughed.

"Please, Professor David," he said reassuringly. "You must not be minding because you are a Christian. I not minding. I am certain that in your next incarnation you will be fortunate enough to be born Hindu."

22

In steamy mid-morning a tired *peon* arrived at Juliet's door with an invitation to visit Matthew Thomas's house.

"Did you come all the way on foot?" she asked with concern as he leaned against the front wall of the house.

"I have run," he said, between deep breaths.

Insane, she thought. Seven kilometers in this heat!

"Come inside. I will get you a drink."

"*Venda! Venda!*" He shook his head, embarrassed and startled. He moved away from her door and sat on the ground, his head between his knees, relaxed.

"Perhaps if the *mem sahib* is so kind as to send her servant with water," he said.

She gave Prabhakaran the pitcher of lemonade and a cup. Matthew Thomas's *peon* did not use her cup – his touch would pollute it – but he slurped the lemonade gratefully from his cupped hands.

They have a way, Juliet thought uneasily, of making my democratic instincts seem gauche and clumsy. In bad taste.

"Tell him," she informed Prabhakaran, "that we will take him back to Matthew Thomas's house with us in the taxi."

Prabhakaran giggled nervously.

"He will not come. He will be afraid."

"Of a taxi?"

"Of Mr. Matthew Thomas."

"Oh nonsense. I will explain to Mr. Thomas. You are coming with us too, Prabhakaran."

"But Mr. Shivaraman Nair has forbidden – "

"Leave Shivaraman Nair to me."

But the taxis were not at Shasta Junction and they had to walk under the punishing sun until a bus came by. At Palayam Market they bought oranges and sucked them to wash the rind of dust from their teeth, to pierce the scummy grit in their throats. Then, after the inevitable haggling with the drivers, they took an auto-rick to Mr. Thomas's house.

His street was so steep and severely rutted that the driver was unwilling to risk his frail vehicle. Again they walked, Mr. Thomas's *peon* several paces behind. Though the road was in a condition of extreme neglect the houses along it were quite imposing, not much different from Shivaraman Nair's house. Children began to cluster at gateposts, watching, chattering, giggling, poking.

There was a break between the houses where a tongue of uncleared forest sprawled out to the road and a massive banyan tree, probably centuries old, stood like a sentinel between civilization and jungle. Its roots radiated out from the huge convoluted trunk like flying buttresses from a Gothic nave, and in the niches thus formed were a number of crude cobra shrines. Some had been carved into the rootwood itself, others were roughly shaped in stone. An old woman, sitting cross-legged in the dust of the road, was rubbing ointment – coconut oil from the smell of it – onto the five hoods and scaly neck of Anantha, the king cobra sacred to Vishnu. A keening chant, the sound of supplication itself, rose from the woman's lips.

She turns to the snake, Juliet thought, because there is power in venom. She is fleeing her powerlessness. Is it a sick grandchild she prays for? Or an erring son? Or an imperious daughter-in-law? Is she caged in a house where she does not feel at home?

As though she heard the thought, the woman turned and looked at Juliet. Her eyes were direct, dark as a hawk's, unnerving. The women held each other's gaze.

It seemed that all understanding passed between them, the knowledge of all women who braid their own years into shackles, who weave with love and resentment the silken cages of their lives.

Then the woman shrugged. Her gesture said: We make whatever adjustments we can. We turn to whatever is available. And her fingers, glistening with ointment, caressed the cobra again.

At the end of the street they came to a high wall with gates. Beyond was a coconut grove, three houses that could be seen, and doubtless more lands and buildings beyond the trees. An estate.

Mr. Matthew Thomas was sitting on the veranda of the closest house, shaded by vines. He saw them as they peered through his gates and came towards them beaming. He surprised and delighted Juliet by greeting her with a hug.

It was not at all what she had come to expect of Indian salutations. Mr. Thomas looked exuberant. Almost young.

He does not seem old enough to be the grandfather of numerous children, she thought.

He patted Jonathan and Miranda on the head, stroked their cheeks, then took them both by the hand and walked back to the house. He nodded to Prabhakaran to indicate that the boy might be permitted to sit under one of the trees, away from the house. He ignored his own *peon* entirely.

Juliet bit her lip.

It was getting harder to remember that Prabhakaran was not actually one of her children. He was almost always with them now, part of what school lessons they still did, part of the bedtime story routine. Part of their lives. Part of the family. She felt personally wounded.

Should she challenge Mr. Thomas's assumption and offend him? Should she meekly accept traditions not her own? She stood irresolute beside Prabhakaran under the trees.

"Venda," he whispered to her. "You cannot take me into the house. *Po, po!"*

But she could not walk away and leave him.

She took his hand and they moved to the veranda. She sat with him on the wooden steps. Mr. Matthew Thomas was confused and deeply embarrassed.

"Please, please," he begged, drawing up a wicker chair for her.

She thanked him and accepted, leaving Prabhakaran on the steps. Mr. Thomas looked uncertainly and uneasily at the boy. It was difficult to understand the ways of Westerners. Surely she could not expect him to offer a chair to a *peon*? He could not do it. It would be, as the Bible itself said, casting pearls before swine.

Prabhakaran fidgeted, rubbing his bare feet on the steps, tense and unhappy, caught between the strange expectations of Mrs. David Juliet and the understandable annoyance of Matthew Thomas.

"Prabhakaran," Juliet said, trapped, conceding herself to be out of depth, "do you wish to play under the trees?"

"Shari, shari," he said with relief, and ran off, the tension broken.

Matthew Thomas called an order back into the house. After a short time his daughter-in-law appeared with tea and cups on a tray. She and Juliet were not introduced.

"I saw an old lady at the cobra shrine down the hill a little," Juliet told him.

"Yes, yes," he said. "This land is sacred to Anantha. My grandfather cleared it after the missionaries helped him to buy it. Before the missionaries, my grandfather was a *peon* on a great Nair estate."

Why then, wondered Juliet, when his own family history was one of upward mobility, did he insist on caste distinctions with Prabhakaran? Were there moral blind spots of her own that seemed just as glaring to Matthew Thomas?

"Did your grandfather choose this land, or did the missionaries? Didn't it seem odd for Christians to build in a grove sacred to the cobra?"

"No, no. For Christians it is safe. When my grandfather cleared this land, he did not find one single snake. But further down the hill there was also a Hindu family building a house. And on the very first night they slept in it, the father was bitten by a cobra and in the morning he was dead. That is why mostly Christians are living in this area. For us only it is safe. But come! I will show you my properties."

And he gave them a tour of his lands, Christian and free of cobras, but in other respects organized and farmed on the same hierarchical principles as Shivaraman Nair's estate.

23

The days crawled by like exhausted sun-stricken travelers who have lost their way. When Juliet climbed listlessly up to the roof with the sandals, she inspected her own hands for mold. She knew she was in decay, a mutant form adjusting to the steamy heat. Sometimes she toyed with the idea of flying home, but she had trouble remembering how such intricate things as airplane bookings and customs clearance were managed. Now when she thought of cities and subways a kind of panic gripped her and she would have to wander around the rice paddy until it subsided.

Occasionally, in a burst of guilty energy, she would organize the three children for school work. Prabhakaran was learning English. He could write his name. Jonathan and Miranda could calculate fractions. For what forgotten reasons? The spasm of discipline would peter out. The children would play on the roof or in the paddy.

A postcard had arrived from Annie. She and Yashoda were going on to Madurai. Another postcard had arrived from Madras. They were going to stay near the fabulous seaside temple of Mahabalipuram for a few days. Would be back eventually.

She heard nothing from the Nair house about the absence of Yashoda. If only they would react, Juliet thought, I would feel less uneasy.

The days crawled by.

News of far events filtered through, weeks late.

"Your Mr. Trudeau has had a scandal," Shivaraman Nair told them. "It is the mistakenness of western marriage. If his parents had chosen wisely...."

In Delhi, Desai was marshaling the courts to proceed against Mrs. Gandhi. There were outbursts of violence around the country. In Bombay. In Madras. In Madurai also, Shivaraman Nair told them. It was getting closer. Something was also happening in Angola, he said.

The days crawled by.

Annie and Yashoda returned. Yashoda, flushed with freedom, looked magnificent in a sari and jewelry bought in Madras. Shivaraman Nair had watched them come through his gates in a taxi. Nothing had happened. Nothing had been said. It was apparent to Yashoda that Annie's presence was better than a sacred amulet. Nothing could harm her.

David, coming home from the university, saw Yashoda drifting through the grove in the murky evening light. She flitted into his senses like a shimmering bird of paradise, insubstantial, graceful as a fantasy.

"Oh Professor David," she murmured, running to meet him. And her eyes were real, her cinnamon-scented breath was real, the hands that he clasped were real. "Oh I am so happy, so free. With Annie it has been as though I were a western woman. I have escaped and yet I am safe. I am being very grateful."

She laughed – it was the sound of Radha's golden anklets – and floated away from him again to join Annie.

He had to lean against a tree, his hands trembling.

She doesn't need me any longer, he thought. And he knew that this was a good thing. Yet he felt as though he had thrown away something of inestimable value. As though for a moment something priceless had been given into his hands and he had fumbled with it carelessly and let it fall through his fingers.

To have her look at him again in that helplessly vulnerable

way! *Professor David, only you can help me.... I want love, Professor David....*

He felt a cold irritation with Annie for her interference and was barely able to be civil to her over dinner. He did not listen to their plans and anecdotes, he fixed his attention elsewhere.

❦

On the second evening after their return, Annie and Yashoda walked together past the Nair house, out of the estate, along the public road to the Junction. They took a taxi in to the Chalai Bazaar, a grotto of color and excitement not far from Palayam Market.

This evening, Juliet thought, they are courting disaster.

"Shivaraman Nair can afford to overlook a trip outside the city," she had said to Annie. "Don't force his hand. If you cause him public embarrassment here in Trivandrum...."

"Of course he'll be angry," Annie had shrugged. "But why should Yashoda submit to that nonsense? And what can he do?"

They had gone, glowing with their own temerity.

Shivaraman Nair sent a note to the house with the evening milk. It was not brought by Prabhakaran, but by a servant they had never seen before. *Professor David*, it said, *please come immediately for discussion of weighty matters.*

"Sounds as threatening as that sign at the railway station," David joked nervously.

It had been one of their private amusements, the large sign in Indian English between the ticket window and the platform entrance: WARNING! TICKET-LESS TRAVELLER! HEAVY PENALTY AWAITS!

"Don't treat it lightly."

"I'm not treating it lightly. I'm worried sick. Though I think... since we were together in the temple, there has been between us...I think we have enough mutual respect.... And she's just

163

a girl really. Surely he realizes – "

"It's very odd that Prabhakaran didn't come."

David left, and Juliet waited apprehensively.

She lit the mosquito coils and read to the children. It seemed strange without Prabhakaran. He had become part of the bedtime story routine. But he would never stay overnight. He had to be near his cows.

The children slept and Juliet sat in the darkness lit only by the glowing red points of the mosquito coils. The palm branches swayed and murmured in the nightwind off the sea, whispering warnings. Heavy penalty awaits! Heavy penalty awaits!

A dead branch fell with a dull boom and Juliet felt the seismic tremors of its landing in the soles of her bare feet. It was astonishing how heavy those lacy-looking coconut fronds were! Tomorrow it would be recycled into thatch and baskets by elderly Harijan women who would sit under the trees, fingers flying, toothless mouths chattering. They would earn a few *paise* from Shivaraman Nair. And the denuded spine of the palm branch would become a threshing flail or the corner post of a servant's hut.

Everything dovetails, Juliet thought. Every tiny thing. There was a link between the vibrations under her feet and tomorrow's dinner – a little rice and tapioca root – for the Untouchable women. A link between the falling branch and the threshing. An endless chain. To disrupt the sequence was disastrous. *When dharma is broken, everyone is suffering.*

"It is not just Yashoda," David said, shaken. "It is Prabhakaran too."

Shivaraman Nair, he said, had been extremely hostile. He had accused the foreigners of abusing his hospitality, of being partly responsible for the bad harvest, of causing disasters which would yet come as surely as planting follows reaping, as inevitably as flooding follows the rains.

"And Prabhakaran?"

"We have corrupted the boy, he says. We have made him unfit to be a servant. He is to be kept up at their house, and a new servant will do our sweeping."

"He can't do that! He can't just treat Prabhakaran like a... like a pawn in a chess game, to be disposed of at his whim!"

"That's exactly what Prabhakaran is. A *peon*. A pawn. It's the same word."

"I won't allow it. It's immoral."

"To us it's immoral. To him the *peon*'s moral obligation is to be a good *peon*. The trouble is," he rubbed his fingers jerkily back and forth across his forehead behind which the intractable dilemma had settled as a clenched knot of pain, "the trouble is I can feel the validity of his point of view. I can see us from a perspective where we look brash and arrogant and meddling and self-righteous."

He pressed the upper bones of his eye sockets with his fingers, kneaded the skin above his eyebrows. "But I can also see... well, Prabhakaran.... It's happened imperceptibly, hasn't it? He seems like part of the family, doesn't he?"

Our moral sense against Shivaraman Nair's, Juliet thought. Absolute against absolute.

"What will we do? And what is he going to do about Ya-shoda?"

Yashoda. How could he speak of Yashoda? It was no longer a question of simply wanting to protect her. It was an obsession to hold, to caress, to recapture a lost moment of power.

"Yashoda," Juliet insisted. "What is he going to do?"

David sighed heavily. "He wants Annie sent away. He does not find it intelligible that I don't have a dictator's powers over her. I tried to explain but he just said contemptuously: 'Is she not the younger sister of your *wife*?' I explained that Yashoda might possibly go back to Canada with us for a visit and I gave him my word that... I said I would take responsibility for her. I promised she would not leave the estate again."

He rubbed his forehead uneasily.

"I don't know how I'm going to tell her that. And I don't

suppose that she'll agree to it. But I don't see what else.... It's the only possible compromise."

"I won't let them keep Prabhakaran away from us," Juliet vowed.

Somewhere in the grove another branch fell, another earth tremor quivered across their nerve ends, another cycle was begun.

24

"You know what it is," Annie told Juliet, as they walked one behind the other along the banks of packed mud threading the rice paddy. "It's standard manic-depressive behavior. There's no other way to explain it. She's still in shock from the death of her husband."

"I don't know, Annie. That sort of explanation doesn't seem to apply easily here. She says she misinterpreted the astrologer."

"Oh come on, Juliet! So. We left on an inauspicious day, she went with the wrong person, to the wrong city, whatever. The magic failed. Her reaction is still neurotically extreme."

They were baffled by Yashoda's excessive guilt and capricious moods. For days she had indulged in an orgy of self-abasement, hiding in her house in the forest, refusing to see anyone, moaning that her wickedness and inauspiciousness would bring disasters to all of them.

"On the other hand, Annie, she may simply be far more conscious than we are of the seriousness of the penalties."

"What penalties? What can they do? All that's happened is a temper tantrum from Shivaraman Nair, and she's forbidden to leave the estate. Which is where we started from anyway."

"She's afraid they'll send her to Palghat. They've done it once already. Before you arrived."

"So? We prevent them. They can hardly drag her out from

under our noses. Look, I know this is partly my fault. I didn't allow for the amount of stress.... Too much all at once. Another little spell of hibernation right now is probably a good thing."

They walked in silence for some time, the warm mud oozing up between their toes, their sandals flapping heavily and making sucking noises.

They had to negotiate their way around a toothless old woman who was squatting on the bank, resting her frail weight on the backs of her heels. She did not look up, but went on picking grass in handfuls from the levee, stuffing it into a sack hung around her neck.

"Why is she doing that?" whispered Annie.

"She is too old for harvest work. She will sell the grass to Shivaraman Nair for his cows. Probably a *paise* or two for a day's work."

"God! One has to make deals with one's conscience all the time here, don't you find? Giving oneself permission to eat."

"Yes." And yet, she thought uneasily, she found it impossible to sustain outrage in India. The energy-sapping heat, perhaps. Or because the sheer quantity of poverty was so overwhelming that it seemed pointless to begin anywhere.

"Fortunately," Annie said, as though reading her thoughts, "there are the Mother Theresas."

"Yes. Even the Shivaraman Nairs. He doesn't *need* any grass for his cows. But he always buys from them. In his own way –"

Annie made a sound of contempt. "Considering his wealth and what he pays his own servants!"

"But that's the trouble, isn't it? Any gesture seems futile and hypocritical and wrong. Take us with Prabhakaran, for instance. We've probably made things worse for him."

"Exactly why I'm not disposed to see Shivaraman Nair in any noble light."

"Me neither, I guess. Yet I can't see him as pure villain either. It would be easier if I could."

What could she do about anything? She had had her moment of moral indignation. (My manic phase, she thought.) She had taken her courage in both hands and confronted Shivaraman Nair. The *peon*, he had said coldly, had been sent on an errand to a nearby village. He would be away for several days. There was much important courier work for him to do. There would not be time for sweeping and bringing milk. Another servant would be sent.

"You are treating him unjustly."

"For the courier work he is receiving more rupees."

Foiled. Or simply in the wrong, perhaps. How could she object to Prabhakaran's receiving a higher wage?

"Nevertheless, this has been done as punishment."

"These things cannot be discussed with a woman," he had said, the matter closed.

Nothing could be done about it. Nothing could be done about anything.

She felt she understood Yashoda, slumped in defeat. Such wilting was surely more logical than extreme. What could be done about rules that had not bent for millennia?

"India makes me shudder at the idea of eternity," she said aloud. "Nothing changing. Ever. Not even the seasons. I wonder if that's why India has always dreamed of escape *from* endless rebirth while the West has been busy yearning for eternal life.

"I can see it has strange effects if you stay here too long. I mean, you, for example. You're so erratic."

"I've always been erratic."

"Not like this. You practically snap my head off the day I arrive. And then you slide into some long hypnosis as though you've been drugged. That's what you mean, I suppose? A sort of timeless drift sets in here. Warning: This country may be harmful to your personality."

"So can small provincial towns, of course. I *do* feel drugged. But then again I've been in some sort of timeless drift for more than a decade."

"You've been muttering that ever since you went to Win-

169

ston. But you never leave and you never push David to leave."

"I'm *always* pushing David to leave. I am endlessly telling him how unhappy I am, how unbearable the parochialism is, how the *blandness* of the place is driving me slowly insane."

"So either he's a tyrant who doesn't care how you feel, or he simply doesn't believe you. And *I* don't believe you."

An echo. One remembered irritation out of many.

"It's not that I don't believe you, Juliet. It's just that I can't take you seriously, my dear."

She had been at a university party in Winston. There had been a cluster of men, a political discussion, and she had pitched in energetically. After her speech there had been a silence – in Winston, it was improper to express strong opinions, a breach of etiquette – and then had come the cheap and patronizing detraction.

The speaker was an associate professor, not in David's department. A conservative man, undistinguished but ambitious, the kind who gravitates to a small college town. The big fish in small pond syndrome. He was not even worth anger.

Juliet had wandered into another room of the house, had stared out of mullioned windows, sipping scotch. This is a new Stone Age, she thought. A just-discovered colony of Neanderthal beings, perfectly preserved.

She pressed her forehead against the leaded diamond panes. Caged! If I were Faustus, she thought, I would not ask for some male version of Helen, but for one genuine bout of intellectual debate, a sword-play of words and ideas, an opponent who would not quail or cheat.

Abruptly she left the party, without waiting for David (an incident that was not to pass without comment in Winston) and gunned her car onto the highway. She would have left right then, eastwards or westwards, it didn't matter, just to put hundreds of miles between herself and this smug mediocrity, fleeing towards her passionate and disputatious past. But then she remembered: there was the babysitter to be taken home. And the children, delicate as espaliered trees, to be nurtured into harvest. She kissed their translucent cheeks, warm with sleep and innocence. What could one do? By morning, when they came pell-mell to breakfast, golden with the day's plans, she was as irresolute as ever.

And David was solicitous and tender as always, understanding. And yet never understanding. We never debate, she realized suddenly. We only share – which is not always enough. He is a gentle pedant, a patient and fascinating instructor; he earnestly absorbs the flamboyant bits of knowledge I offer. He considers, he concurs, or he quietly disagrees.

But I'd like a rapier in my hands again.

That afternoon, she had called Jeremy and picked up the threads of a five-year-old argument about Marcuse. Therapy, full of sound and fury, signifying a need for battle. As she hung up, vital again, she made herself one promise: No more university parties that had nothing more to offer than scotch and sanitized conversation.

"Annie," she said, tossing a stone into the paddy water. "You've got to believe me. Winston is impossible. I don't think I can bear to go back, I'm sure I can't. Which means, I suppose, that I'm entertaining the idea of leaving David. I know," she grimaced sheepishly, "that I've thought, and maybe said, this before. I know I think it every year."

Annie sat down on the bank, removed her sandals, and lowered her feet into the water of a harvested terrace. Green shoots of new rice, planted only a week or so earlier, came up between her toes. She leaned forward and examined her muddy reflection. There was a long silence.

"Look," she said finally. "I've got to admit I couldn't live in a small place like that myself. I'm not dismissing it as a problem. But if *you* really found it as terrible as you claim, it would have poisoned everything, including your marriage, and you would have left long ago."

"That just doesn't seem to be true. I shuttle between impossible situations. I can't stand living in Winston, and I can't stand the thought of living without David and the children. I'm shackled to a swing that I can't get off."

"Whenever I've visited you there, I've felt sick with envy. You can't fake that domestic contentment, so you'll have to pardon my difficulty with believing in all this Sturm und Drang. And that lovely old house, and the lake – "

"Oh yes, the house and the lake are consolations. And the family itself." (Why was she so insistent on her unhappiness, licking it over obsessively like an oyster: embroidering the grit of dissatisfaction as though it were her costliest treasure, her pearl of distress.) "It was the suddenness, I suppose. The total wrench from the track of my past, like a dislocation. I've led a sprained life."

"You *chose* that. Freely. And ecstatically ad nauseam, I recall. God, you drove the family crazy about David. It was embarrassingly uninhibitedly romantic."

"I think I must simply be voracious. A glutton for living. I want to be you *and* me." (I want urban yeast but also family epiphanies on the empty frozen lake. I want David *and* Jeremy. Oh yes, I want Jeremy too, which is perverse and rapacious and irresponsible.) With her feet she sent tidal waves through the young shoots of rice. "So I play with other possibilities all the time, it's a tranquilizing game. I could play it forever, I suppose."

"What about that guy you used to live with in Toronto?"

"*What*?" The unnerving thing about siblings is that it is dangerous to think in proximity to them.

"I can't think of his name. The politico with charisma. What was it? Jim? Jeremy! That was it. Jeremy!"

Oh Jeremy.

This had happened a week ago: feeling desolate (Annie and Yashoda still away; David roaming the villages with his tape recorder), Juliet had conceived the radical idea of telephoning him.

It had been delicious, sitting beside the rice paddy, to imagine the conversation. It had been like having a glass of wine in Place Jacques Cartier.

"Juliet!" he would say. "I thought you were still in India!"

"I am in India. I'm slithering into a swamp. I'm about to be swallowed up by vines or ants."

"You sound so faint."

"Only my voice is left. I've dissolved in the monsoon, I'm dispersing into the elements."

"Listen!" he would say, conspiratorially urgent, sending western adrenalin along under-ocean cables. "I haven't been able to sleep since I was with you in Montreal. I've accepted a position at McGill. I've taken an apartment there and it's waiting for you to move in. Come back. Please come back."

She had tried very hard to get away with this script but reality always intruded. What he would actually say, his voice puzzled and far away, would be: If you want to leave, then leave for heaven's sake! I'll meet you at the airport. But then I'm afraid I'll have to drop you and run. The woman I'm living with at the moment....

Nevertheless, with children in tow, she had even gone as far as asking Mr. Motilal whether she might make an overseas call from his telephone at the emporium. He had been dumbfounded. She might have asked for his rocket-launching pad. His phone had never been used for such a purpose, he was certain it was not possible. He suggested she inquire at the post office. Which she did. Ahh, they had said, flustered. Such calls are very complicated, very complicated. This will take many weeks. You must make a reservation for your phone call. We will send a postcard at the appointed time.

And so of course Jeremy had receded to his usual status: a tantalizing mirage, remote as snow, forever just out of reach.

Reality was always intruding.

"Wasn't that his name?" Annie persisted. "Jeremy? Did you ever keep track of him?"

"For god's sake, Annie! Twelve years ago. What on earth made you think of him? Can you remember the name of whatever man *you* were fooling around with twelve years ago?"

Annie said nothing, but stood suddenly and waded out into the paddy, sinking rapidly to the knees. Paddy mud, shifting, uncertain, pungent with decay, crawled up her legs.

She thinks I am implying flightiness and promiscuity, Juliet sensed suddenly. When I am only defending myself.

She got to her feet unsteadily and slid into the paddy water, lurching towards her sister. She pushed through the warm stinking water and the sucking mud like an ice-breaker smashing a ferry channel in the St. Lawrence River.

"Annie, I didn't mean anything by that!"

"It's okay. It's nothing. I'm jealous of all the permanence in your life."

"That's crazy, you know, when you think of how I get into a rage about the lion's share of freedom you have."

They waded to the edge of the paddy, getting on with the normal business of envying each other's life.

174

25

"Couldn't we take a taxi?" the children pleaded.

But the taxis were not at Shasta Junction and they stood waiting for the bus for nearly an hour in the mid-afternoon heat, without benefit of shade. Consequently they missed Anand who had gone to their house with the news that had come over his father's radio.

It is not a good day to be entering the city, he thought when he found their house empty. No. The time is most inauspicious.

The bus ride was overcrowded and uncomfortable, not unlike any of the others. But something was different about the arrival. The streets were full of movement and chanting, of marchers and banners. That in itself was not unusual, demonstrations being as common as buffalo carts. But it was as though the entire city was involved, seething and clustering in rival factions.

As people dropped from the sides of the bus, Juliet could see out the window. Stores were boarded up, some had been smashed and looted. Carts laden with plantains and coconuts and obviously destined for the market were standing abandoned and at the mercy of pilferers.

People in the bus were calling to people in the street. The passengers broke into agitated high-pitched jabbering. A message was flying from mouth to mouth with ripples of shock and excitement.

"What is it? What is it?" Annie asked everyone at large.

Someone eventually answered her in English: "Mrs. Gandhi has been arrested. Janata groups are celebrating. And Congress groups are protesting. They are fighting each other."

Anxiety closed in on Juliet's heart like a cramp. She and Annie were sharing a seat close to the back on the far side from the door, the children on their laps. David was out of sight somewhere at the front in the men's section.

"We've got to get off," Juliet said urgently.

But of course it was impossible until the terminus was reached. Or until the same desire was felt by the mass of bodies between their seat and the door.

Annie seemed lit by inner excitement. "Think of it!" she bubbled. "We're right in the fist of history."

Juliet was thinking that it was not, after all, so pleasant to be caught in the clutches of history, that she would prefer to be watching it, abstract and detached, on a television screen somewhere in the suburbs of another world, where the children were safe from harm. Or to have been marooned in the vegetable safety of her rice paddy, oblivious to large events.

The bus was creeping slowly forward as a sea of demonstrators massed around it. Juliet looked out the window again, and promptly covered Miranda's eyes.

A man was lying writhing in the middle of the road, bleeding profusely. The crowd stood around him in a circle, watching. No one came closer to him than about six feet. They just stood there, staring, staring.

Monstrous, Juliet thought, sick with horror. Inhuman! She pressed her head against the bars of the window and screamed to the man: I'll help you! But no sound came out of her throat. A jab of realization came to her: A dying body must not be touched. The Hindu prohibitions against pollution.

She could feel panic, hysteria, coming upon her like a tidal wave. She held it back with the wall of her will. One thought staccatoed across her nerve ends: Get the children to safety.

And then came a sudden lurching sensation of seasickness.

The bus rocked from side to side and its cargo erupted into a conflagration of screaming. So this is death, Juliet thought, as the road rushed up to her eyes.

And what she felt was not fear, but rage, a rage so vast and violent that she knew, for an instant before the blackness swallowed her, that she would be able to tear the bus apart like tinfoil to get them out.

Her head hurt abominably and there was an enormous crushing weight on her body. She could hardly breathe. Where am I, where am I? she wondered frantically, feeling panicky, claustrophobic. A coffin, she thought. Buried alive. And she passed out momentarily again from the horror of it.

When she came to she could smell her own blood and felt it wet and sticky on her face. Then she realized that Miranda's hair was in her mouth, that Miranda was packed tight into her arms like a leaden doll. And everything came back like the dark sudden swoop of a crow. Her mind tensed and coiled like a cobra about to defend itself.

The door must be above us, thank god, got to heave off the weights, climb out, thank god we're at the back, door almost directly above.

"Annie!" she bellowed, the cry muffled by Miranda's hair, the road and the bars against her cheek.

Got to heave off those bodies like a whale surfacing, got to climb out the door, lift out the children, and all the people one by one until I find David. She sobbed and heaved.

"Juliet!"

"Mommy!"

She heard them both muffled above her.

"Jonathan!" She shouted and wept and laughed. "Oh Annie, can you move? Climb on me! Get to the door!"

"I'm trying, I'm pushing, it's giving, it's beginning to move."

"Stand on me!"

"I'm trying!"

She was being pummeled by layers of bodies gyrating,

pushing, kicking. She could take it, she could take anything, a belting, a kick in the teeth, thank god for movement. She felt the stab of a heel on her spine, Annie's, please god.

Then an easing. Jonathan somehow standing on the window bars beside her head, bending over her, crying and stroking her sticky face, murmuring Mommy, over and over. Miranda still leaden and silent in her arms.

"Juliet!" A shriek of triumph. "I've done it!"

She looked up. She was in a canyon, bodies banked up on either side. Annie's feet swung wildly above her. Thank god for brash cultural indifference, Juliet thought. Thank god for jeans. Annie's hands were curled round the bars of the window above. She hefted her body along, monkey-walking hand over hand along the bars.

"I'm there!"

Her legs swung back and forth, up. Missed. A backward lurch. Up, up, a foothold. The silhouette of Annie against the sky. Someone else, a man, joined her from outside. The two sat astride the step, their legs hooked around it, and reached down inside.

Arms, arms, arms, stretched up to them. They lifted, hoisted, a body rose. Then another. Another. They were passing people out. Ten bodies. Then Jonathan. He stood on the edge of the seat reaching up across the aisle. They leaned down to him. Juliet kissed the calves of his legs.

"Hang on tight, darling!"

He arced up, poised in the doorway, was over.

"Juliet!" Annie was screaming over the rolling waves of moaning and wailing that filled the bus. "Juliet! Hand up Miranda!"

Miranda was a dead weight. Juliet heaved, pushed, she thought her blood vessels would burst. She was sitting at last, cradling Miranda, seeing her face for the first time. It was covered with a network of red rivulets spiraling out from a gash on her right temple. Her skin was white, her lips bluish.

"Oh god," Juliet whimpered, kissing the blue lips, the white cheeks, with a life-giving frenzy. Miranda's eyelids flickered, gently as a funeral shroud stirs in the flames. And Juliet sobbed and laughed and goaded her aching body to further action. She slung Miranda across her shoulder, stood on the seat edge, reached for the seat above her across the aisle. Her arms threatened to buckle.

Annie descended, agile and divine as Hanuman the monkey god, took Miranda, passed her up to the man in the doorway. Miranda disappeared over the step, handed down to the magical outside, to life.

Juliet and Annie, suspended from seat backs, spanning the aisle, hugged each other with their legs. Juliet's skirt ripped sharply from ankle to thigh. She was free to move. There was more reaching and straining and muscles roaring with pain. And Juliet sat finally across the door step, only the sky above her.

Like resurrection, she thought, breathing deeply.

It was a seven-foot drop to the ground. A man was waiting to catch her. It was David! She jumped into his arms and they clung together, kissing.

The rhythm of rescue went on and on.

Juliet, sitting at the roadside with Miranda in her arms, watched as Annie and a young man reached and pulled and swung over to David. The young man...? It was Prem again! The Marxist student, the specialist in market-place disasters.

Near the front end of the bus, slowly and fitfully, a trickle of men were clambering awkwardly out of a smaller space where the window bars were broken. And she realized that was how David must have escaped.

There were no ambulances in Trivandrum to come sirening to the rescue of the wounded. People helped one another as best they could. A couple of doctors, who must have been in the crowd when the bus went over, were moving among the worst cases, staunching heavy bleeding with bandages. Juliet went on rocking the children, crooning to them. The afternoon sun dipped towards the horizon.

Finally Annie and Prem lowered themselves into the bus, then reappeared in the doorway and called instructions to David. After a time, with people scurrying into boarded-up stores, a pulley of cloth and rope was set up. A number of elderly people were ferried to the outside by this method.

Then Annie called again from the doorway: "David, there are ten dead. I'm going to stay and help but there's no point in your staying any longer."

David nodded and went to his family.

26

Mr Matthew Thomas's daughter-in-law was bringing tea. The doctor, Jacob Mathai, was cleaning the gash on Miranda's forehead and the cuts and grazings on the side of Juliet's face. He had been fetched from his house, a few streets away, by Matthew Thomas.

It had been impossible to find a taxi or an auto-rick, and they had walked all the way, David carrying Miranda. It was only now, in the security and peace of the doctor's presence, of sipping tea, that they began to speak of the bus.

"I couldn't understand how you got out before me," Juliet said. "But then I saw that one set of bars was broken. Thank god for that!"

David stared at her, arrested by a singular thought, like a pilgrim suddenly surprised by illumination. "I did that," he said with a slow dawning of wonder. "I broke those bars."

"*You* did?"

"I hardly noticed I was doing it, isn't that amazing? I was next to that window when the bus went over and I never let go of it. I was so frantic to get to you and the children, I just ripped.. They were in the way."

He looked at his hands, holding them out in front of him, turning them over wonderingly, incredulously. They seemed to him invested with miraculous powers, quite external to himself and his own knowledge of his body. He felt an overwhelming respect for them, as for something apart, separate beings.

"I was standing on something," he said, puzzled. "I kept digging in, to get a better grip on the bars."

He closed his eyes, his forehead creased in concentration.

"Bodies! Faces! I was standing on faces. I remember looking down and seeing mouths and eyes!"

"I am going to give everyone tranquilizers," the doctor said.

It was already dark. The doctor took Matthew Thomas aside to give certain instructions, and then mercifully they were in the car retreating to the calm of their coconut grove.

Prabhakaran came running out of the darkness as the car wound slowly through the trees.

"*Apāyam*," Juliet told him. Accident. Disaster. But she could not think of any other Malayalam words to explain what had happened.

"Mr. Thomas," she begged, her speech blurred off into sleep. "Tell him."

The car was still moving slowly and Prabhakaran bobbed along level with them, conversing through the window with Matthew Thomas.

"*Ai! Ai!*" he kept exclaiming with alarm as he heard the story.

Then he went running off in the direction of the rice paddy.

"He says he is going to bring someone to help," explained Matthew Thomas.

Yashoda, Juliet thought drowsily.

෮

When Annie jumped finally from the bus doorway to the ground she was surprised by the way her legs crumpled under her like rice before a scythe. She was surprised by the trembling and the aching of her arms when she tried to push herself upright again.

Someone, the young man with whom she had worked side by side for hours, leaned over and helped her up. He steadied her with his arm, keeping it around her waist. She laughed shakily, looking up at him.

"This is crazy," she said. "Do you realize that after all these hours we don't even know each other's names? I'm Annie."

"My name is Prem." He smiled. "You are most remarkable, Annie. Very brave and strong."

"Thank you. Right now I feel horribly weak."

"We are needing sleep. I will take you to the house of my family. You will come?"

He did not wait for an answer but propelled her from the lee of the bus's underbelly into the human mêlée. She moved meekly along with him, though it was difficult to make any progress through the crowd. Here and there flares stabbed the darkness, illuminating the chaos. Somewhere further down the road a building was burning like a monstrous torch. A line of police, *lathis* flailing, was advancing down Mahatma Gandhi Road from the northern end where the police barracks were situated. Annie remembered, with a flash of amusement, having noticed the sign from the bus on the way in. *Commissionerate of Police* it had said in Indian English.

Retreating from the police *lathis*, the crowd was becoming more dangerously and explosively compressed around the market entrance where the overturned bus and stalled cars, taxis, carts, buffaloes, jammed the street.

Prem held Annie firmly by the arm and rammed his way through the mess. Quite suddenly they broke through its farthest reaches into the deserted market. He led her down the labyrinth of bypaths between the empty stalls, out into a back road behind the bazaar. They seemed to walk for a long time on endless alleys as narrow and unpaved and rutted as the little country thoroughfares that linked the houses and estates out in Krishnapuram. Annie was surprised to find such roads so close to the center of the city.

The houses which lined the alleys were mere hovels, packed

mud huts with low thatched roofs. Prem stopped in front of one, beckoned her to follow him. They had to stoop to enter the door which had no covering. He put his finger to Annie's lips to indicate silence and crept into the black recess.

As her eyes accustomed themselves to the darkness, Annie could see that there was just one room. Two shapes were curled on sleeping mats at one end, three smaller shapes at the other end. At the back of the room was a low platform with a few cooking vessels on it.

Most people, Annie remembered, went to bed at nightfall and rose at dawn. They could not afford the coconut oil to burn lamps after dark. Blessed are the poor, she thought wonderingly, overwhelmed by the poverty and the soft sounds of slumber, for they shall sleep peacefully through the upheavals of history. But then she felt glib, seeing the starkness of the little hut, remembering the bruised and shattered bodies at the bottom of the bus, and she thought instead: for they are the wretched of the earth.

She felt suddenly that she might vomit and hurried outside. When Prem tiptoed back with two rolled mats under his arm she was leaning against the wall of the hut, shivering and drenched with sweat, retching in dry convulsive spasms. Prem dropped the mats in alarm and took her in his arms. He set her on the grass, a rolled mat under her head, and went back into the hut for a small vessel of water.

Gently he bathed her face. The night breeze and the water refreshed her.

"I'm all right now," she said, sitting up.

"There is not room for us to sleep inside," he whispered. "And outside it is cooler. Always I sleep outside when I come home."

"Where do you sleep when you're not at home?"

"At the university I have a room."

Behind the hut there was a circular clump of banana palms. The parent tree had been removed leaving a ring of young palms like a living picket fence. Prem pushed through an opening and spread the mats on the grass inside.

Like a secret turret, Annie thought, gazing up through the broad plantain fronds at the night sky luminous with stars.

They lay on the mats facing each other, holding hands, and fell promptly into a chaste and exhausted sleep.

∽

Matthew Thomas was gently carrying Jonathan from the car. He had already settled Miranda on her bed. Both children had fallen asleep in the car. Juliet and David, heavily drugged by Jacob Mathai, had barely managed to get from the car to their bed, and were sprawled across it fully dressed, in a deep sleep.

Matthew Thomas lowered Jonathan onto his bed, stumbling a little in the dark. He had found the switch but the power was off, and as he felt his way back to the main room his bare foot squashed something slippery and cold. Frog, he thought. They were always hopping around the cool floors of houses in the evening. Poor little fellow, he murmured, reaching down and picking it up. It seemed all right and he put it on the window-sill.

Then he bumped against the rim of a wall niche and something fell to the floor. He felt for it with his hands and found broken pieces. Sandalwood! Its bruised fragrance bled into the room. He was appalled.

He took the pieces to the window and held them up against the moonlight.

It was the flute player; it was Krishna himself! Matthew Thomas felt ill with the inauspiciousness of the accident. Had he broken a household image of the Nairs? Or something belonging to Professor David and Mrs. Juliet? It was impossible to tell since the Westerners, he had observed, had a strange habit of buying sacred objects of other faiths as though they were souvenirs. He hoped the statue was theirs because it would be easier to make amends. If he had desecrated a Hindu shrine, he trembled to think of the consequences. In either case, he would buy the costliest replacement he could find.

He could hear the boy now, moving around in the dark kitchen.

"What are you doing?" he called softly.

"I am searching for Mrs. Juliet's oil lamps and matches," the boy replied. "I have brought the lady of whom I spoke. She will sleep here tonight to watch over the children."

He emerged from the kitchen bearing two small brass lamps, the glow from their wicks casting a pale halo around him. In that soft golden light Matthew Thomas and Yashoda first saw each other. They made formal greeting.

"*Namaskaram.*"

"*Namaskaram.*"

She was the age of his daughter Kumari, and as beautiful. Perhaps, a disloyal thought surfaced, even more beautiful.

"I am Matthew Thomas," he explained. "I am a friend of Professor David and Mrs. Juliet and the children. After the accident they were walking to my house. The doctor has given them sleeping medicines."

"Prabhakaran has been telling me," she said.

Her voice was like nightwinds in jasmine bushes, filling the air with a lilting sighing fragrance. "My name is Yashoda. I also am a friend of Mrs. Juliet and of Annie. Please tell me, where is Annie? Is she hurt?"

He did not answer, caught in the spell of her almond-shaped eyes. I should not be here, he thought nervously, alone with a Nair lady. Where is her husband?

"She is hurt," faltered Yashoda. "It is my fault. I am inauspicious, I am bringing misfortune…oh Annie…I am so evil, so evil." She began to weep. "Annie is not…? She is not…?"

"No, no, what are you saying?" he asked, terrified.

Prabhakaran ran to Yashoda, flinging his arms around her.

"I do not know Miss Annie," Matthew Thomas said with alarm. "Professor David has told me she is not hurt."

"Oh...oh...." Yashoda was half laughing with relief, half crying.

She ruffled Prabhakaran's hair abstractedly and he looked up at her with adoration.

Matthew Thomas felt like new green rice bowing before the monsoon. He swayed with emotions he had forgotten he ever felt. Far too many things had happened in one night.

"I am happy that you have come to take care of everyone," he said awkwardly. "Now I will be returning to my house."

"Yes," she said. "Thank you."

They bowed to each other. They murmured *namaskaram*.

He was just slipping his feet back into his sandals at the door when Jonathan screamed. Matthew Thomas and Yashoda both ran to the bedroom. Jonathan was writhing and raving in the grip of a nightmare. He ran back and forth in jerky little lines, his steps erratic and frenzied as though he were on hot coals.

Shaking with fear because he had never seen such a thing before, Matthew Thomas tried to lift him. He wished he had paid Jacob Mathai to come with them. He had his arms around the child but Jonathan, whose eyes were open but blindly glazed, screamed piercingly and beat him off with a terrified flurry of his arms. He was jabbering incoherently, an occasional word intelligible: "Mommy, Mommy...taxi...yes, yes, holding tight...."

Every time Yashoda or Matthew Thomas tried to calm him, to hold him, he screamed and beat them off in a paroxysm of panic. His cries pierced the heavy sleep of David and Juliet. They half woke, tried to get to his room, bumping into walls. Yashoda went to them.

"We are here, we are here," she said. "We will take care."

She led them back to bed.

Jonathan's night terror lasted about four minutes, though it seemed endless. Yashoda and Matthew Thomas stood as near as they dared, helpless, trying merely to guide his staccato steps away from walls and beds. The screams faded to whimpers, he collapsed suddenly into Yashoda's arms, exhausted. She tried to lift him, Matthew Thomas helped her, and together they got him back to bed.

"I think I should stay," he said.

She nodded assent.

She sat on the edge of Jonathan's bed, taking the sweating little hand in hers, stroking his arm. Matthew Thomas sat on Miranda's bed. Every few minutes he felt the sleeping child's forehead, ran his fingers lightly over her cheek and hair. Prabhakaran set the oil lamps on the window-sill and sat cross-legged on the floor in front of them. Whenever the flame dimmed he would trim the lamps with more coconut oil and fresh wick.

Hours passed. Jonathan had two more night terrors, similar to the first one. Each time Miranda stirred and tossed and moaned but did not wake.

In the lulls between nightmares, Matthew and Yashoda talked softly, partly to keep themselves awake. Perhaps it was the privacy of the darkness, perhaps the shared intimacy of anxiety and helplessness before the frightfulness of Jonathan's dreams. Perhaps it was even because of their different castes, different faiths, different ages. The intimacy of travelers, strangers who never expect to meet again, whose social spheres will never intersect. And there was nobody to eavesdrop, to carry reports. There was only Prabhakaran on whom Yashoda smiled fondly whenever he moved and reminded them of his presence.

Matthew Thomas told her of Kumari, of his newest hopes, wild thoughts only, of visiting her in America. She told him of her widowhood and her loneliness. He spoke of his wife, long dead, whom he had loved dearly. She spoke of her fears, her own dreams for a future, her longing for love.

The night passed. Sometimes they drowsed. Just before dawn Matthew Thomas stirred, started, remembering where he was. The oil lamps had burned out. There was no sign of the boy. Yashoda was lying awkwardly across Jonathan's bed, one arm under her face like a child, sleeping.

Matthew Thomas bent over her, placed his hand lightly on her shoulder, and kissed her, the merest chaste whisper of a kiss, on the cheek. Because she reminds me of Kumari, he told himself as he slipped quietly outside to his car.

27

Annie woke first. Dawn was slipping down through the canopy of plantain leaves discreetly as a kitchen servant kindling the day's fires.

She sat up and looked at Prem. His long dark lashes brushed his cheeks, his black hair was slicked around his face in damp tendrils. He is like a figure from Botticelli, she thought. Perfect as a child. Almost too beautiful for a man. There was a certain appealing androgyny about Indian men, she thought. It was apparent in their painting and sculpting traditions. The only way one could ever tell Radha's face from Krishna's was that his was always represented as blue.

Dinesh's body had been delicate and hairless as a woman's, but possessed of an extraordinary muscular agility and strength that was indisputably masculine. Dinesh, movie playboy, connoisseur of European and American cities and women, peaceful conformer and discreet subverter of Indian family expectations, author of a thousand and one sexual delights. Annie sighed in fond and regretful memory.

She watched the frisky newborn sun playing across Prem's face. She looked up through the turret of leaves at the light, and folded her arms across her breasts, hugging herself with pleasure because life was so unfailingly intoxicating and infinitely variable.

I am a princess in her round tower, and I am about to waken

the Sleeping Prince with a kiss. She leaned over towards Prem's lips which were as full and sensuous and inviting as Krishna's, but just then he woke and sat up abruptly, startled, embarrassed.

Annie smiled at him, her lips still slightly parted, unabashed. Prem felt as though his entire blood supply had raced to all the extremities of his body at once, leaving a terrifying vacuum in the region of his heart which seemed to be careening down some newly opened abyss within him. It seemed in fact to plummet to his loins, on a collision course with the rest of his blood. He drew his knees up to his chest, wishing desperately that he had worn his loose pajama *lungi* as usual instead of remaining in his close-fitting daytime western pants. He had no idea what to do. He had never slept with a woman. He sat hunched tight in embarrassment, afraid to move and expose the roaring confusion of his blood and his emotions.

Women were so very unavailable in India. Even at the university, where one could meet young unchaperoned female students, the girls stayed together in nervous giggling clusters. They would not risk being hurled from the family circle in disgrace, permanently debarred from marriage. Occasionally there would be a celebrated scandal and two students would marry secretly without the consent of their parents. The repercussions were always disastrous, the couple either reduced to utter poverty by withdrawal of all family monies, or taking their chances as hopeful emigrants to England or America. Provided they could survive the long wait for visas.

There were prostitutes of course, low-caste women, Untouchables, driven to desperate measures to feed their children, or to support parents who cursed those very daughters if the source of the money was ever discovered. Many, perhaps most of the students, had slept with such women. But Prem considered them to be of his own kind, his own people, the poor, the spurned, the wretched. He would never exploit them for sexual pleasure.

He imposed on himself a rigid political ethic. And he understood the intricate international web of forces that made it possible for a young Canadian woman to take a vacation for pleasure in India, while his mother and brothers and sisters – at least, until he had been able to provide some money from his university scholarship – were sometimes kept alive only by the water in which his father's rice had been cooked. That was standard on Prem's street in the desperate weeks before the rice harvest. The men ate what meager grain was available, the women and children drank the cooking water. Meanwhile Canadian women daily threw out scraps that would feed his family for a week. And the servants of Nair landlords, given food scraps to bury under trees, came home with what prizes they could – bones, intestines, the clawed feet of chickens on which the children sucked and chewed.

And now Prem was facing the enemy who leaned towards him with parted lips and golden hair, beautiful as Radha. He was in a chaos of contempt and desire, anger and hatred and yearning. She was woman. He had gone to sleep holding her hand. Last night he had thought of her as a fellow struggler against Congress Party hooliganism. This morning she was a Westerner. He was in anguish.

"I have upset you, Prem," she said. "I'm sorry."

In some subtle way, though she barely moved, she withdrew physically. She extinguished the luminous sexual aura that had surrounded her.

As soon as she did that he cursed himself for not having responded. His blood flowed cowed and dejected back into its habitual channels. He felt arid and miserable and infinitely lonely. But what could he have done? What should he have done? He simply did not know.

"Come," he said gruffly. "I will show you where we bathe."

He led her down to a muddy canal that flowed behind the row of huts. It linked two reaches of the vast network of Kerala backwaters. Children were frolicking in it. Buffaloes were being swabbed down by their drivers. Prem walked into the water and sluiced it vigorously over his face and body, through his hair. Annie hesitated a moment, recalling all the dire warnings about polluted water, about hepatitis and malaria.

Prem noticed her reluctance.

"We do not have bathrooms," he called back savagely.

A silly jingle occurred to Annie, and she found herself singing it silently, mindlessly, to cover her hurt. *This is the way we wash ourselves, wash ourselves, wash ourselves.* She entered the water quickly and began to swim in order to wet herself totally without having to think about it. She stood up and filled her cupped hands with water and splashed it over her face.

Prem was dazzled. The thin muslin smock clung wetly to her breasts, her hair licked her face and shoulders like tendrils of pond weed, her cupped hands were full of sunlight. He thought of the carved stone maidens who held out their oil lamps in the temple courtyard and he was ready to worship her. He felt again that involuntary rush of blood, felt himself swelling and pulsing under merciful cover of the muddy water, felt himself climax suddenly and helplessly and uncontrollably. He dived shallowly and swam violently away from her, churning the water to disguise the sobbing and spluttering of his humiliation.

Annie became conscious of the staring of the children and the buffalo cart drivers. They pointed and giggled among themselves.

She felt as though she were naked.

It was one of those moments when she sensed the knife edge of doubt and uncertainty, when she knew afresh that life was not entirely pliable to her touch. She swam sadly and slowly after Prem, joining him downstream on the far bank where a small grove of coconuts and areca palms and mango trees began.

"This is the way we clean our teeth," Prem said, not looking at her. He snapped a green twig from a mango tree and frayed one end of it with his thumbnail. He used the bristled end on his teeth like a whisk. Annie copied him. They sat on the grass in the sun, the dampness steaming and eddying upwards from their clothes and bodies. Prem was very thorough and absorbed with his twig. Cleaning teeth in this fashion was clearly something more than simple hygiene. It had perhaps the function of morning coffee or a morning pipe or reading the morning newspapers.

Gradually, it seemed to Annie, the strain and hostility seeped away into the mist that rose from their bodies. When Prem stood to leave, her shirt was dry but she knew it would be several hours before the heavy denim of her jeans dried completely. They felt weighted and soggy and rather uncomfortable. Did one catch cold from staying in wet clothes, or was that an old wives' tale? She had the unadventurous desire to take a taxi to Krishnapuram and change into something clean and dry, but instead she followed Prem.

They sat in a little restaurant near Palayam eating *masala dosai* and drinking strong black coffee. Prem was reading the Malayalam newspapers, Annie the *Indian Express*. It was the Madras edition that Annie had, so the headlines concerned Tamil Nadu. INDIRA ARRESTED. DESAI BUNGLES. RIOTS, DEATHS IN MADRAS AND MADURAI. The Kerala news was in the lower right quadrant of the front page. Its headline was in smaller type: ARSON AND STABBING IN STATE CAPITAL. STUDENTS AND POLICE CLASH IN COCHIN. Thirteen dead in Trivandrum, nine in Cochin. She showed Prem.

"Malayalam papers are saying twenty dead here in Trivandrum," he told her. "We can conclude in reality thirty to forty dead."

"I personally saw eleven dead," she said, thinking of the man bleeding on the road (the stabbing of the headline?) and the corpses in the bus. She winced, squeezing her eyes shut against the memory, her stomach queasily rebelling against breakfast.

They had both been shying away from the thought of those bodies crushed between seats and window bars. Prem reached across the table and touched her hand.

"If we had not been there, there would be many more deaths."

She smiled wanly.

He smiled back, seeing again his partner in the rescue work. She had been so magnificent. She was so beautiful. It was so pleasant to work with her, to have breakfast with her, to talk with her as an equal and a friend. Not to think of her as a woman and a Westerner.

"Annie," he said suddenly. "The other western woman and her children...?"

"She is my sister. How did you come to be there when the bus tipped over?"

He smiled sourly. "I was already a victim of Congress Party hoodlums. We would not close the Marxist Book Store to please them. They smashed our windows and threw our books in the street and beat us with *lathis*. But I escaped into the market. And then I saw the bus."

"Thank god you were there! So you are on the Janata side, celebrating the arrest?"

"I am happy with the arrest, yes. But I am not with Janata. Desai is really no better than Mrs. Gandhi. He also is an elitist. He is wealthy and corrupt. He speaks much of the evils of casteism but he is doing nothing." He tore angrily at his thin rice pancake and scooped up the fragrant curry in agitated jerky motions. "So what is different?" he asked bitterly. "For the poor, nothing is different. Our families will still go hungry, and the rich imperialists will still take pleasure trips to India."

She saw him as a prophet, burning up in the twin flames of idealism and hate. He saw her as the enemy. They stared at each other, riveted.

"Prem," she said shakily. "I care about these things. You should not hate me because I am Canadian."

His quick anger was punctured. He lowered his eyes.

"I'm sorry," he said in a low voice, "but still, Annie, this is making a very great difference between us."

"Yes," she said humbly. "I understand that, Prem."

But she felt glib, guilty of cheap sympathy. She would have liked to tell him that she was a law student, to have pleaded, in extenuation of her affluence, her idealistic hopes, her store-front lawyer plans. But it would have sounded shallow and self-congratulatory. Instead she said abruptly: "I have to go now and see if my sister and the children are all right. They'll be worried about me."

"I'd like to come with you. To see the little girl. I have met your sister and the children before."

"Really? You didn't show any sign last night. But then, I guess we were all in shock...."

The waiter came and left their check.

"Please, Prem," begged Annie. "Let me pay."

He was instantly furious with her again, caught between male pride and political justice.

"This is hopeless," she told him ruefully. "You might as well go ahead and hate me. But I'm doing it for your family, for those children I saw sleeping in your house last night. It's a fair exchange for your concern about Miranda."

She cared about his pride, however, and passed him five rupee notes under the table.

He took them, resenting her.

28

The tunnel seemed to be contracting, to be closing in on Juliet, suffocating her. She was crawling on her hands and knees towards a remote circle of light. With every yard she gained, the light receded further into the distance.

This tunnel is my life, she thought. I am trapped in it.

Furry things brushed her in the darkness and she shuddered. Sewer water, a warm slime of it, flowed around her, and cobwebs dangled like ropes. Not cobwebs. Creepers! Snakes! The tunnel was India and she would never get out alive. A mere pin-prick now, the light was dwindling, dwindling. The creepers had sprouted hands that throttled, she could not breathe. The hands had grown arms and bodies. The bus rocked, lurched, went over. She screamed....

And was awake, trussed like a mummy in the bedsheet, sodden with equatorial dampness and sweat.

Alive, she remembered. We are all alive. And she bent to kiss David who tossed fretfully; she padded barefoot into the children's room. They were there. Sleeping. Safe. She touched them, she touched the window bars. She walked about the house, trailing her fingertips along walls, over wicker chairs. Everything was solid, in place, reassuring.

She came to the shrine niche and saw the flute player's delicate shards. Chill. The seasick pitch of nightmare. She leaned against the wall, queasy, and closed her eyes tightly against the crumpled bodies in the belly of the bus.

Take deep breaths, open the eyes on an ordinary casual mishap.

Her fingers hovered, touched the splintered edges: braille of a normal occurrence. And such an aromatic accident, the room rich as a temple with incense. A sanctuary. They were safe, they had escaped from the bus, it was all behind them now. It was not so different from witnessing a pile-up on the highway back home. One shivered a little, perhaps, but drove on by, forgetting everything within the mile.

She walked out into the wet, still air, and raised her arms towards the umbrella of the coconut grove that had never known change or harm. She was startled to see how high the sun was. Their drugged sleep had beached them on the shores of noon, the drowsy air was silent of bird calls, the palm trees limp with the stupor of centuries.

It was not possible to believe in the cracked ribs of buses and history, not possible to believe that only seven kilometers and one night away, dread things had happened. Or that Annie, of white-water ways, might even now be sluicing through political rapids. No, it was not possible, any of that.

I am dreaming my own life, Juliet thought. It is as still as paddy water.

Into which, at that moment, the outside world cast a pebble. A taxi, bearing Annie and Prem, was easing itself between the trees. And from the direction of the forest, Yashoda approached in the full plumage of usefulness and defiant silks and jewels.

I would have preferred, Juliet thought, to keep the illusion of changeless peace a moment longer. But she hurried inside to drag her family from the country of oblivion into the ragged present.

Prem was noticeably ill at ease, Juliet saw. His angry eyes swept over the expanse of coconut grove and paddy. He took stock of the tiled roofs and marble floors.

He greeted her with some warmth, was polite with David,

gentle and solicitous with the children, curt with Yashoda.

He asked about Prabhakaran. "Your other child," he reminded Juliet. There was a note of sardonic challenge.

"Prabhakaran is a *peon*," she said heavily. "He has been removed from our corrupting influence." Last night, she explained, he had appeared miraculously out of the darkness. But he had been gone again when she woke. "Probably he is being punished for coming here again."

"That is the way of the Nair landlords," Prem said bitterly.

A moment of empathy, of shared anger, bound Prem and Juliet.

Only a moment.

"They are also punishing Yashoda."

But that, he thought, with a hostile glance at the gold bangles and jeweled rings, is different.

Juliet saw the curl of his lip. Their eyes met again. Held. A moment of mutual distrust and annoyance bound them.

Prem turned abruptly and left the house.

Annie was clearly eager to get away again. It was obvious that she found the quiet isolation of the house anticlimactic and stifling, that she was restless to return to the chaotic and colorful hub of the city, to be at the pulse of things. She said goodbye and joined Prem in the waiting taxi.

As the car emerged from the grove Prem said: "I do not want you to think that I hate all Nairs. Or all Westerners. I like your sister. You also," he added as an afterthought.

She grinned and rested her hand lightly on his, companionably. He withdrew his sharply and instantly regretted it. For one thing, it seemed to contradict what he had just said. For another her touch had given him pleasure. But the movement had been a panic reflex.

Annie sighed and looked out the window. This is hopeless, she thought impatiently. For Prem I can only be a sightseer of injustices. His angers and bridlings made sense but it was uncomfortable to stay within their prickling reach. She was not going to waste her time making endless futile apologies for being white and western and middle class.

As soon as I can do it graciously I will say goodbye, she decided.

But they spent a pleasant day together, full of lively discussion and free from further hostility.

By dusk Mahatma Gandhi Road was ominously quiet. The market stalls were empty, the shops boarded up. Crows, black and huge and grotesque as death, wheeled above an overturned cart of ripe plantains. Every few minutes they swooped down to rip at the soft fruit with their vicious beaks, their vast wings flapping slowly and arrogantly. Rice had spilled onto the road from the burst sacks of another cart and rats could be seen heaving and burrowing through the mounds of grain.

To those who owned radios, word had come that Mrs. Gandhi had been released and the news was spreading by word of mouth with the speed of the southwest monsoons rolling in off the Arabian Sea. The factions were gathering for the second day in a row, but this time the roles were reversed. Congress Party supporters were celebrating, Janata supporters were massing in angry protest.

"It will be even more violent tonight, I think," Prem said.

"I should leave now," Annie said.

"Where will you go?"

"To Krishnapuram. I should be with them."

"Yes," he agreed miserably. "It is best."

"Goodbye, Prem. I am glad to have met you."

"Please, Annie...." he entreated.

"Yes?"

"Don't go. Stay with me."

She smiled, radiant as sunlight.

The tumult could barely be heard, the merest whispering echo, inside the clump of banana palms down the green funnel of which the moon poured its white light.

Prem felt as nervous as a boy on his first day of school.

Terror and excitement washed over him in chaotic alternation. His skin tingled with burning flashes of anticipation and chilled in the cold sweat of his fear of failure. But she is gentle, I like her, I can trust her, he reassured himself.

They were sitting facing one another on the sleeping mats.

"Annie," he said in the voice of a child, in the voice of an acolyte waiting to be inducted into the mysteries, "I have never slept with a woman."

He did not need to ask if she had known other men. Western women lived differently from the rest of the world's women. They were unrestricted, they engaged in insatiable and notorious sexual adventures. It could be seen in the movies. It was well known. He waited trustfully for the key to the great secrets, for her to endow him with miraculous potency and knowledge.

She took his hands in hers and smiled, the high priestess of fertility, the mother goddess.

"It's like breathing, Prem," she said gently, easily, companionably. "It is like waking up in the morning and seeing the sun. There is not a wrong way to do it. You do whatever you want to do and it is always right and beautiful."

He could not move. He sat waiting expectantly like a child. Not even the morning's hammering turbulence of drunken blood came to his rescue to spur him to blind and instinctual action.

Annie undid his shirt buttons and ran her fingers lightly down his chest to the navel.

"Your body is beautiful, Prem. Like a young god's."

He closed his eyes to luxuriate in the delectable sensation of her touch. She slid his shirt off his shoulders and ran her hands playfully, caressingly, over his shoulders and back, his chest, through his hair. Her finger followed the outline of his eyebrows, his lashes, his lips, with the feathered lightness of a *chakora* bird following a moonbeam. He felt like laughing and crying, he felt as safe and blissful as a baby in its mother's arms.

Tentatively he placed his hands under her loose smock and

stroked the skin of her belly. It was as firm and smooth as the skin of just-ripened papayas. He slid his hands upwards, shyly as fluttering doves, until he felt the soft arcs of the underside of her breasts. His hands stayed there, cupped, brimming with softness, and he leaned forward, burying his face against the swelling cargo of his hands, overcome.

Annie gently raised his face with her hands and kissed him on the lips and pulled her smock quietly and deftly over her head, tossing it onto the grass. Then he felt again the leaping in his blood, the crazy thumping and throbbing, the needling itch of ecstasy. He pulled her towards himself, cradling her in his left arm, fondling her breasts with his right hand.

He ran the tip of his tongue around one nipple and laughed with pleasure at the way it stiffened and stood erect. He bit it gently and experimentally, nuzzling it with his teeth.

He felt ravenous for the taste of her breasts, like a hungry infant. He sucked them, nibbled, ran his tongue greedily over and around them, buried his face in the soft valley between them.

His right hand was spread across her belly. He pressed it hard against that smooth firm surface and she moved into him somehow, curling one leg across his body, making little sighing sounds. It gave him an intoxicating sense of power and possessiveness.

He realized that he could slide his hand down under the waistband of her jeans. He could feel the flimsy little undergarment that western women wore. He eased his fingers under the elastic line of resistance, felt the soft fuzz of hair. Further, further, while he sucked and sighed at the delicious yielding ripeness of breasts. Then he felt the swollen skin beyond the hair, warm as fire, soft as silk, wet and flowing as the flesh of a green coconut oozing milk.

He began to tremble violently, fearing he would not find her in time before he exploded in his own excitement. He unzipped her jeans – he would not have believed he could be so confidently aggressive – and tugged at them with ragged energy. He pulled off the little underthing.

But the fastenings of his own clothing were perversely clenched against him. His hands shook with frenzy, he was almost sobbing with frustration and anxiety.

Annie sat up swiftly and pushed him gently back onto the mat. She knew it would have to be fast, this first time.

"Whatever is done is right, Prem," she murmured, leaning over him so that all her generous softness tumbled down on him like jasmine petals from a festival palanquin.

She knew it would be fast and urgent as a waterfall this time, but she wanted him to give himself to his own tides, to sway with them, to trust them. Not to fear. She laid her cheek on his chest, stroking him, kissing him, calming him. She eased him from his clothing and rested her hand gently on his genitals. He quivered in delectable pain.

She knelt between his legs, looking at him.

"Ah Prem," she said.

It was always wonderful, always exhilarating and splendid as creation itself. She felt rich and fluid with love, peaceful as the earth at springtime.

She cupped his testicles gently in her hands and played with her lips along the length of his penis, kissing and licking with teasing darting movements of her tongue.

He jack-knifed upwards, spared one proud and startled glance for his own magnificence, and entered her as they rolled backwards, coupled in explosive joy.

She cradled his seismic body against her own, stroking him, murmuring to him. She received his wild brevity as a tribute, as a mother receives the first jumbled rush of words from a child, with infinite tenderness, with loving pride, with faith in beginnings.

There was an entire night for the discovery of procrastination and delay, the exquisite torment of lingering, the delights of dalliance.

Along Mahatma Gandhi Road, by Palayam Market and Chalai Bazaar, in front of the police barracks and the Secretariat and the post office, there were convulsions of violence throughout the night.

Annie and Prem, oblivious to the tempo of history, moved to rhythms of their own till daybreak.

29

Retribution and grace.

The words presented themselves to David as newly minted, newly imbued with meaning. He felt a deep, almost superstitious sense of the intricate connection between his fascination with Yashoda and his family's brush with death.

The wages of sin.... *When dharma is broken....*

One could relativize and rationalize. One could be a scholar, an observer of cultural differences. But one could not escape an age-old conviction of wrongdoing. And of retribution.

Nevertheless there was also grace.

They had survived. They were alive. They were together.

He thought of beginnings and of innocence. He remembered Jonathan new born, a wonder, he and Juliet leaning over the crib in awe. Such tiny delicate fingers, such complexity in the whorl of his ear, in the blue vein under his cheek. He remembered how they had touched hands and had stood guardian for hours, amazed, keeping watch over the sweet fragile breathing. Can it be that we are responsible for this life, for this tiny perfect thing?

In the evening, when the mosquito coils were lit, he sat with a child on each knee. And they – so conscious usually of the dignities and perquisites of growing older and bigger – did not object. He told them stories, stories they had not heard for years, stories his father had once told him, stories of his own childhood.

"Tell us about the time you and Grandpa were riding your bicycles out in the country and the storm came...."

"Tell us about the time you ate Grandma's raisin cake that she made for the party...."

"Tell us about the time your dog Nip got lost...."

In the morning he fished with the children in the irrigation ditches.

"I wish you wouldn't," Juliet demurred. "There's still hepatitis and malaria to worry about. I don't think you should act as though we have charmed lives."

"Oh but we do!" he laughed, catching her in his arms and kissing her. "We do!"

It was then that he saw, through the golden network of Juliet's hair, Yashoda coming silkily through the trees towards them. An interior fluttering, some nerve-end recoiling like a snapped thread, disturbed him and he held Juliet fiercely to himself. Yashoda paused, watching. Even when still she seemed to quiver. Like a hummingbird. Like a petal in the wind. It was her eyes that unnerved him. (*I want love, Professor David....*)

Perhaps if like Odysseus he stopped his ears...?

Then she turned and walked quickly back towards the forest.

It should be easy for women to give themselves fully to the present moment, Juliet thought. They have had such lifetimes of practice.

She scraped away at a coconut, strafing the soft white pith into shavings for the curry paste, glancing up occasionally to watch the children at their school work, to see David making notations on the manuscript of his book.

And so they lived happily ever after, she sighed to herself. Returning eventually to the small provincial town of no opportunity for adventurous educated women. She took up her stone roller and leaned over the granite slab. Piquant and greenly bleeding, the curry leaves snapped and shredded themselves beneath her pounding, darkening the coconut flesh, absorbing cloves and turmeric. Juliet leaned over the golden paste and was assailed by the pungent fragrance, a shock of pleasure. Dazed, she dipped her finger into the mix, and smeared a thin ochre line across her forehead, an anointing of sorts.

Nothing gold can stay, she reminded herself. Neither one's gilded myths of the self, nor the luminous green-gold growing of one's children, nor the sweet bruising of living things that bleed perfume and curry.

Her gaze rested like a benediction on her family, and, remembering the abrasion of road grit and window bars against her cheek, she thought: It is a rich moment, the present one. I should be totally content.

Perhaps she had been born at a fractious moment, when colliding stars competed for the same orbit. It was certainly perverse that she should feel a prickle of unrest like a congenital rash; that she should be yearning even now to transplant the family, so recently snatched from destruction, to city soil; that she should be dreaming of the ferment of a circle of argumentative friends; that she should feel, even, an urge to contact Jeremy – to note his quick alarm, to feed on his relief that she had won in a brief skirmish with death.

Yashoda and I, she thought, we want everything. We swing between worlds, always in conflict, always looking for impossible resolutions, destined to uncertainty and dissatisfaction. She bent over the curry paste again and closed her eyes, imagining herself and Yashoda side by side on the ivory swing, their vacillations preserved as art. There would be a kind of immortality to it – the immortality of the bronze dancer in the museum case. As long as one did not mind an eternity of going nowhere.

David leafed through chapters and months of research. And Yashoda moved back and forth across the pages like a pendulum. Like a maharani – or a *yakshi* – on an ivory swing, trailing silk and temptation. He closed his eyes, only seeing her face the more clearly. He opened them and read determinedly, making notes.

He glanced at his wife, who was absorbed in the making of curry. She had paused, she was bending over the stone roller, she had that abstracted, excluding air. She was distant from him, moving on a private path.

He looked out the window at the green maze of palms and recalled Yashoda standing there, her eyes luminous with want.

What you are obsessed with, he told himself sardonically and analytically, is a perception of omnipotence. There was a moment when you tasted a kind of power you had never experienced before. You are drunk with the memory of it, intoxicated with its possibilities. You cannot bear to lose it. You want to convince yourself that it is still there for your taking although you choose – nobly, of course – not to exercise it.

Yes, that was it. Simply that. Nothing unnatural, not even very unusual, just an ordinary human weakness. And if he were to talk to her again, simply talk and comfort and explain – as an ordinary sympathetic benefactor – then this false tension, this arbitrary and guilt-induced intensity, would dissipate. He was, after all, just as cunning and wise as Odysseus, secure in the ship of family, safely lashed to the mast of rationality.

He would come home unscathed.

He looked at Juliet again. She was now moving the stone roller back and forth with a snap of her wrists, fragrance rising around her like a fog. The hint of a smile played about her lips. She is contented, he thought. And so self-sufficient. We are in no danger at all. He would come back to her without mishap.

"Don't you think," he asked Juliet, "that you and the children would enjoy the beach?"

She flicked her eyes towards him in surprise and considered it.

"They're bothering you. You should have gone to the university."

"No, no. I just thought you might like...."

She remembered the red sand and the lush green line of palms and the fishing boats with prows like curled ferns. She thought of the way a shoreline pried a country open so that it flew out in a rush to the universe, sibilant as waves.

"Yes, it's a wonderful idea."

And they set off, Juliet and the children, to hail an auto-rick on the main road.

Beyond the paddy the forest seemed full of shadow and murky intent. There was a sweet heavy smell of decay. David, buoyed by centuries of leaf mold and probity, rehearsed both sides of a conversation.

Yashoda did not see him immediately. She was sitting on the grass beside the pond, bending towards him, her tilted face half-hidden behind the black waterfall of her hair. And languid as the slow-swaying lotuses, she combed it with an ivory comb. The deliberate strokes descended like costly jetsam sliding down a cataract and she sang softly and rocked backwards and forwards to the rhythm of her music and her combing.

Once she paused and tossed the long hair away from her face as though it were a mane and then she saw him. She startled like some animal that is wild and skittish and vulnerable.

David made a gesture of reassurance, of benefaction. There was so much he was going to say to her with avuncular gentleness but when she continued to sit there staring at him, when she simply offered him her comb, he could remember none of it. Nevertheless, he thought, the most delicate gestures are wordless, and solace has more faces than one would dream of.

He took her proffered comb and it moved through her thick black hair like a frail dove in his hand. He did not know how long he sat there combing while Yashoda sang, but when she turned to face him, when she held her hands out to him like a princess begging, he heard again that wild high note of absolute power, felt himself to be straining against the bonds of his entire life and culture.

"No," he whispered, kissing her hands. "I cannot." He stood up, feeling as self-disciplined and as foolish and as life-denying as a monk.

When he looked back from the edge of the forest she was still sitting there, staring after him. He walked on through the forest and the paddy and the grove, seeing nothing. The empty house surrounded him like a hair shirt. He paced it erratically, entering the bedrooms, the kitchen, the porch, the kitchen again.

In the great mortar anchored to the floor, the rice waited to be ground into a mush for cakes. He seized the heavy pestle and began pounding, astonished at the energy it required, at its single-minded thought-numbing demands.

How simple it must be for women to hammer out their own tranquility!

That night he made love to Juliet with a guilty passion of transposed desire.

30

Shivaraman Nair stood moodily in his courtyard watching Prabhakaran feed rice mush to the two new calves. The animals were still unsteady on their feet, their velvety flanks trembled, and periodically they would pitch forward onto their knees. Prabhakaran crooned to them and fondled them, coaxing handfuls of mush onto their pink tongues. And they looked up at him out of their huge luminous eyes and licked his hand and sometimes his face. His low laugh of pleasure filled the courtyard.

For some unaccountable reason, Shivaraman Nair found himself growing sexually excited and angry at the same time. Ever since he had seen the boy, eyes dilated as a calf's with excitement, come flitting through the forest from Yashoda's house, he had been tormented by his own imagination. What had happened between the two?

He was unable to block out a vision of his kinswoman, warm and liquid-eyed and vulnerable as a newborn calf, trembling at the touch of the *peon*. The boy would have bewitched her with his flute, of course, and since women are mere petals blown on a wind of passion, since widows in particular are known to be unappeasable in their hunger for a man, she...she would have.... It was unthinkable, what she might have done.

He gave a sudden bellow of rage, strode across the courtyard, and savagely kicked the calf from Prabhakaran's arms.

211

"Go to your work, lazy boy! You waste time. You are too slow with the calves."

The boy had quailed back in shock and instinctively raised an arm to ward off blows, but his horrified eyes were on the animal.

Mrs. Shivaraman Nair and Jati came running into the courtyard in alarm.

Shivaraman Nair's rage mounted. The *peon* had caused him to be guilty of rash and terrible action. He had injured a cow. Never before had he done such a thing. The *peon* was responsible. And that woman, that temptress.

His wife ran to him, whimpering and solicitous. Though she was a good woman and he was fond of her, the sight of her tears trickling through the folds of chin, the heaving of her ponderous body, served only to exacerbate the sense of unbearable wrongs having been done to him. He turned from her in disgust and stalked furiously out through his coconut grove.

The peaceful green of his paddy calmed him. His lands always comforted and sustained him. They reminded him of his power and of his responsibility to direct in proper paths the lives of those who, by the natural ordering of the universe, were subject to his command. Before he had really noticed where he was going he found himself drawn across the terraces towards the tranquil seclusion of his forest.

The shadowy fungus-perfumed retreat seemed imbued with the presence of his kinswoman. He thought of the cascade of her hair, her almond-shaped eyes, the way she walked, the way the taut brown skin of her midriff (she wore her sari scandalously low on her hips) always made him want to brush against her in passing.

It was undeniable that she flaunted her beauty shamelessly. She was indifferent to family honor. And yet after all, she was woman. What could one expect? Can a tiger change its stripes or its hungers? Such a widow drew scandal to herself as inevitably as ivory drew thieves and honeysuckle lured bees.

But he would be, as it were, the aristocratic bee, who would keep the honey of her youth pure and free from contamination. He would offer himself to her in a gesture of noblesse oblige, for the sake of her need and the honor of the family name.

He came to the clearing and heard the sound of voices. Western voices. Always that family interfering, he thought with anger. He remembered that Mrs. Juliet had been present on the occasion when the *peon*.... And there was the younger one, her sister, who knew nothing of moral behavior. Such women told one another their secrets, wove together their carnal nets.

He backed into the cover of the trees and vines, but his thighs were burning with frustration and he was in physical pain. He leaned against a tree, trembling.

It is the fault of the *peon* and of the foreigners, he told himself. I will not forgive them.

31

Night had fallen and Matthew Thomas was driving out to Krishnapuram with a replacement for the broken flute player. It was the costliest and most intricately carved sandalwood Krishna that Mr. Motilal could supply and he was anxious to present it to Mrs. Juliet. Also he wished to see them again, not having had a chance since the terrible night of rioting. He felt too that it would be fitting to meet the beautiful young widow again in the legitimate company of others. He would be able to express, by his eyes perhaps, his quite polite and honorable friendship, his concern for her welfare. Without impropriety. He had been unable to stop thinking about her. Because, of course, she reminded him of his daughter.

It was true that the lateness of the hour might present a problem. Because the days were almost unbearably steamy most people did their marketing or browsed through the flare-lit bazaar in the cool evenings. It was quite probable that the family would not be at home. But still the matter of the flute player was urgent. This accounted, he felt, for his considerable restlessness and agitation. The drive would calm him, even if it should prove fruitless.

His headlights lit up the coconut grove as he eased the car along the track towards the house. It seemed to be in darkness.

He clanged the front grille but there was no answer. It was just as he had feared. They have gone to Palayam or the bazaar, he told himself regretfully. He would have to come again the next day.

But it seemed to him that the matter of the statue was pressing. It would be inauspicious to leave with it again when he could give it safely into the hands of the young widow.

She had told him that she lived in the forest beyond the rice paddy. The moon was almost full and by its light he made his way past the house and out onto the levees.

It was not difficult to see the track that went into the forest, though once he entered the dark tangle of trees and vines he became a little nervous, almost turned back. He wished he had thought of bringing the flashlight from his car. He stood irresolutely at the shadowy line between the paddy and the curtain of creepers and leaves that swayed and whispered over his head. Then, with his arms stretched out to the sides, he began to feel his way along the cleared space, helped every now and then by spills and splashes of moonlight that leaked through the leaves.

In the quietness he could hear the sounds of insects and the soft stirring of ferns and then the gentle lapping and swishing of water. He came to the edge of the clearing where the moonlight fell golden and unchecked and stepped quietly out from the trees. But then he stopped, hypnotized, as though bound by the invisible threads of an enchantment. Afraid to move, afraid to breathe.

The water lapped the edges of his vision, the pond lilies swayed in his veins. And slowly as a swimmer in a dream a woman moved among the lotuses. He could see the soft shimmer of her skin disturbing the water, the leisurely arc of her arm as it cut cleanly down between the lily pads, the dark trailing seaweed hair. She was pure and naked as Eve.

No thought jarred the bewitched sleep of his mind. He was his five senses. Time stopped. She swam in slow circles, and then she turned languidly and floated on her back, motionless except as the water rocked her lightly, offering herself to the moon and the stars, solitary as the first woman in the universe.

He could see the dull gleam on the delicate gold chains around her throat and waist and ankles.

He had no concept of how many minutes passed before she slowly raised one hand in a silver shower of spray and began to caress herself. Lightly as moonbeams her fingers stroked her breasts, her stomach, the little tuft of wet hair through which the water gurgled softly as rainwater through mosses.

Thought returned to him then. And desire and anguish. Lord God, he prayed desperately, lead me not into temptation. Deliver me from impure thoughts. But he could not turn back into the forest. He could not move.

He stood there until she came slowly up out of the pond, water glistening and falling from her body in careless splendor, the tiny gold bells on her waist and ankle chains chiming and sighing. She saw him and gave a small startled cry, her hands hovering like frightened moths to cover the triangle of hair between her legs.

They stood looking at each other. Nothing moved.

And gradually he became aware that her eyes were filled not with shame but with a shy and steadfast entreaty. It seemed to him that it would be cruel, even sinful, to turn away from that plea. So he placed the sandalwood flute player gently on the grass and went to her, moving as in a dream, and took her gently in his arms and stroked her long wet hair.

Then, as the night rains began, she led him into the little house.

32

The rains had begun again in earnest. It was the season of the second monsoon, though the gap between monsoons had scarcely been noticeable to the Westerners. It had been raining almost every night since the first monsoon officially ended in mid-July. But now the skies flooded and thundered into the days as well.

The roof of their house, with its tiled parapet, was a catchment area, a veritable lake, and water gushed in torrents from the outlet holes in the eaves so that they seemed to be living in a grotto under a waterfall. Now it was impossible to keep the shoes from molding and the books from swelling and warping. Clothes and sheets were spread across chair backs like tents in an attempt to dry them under the ceiling fans – during the brief spasms when these worked. Unfortunately power failures were even more frequent during the rains.

Several times an hour dead palm branches came crashing down under their own soggy weight, sending earth tremors through the house.

One night, battered by rain and banked-up flooding, a levee burst in the paddy. The unprotected section emptied its water in a cataract onto the next terrace. Five-inch stalks of young green rice on the drained terrace faced the morning's sun as naked and bedraggled as newborn babies still sticky with birth fluid. Out of their rightful element, like fish out of water, the fledgling plants gasped in agony. Incredibly, in the blazing space between showers, as the ground hissed and steamed and fogged sunwards, as it fissured and cracked in the grip of that ruthless solar magnet, in those few disastrous hours while the monsoon paused coquettishly, a whole terrace was ruined.

It was considered a catastrophe of more than economic proportions. Such an inauspicious event must have a cause. Someone had broken *dharma*.

Somewhere in Palghat district a child died, a grandson of one of the Nair uncles who were visiting Trivandrum for the impending *arat* festival. They were staying with Shivaraman Nair. When they heard of the broken levee it was apparent to them that the two events were linked. There was a disturbance in the cosmic ordering of things. Unless the disorder was rectified, unless propitiation was made, the full chaos of the *Kali Yuga*, that last age of dissolution and decline, would come upon them.

It was not difficult to ascertain the source of the trouble. The Nair uncles had seen for themselves that scandalous young woman flaunting her jewelry. The men of the extended Nair family convened in solemn assembly.

Item after item of evidence against the widow was considered. There could be no question of extreme guilt. Anand requested permission to speak to his elders. He reminded them that his cousin had been led astray by a young Canadian student of whom no propriety could be expected. His kinswoman had not appeared in public beyond the estate since she had been rebuked for her wrong actions. And on the matter of her refusal to dress as a widow, he pleaded, since she had been in part educated by Westerners (which was not her own sin, but that of her father), since she had suffered the misfortune of a mother's death early in her life, since she had been raised by a father who himself strayed from right actions, since she was so young and beautiful, and since her jewelry could no longer be seen by anyone outside the estate, might she not be forgiven? Might it not be concluded that no further harm would affect the family or the harvest?

There was considerable disagreement and anger voiced among Anand's elders in response to this plea for clemency. During the noisy debate one of the servants entered to inform Shivaraman Nair that his daughter Jati wished to speak with him urgently.

A short time later Shivaraman Nair returned to the family council, his face pale and ominous as that of an astrologer who has dire things to reveal.

His daughter, he announced in a low and savage voice, had seen things which were unforgivable. She had seen a car driven by a stranger, a man not of the Nair caste, enter the estate. At that time, as she well knew, the Canadians were not in the house. She had seen them leave early in the evening on their way to the taxis at Shasta Junction. Nevertheless nearly two hours had elapsed before she heard the stranger's car pass again through the gates of the estate.

Perhaps, Anand suggested, the man had simply been waiting for the return of the Canadians.

To his elders, however, the situation was clear. It was as the ancient Law of Manu warned: A woman not in the custody of a man is an abomination. Degradations will multiply in her courtyard as rankly as weeds. If she is widowed, she must be placed in the custody of her son; if she has no son she must revert to the custody of her father or father-in-law. This had not been done, and now the bitter fruit was being harvested.

The infamous young widow had become a common harlot, receiving men of low caste indiscriminately, desecrating the estate, jeopardizing its fertility, bringing calumny and divine wrath upon the family. She had placed herself outside the rights and privileges of a Nair woman, she was out-caste. It was no longer a question of tutelary discipline. The evil had to be cauterized before its infection spread throughout society and the natural world.

∽

Prem had begun frequenting the toddy shop that stood beside the road between Krishnapuram and Shasta Junction. His ostensible reason was political. All the low-caste laborers from the surrounding Nair estates gathered there in the evenings to squander their few *paise* on the heady sap of the palmyra palm. The institution of the toddy shop was cohesive, warm and rollicking, a community of the kind of abandoned and drunken revelry that only the truly despairing of the world indulge in. It was an opportunity for Prem to talk easily with the men, a forum for sowing political seeds.

It was also a calming and numbing foil to the tumult of his relationship with Annie, and he would call in there on his way back to the university after visiting her on the Nair estate. He did not know how to handle the possessive passion, jealousies, doubts, ecstasies, humiliations that buffeted him like an endless surf with a deadly undertow. She was bewildering, cavalier in her attentions. Sometimes she slept with him inside the ring of banana palms. Sometimes she disappeared for a day or so, sightseeing. Sometimes, without explanation, she left him abruptly and stayed at her sister's house. And so he had come to value the instant anesthesia, the prompt camaraderie of palmyra toddy.

One evening shortly before the *arat* festival he was listening to the talk that flowed around him warm and blurred as a canal spilling over its banks in monsoon time. There was much bawdy joking and lecherous guffawing about a woman who had been seen bathing naked in the forest. One of the workers had seen her by accident when he had crept back at night to retrieve a cache of rice, an illegal bonus that he had hidden on an estate during harvest. At first he had thought that the woman was *maya*, illusion, that he was under the enchantment of some demon of the forest. He was still not sure. Because who had ever known of a human woman who would do such a thing? Perhaps she was a *yakshi*.

He had gone again with friends to investigate. It was not a place to be alone. On several nights they had hidden in the forest, waiting. On some nights nothing happened; on other nights she would be there, silently bathing, naked. She appeared and disappeared like a spirit. Who could say where she came from? Undoubtedly she was a *yakshi*.

Might she not be the cause of the local troubles? An evil spirit ruining the rice? The harvest had been poor – did they not all know it from the distended bellies of their children? Contrary to nature the rains had never stopped properly for the harvesting. And now the second monsoon was excessive. Levees had broken on a number of estates. There would be suffering for all.

Perhaps the *yakshi* should be killed? No, killing was an unlawful act, one which, according to the Brahmin priests, would condemn the murderer to many more lives of suffering and destitution. But if the woman were evil, if she were in fact not a woman but a *yakshi*, then the killing would be an act of deliverance, as when Krishna had killed Kamsa. It would mean salvation. One might leap along the ladder of rebirth to higher rungs.

It was decided that at the very least the matter should be reported to the owner of the estate and his advice sought.

"The Nair landlords are your enemies," Prem told them angrily. "Do not tell them anything you have seen. Perhaps it is only some poor servant girl who will be destitute if the landlord is informed."

The Nair landlords are also our protectors, they told him. Who else will give us work and food? Also they have read the Vedas. They are better able to judge in the matter of demons. They can make decisions. We will tell Shivaraman Nair.

Prem was alarmed. Some woman was in danger. Could it possibly be the widow? Perhaps it is not merely a question of jewelry, he thought. Perhaps there are other dangers besides poverty, other wrongs besides hunger.

He went to visit Annie on the Nair estate.

33

Matthew Thomas's son, Devadasan Thomas, watched his father wandering between the coconut palms on his estate like a madman. The older man was without an umbrella and his aging body was buffeted by the rains as a straw basket is tossed about by flood waters. Devadasan Thomas was afraid that his father would be hit by a falling branch.

"It must be the letters from my sister," he said to his wife. "He has not told us everything. He has a sickness of the mind."

"If your sister has caused some scandal, it is well to leave him alone with his thoughts. The rains will cleanse him."

Weaving between his trees, Matthew Thomas felt something akin to seasickness. His sodden clothing was not as heavy as the weight in his chest. He could feel some tangible knot in there, jagged-edged and constricting, upsetting his balance, causing him to flounder and stumble in the sticky red clay. The rain battering his head and shoulders was soothing to him, so much less turbulent than the swirl of his emotions, that churning surf of excitement with its dizzying undertow of guilt.

What shall I do? What shall I do? he asked himself. An old Kerala proverb came to him. Yes, he thought, I am like a man with his feet in two boats. I will surely drown.

A branch fell not far behind him and he felt its jarring impact along the fault lines of his body. Just ahead of him another branch, disturbed by the vibrations, descended before his eyes like the *lathi* of an outraged god. The boom of its landing was not as loud as the thudding movement of his blood.

I am trapped, he said aloud. Caught between two torments, between destruction and damnation.

When he thought of Kumari, of his other children, of his grandchildren, he knew that the family was inviolable. He could never cause scandal or disgrace to come upon it. When he thought of Yashoda he knew he was already lost, the die was already cast, there was no decision to be made – and his wretchedness would recede momentarily. A sensation of ineffable peace and gentleness, unearthly, divine, surely divine, would wash over him. And then he would see the shocked eyes of his son, Devadasan, the dismay of his daughter, Kumari, and the pain would swamp him again.

He tried to pray, but he had little confidence that God would fully appreciate the complexity of the situation. God was, after all, a Westerner. His missionaries had never managed to unravel the intricacies of caste. Mrs. Juliet seemed unable to comprehend either its convolutions or its importance. Of what sins must he be guilty, that his passions should shame him in this way, wandering like errant children across forbidden boundaries? Why had he not protected himself from so many years of deprivation by marrying one of the widows in the church, good Christian women of his own caste?

I kept myself free for my children, he remembered. For Kumari. So that there would not be the children of a second wife to claim my attention, to divide my inheritance.

But Kumari herself was distant and changed, wearing strange clothes, following other rules.

I am glad I am old, he thought, shading his eyes to deflect the blinding waterfall of monsoon. There is too much change in the world. It cannot be understood. I have lost my way. I am glad that I will die soon.

❧

Yashoda sat on the wooden porch of her house threading ropes of jasmine with restive fingers. She could see, beyond the curtain of water that unfurled itself from the thatched eaves, the pond lilies flattening themselves before the passion of the monsoon, soft and receptive as a woman ready for her lover.

The astrologer had promised this – the coming of a great love. A smile played about her lips, the chain of flowers fell from her hands, and she drew her legs up against her body, hugging them with her arms, leaning her forehead on her knees. She laughed softly with pleasure, remembering again the strong cradle of his arms, the dazed wonder in his eyes.

The gods smile on me, she thought. Especially Lord Krishna. When he sees me he remembers his passion for Radha.

The old rules did not apply to her, as they had not applied to Radha and Krishna. The old rules had never contained her. She had always been different. Had not her father loved her even above his son? It was not only my brother's *wife* who drove me out of my father's house, she thought.

Since childhood other worlds had been laid at her feet – foreign tutors and visitors, travel to distant lands, banquets where she served fine western wines. She had never belonged only to the Nair world. She could not be contained in the ways of the Palghat uncles. The area of darkness spoken of by the astrologer, that dead dark space of isolation, was over. She was warmed by a new sunrise, full of light.

She trembled, feeling again the gentle stroking of his fingers over her breasts, feeling herself fluid and throbbing as the weather, her thigh muscles tensing rhythmically to the wild tempo of the rain on the roof. Ah, she sighed, ah, my love my love my love, ahh! She gave a sharp laughing cry, remembering his huge ragged thrust, sobbing for her hollowness, her emptiness, sucking him back to herself. She touched the small mark his teeth had left on her breast, craving for him.

She began to sing softly to herself the ancient and haunting melodies, the love songs of Radha calling Krishna to her bower.

And he was coming to her. Through the prisms of rain she saw the blurred shape emerge from the forest and held her breath, waiting.

But it was only Annie. And Prem.

She greeted them dreamily, reluctant to leave her private world, but translucent and generous in its afterglow.

"Come in, come in. You are so wet. You must have some tea."

"No, no. This isn't a social call, Yashoda. This is urgent. There may be trouble from Shivaraman Nair. Prem overheard some laborers talking."

"How can that concern me?" Yashoda asked from within the magic circle of her secret.

"Someone has been seen bathing...at night," Prem said, embarrassed and awkward. "In the pond. You were...it is said a woman was.... It is being told to Shivaraman Nair."

Yashoda had a sensation of being hit violently and suddenly. Of being winded. Of shattering. It vanished into thin air, that beautiful fragile bubble of love in whose permanence she had so ludicrously, so wantonly, allowed herself to believe. Abruptly the golden light within her was extinguished. She felt safety and happiness leave her like an ebbing tide.

Lord Krishna had turned away his face and she felt the chill of his frown. She was not as his beloved Radha, but as the evil Kaliya whom the Lord trampled beneath his feet. Kaliya, that serpent of overweening pride and rebellious arrogance. Yashoda writhed, snake-like, in shame and fear.

"Come back to the house with us," Annie said gently, conscious of Yashoda's anguish. "We're not leaving you here alone. David will speak to Shivaraman Nair. You and I could leave for

Madras immediately, if we need to. We can stay there as long as it's necessary."

Yashoda felt exhausted, as though she had arrived at the end of a long and dizzying downward slide from a mountain peak that had been exhilarating, Himalayan, but fraught always with the terrors of falling. It seemed to her that it required immense energy to shake her head, to tell Annie no, it was too late. She had fallen back into the world of stern uncles. There was no escaping. She had always been part of that world too, and she had violated its terms. For great sins there were great penalties. Only by submitting to the will of her relatives, to the ancient expiatory laws of Manu, could she hope to erase her wrongdoing, to preserve herself from sliding back still further into some lesser and unhappier life in her next birth.

Annie pleaded, scolded, became exasperated.

Prem reasoned. "Shivaraman Nair cares only about his wealth and reputation. He will punish you for no other reason than offended pride. You do not owe him obedience. Even my professor, and he is a Brahmin, a *Brahmin*, even he says that justice is greater than the laws of caste and family."

But Yashoda was unreachable, locked inside her shame and fear and loss, the ravaging underside of her euphoria.

"Go away, go away, go away," she murmured, sitting on the wooden floor and rocking herself like a mother by her son's funeral pyre, like a pond lily battered and torn by the rains.

They will come and take me away to Palghat, she thought, sitting waiting on her porch, passive, her legs folded in the lotus position. I will work as a drudge in the house of my mother-in-law. They will take my jewelry and I will wear drab cotton. I have been as vain and as foolish as the peacock and now I will become my own shadow, brown and unnoticeable as the peahen. No one will speak to me. In a mountain village in the Ghats I will live and die in silent disgrace, the subject of warning tales to children.

None of this mattered. It fell from her as easily as rainwater slid from thatch, irrelevant beside the awesome impossibility of love.

And yet, she thought, I have known it. This once I have felt the great passion that all the poets sing of. It is something. It can never be taken from me. It is worth everything.

The rain slackened like a weary *peon* who has run many miles on his master's business, faltered, paused for a brief respite. In the stillness Yashoda waited, rocking herself slowly, looking towards the forest which sighed and dripped and gurgled.

When it happened it was quiet and orderly. A small group of women, Jati and Mrs. Shivaraman Nair and several older relatives, emerged from the trees with slow dignity, imposing in their moral authority.

They surrounded Yashoda who sat motionless as a *sunyasin* in meditation. They sent away her servant, who was old and frightened, who whimpered as she limped away through the forest.

They removed all her jewelry. She watched, impassive, as the bangles and rings were smashed with rocks.

Then the oldest of the women withdrew from the folds of her sari a long-handled razor. Yashoda gave an involuntary cry of dismay. "Oh please!" she begged. "Oh please! Not that! Jati, Jati, my cousin...."

But Jati joined the other women in pinioning her arms, holding her down.

Yashoda felt the insolent scrape of the razor on her scalp. She sat perfectly still, her eyes dilated and dry, as her lustrous black hair fell from her like a dark rain.

34

A foolish hope, Juliet knew, as she spread the sodden sheets over the coir rope between the bamboo poles. Foolish to think they would dry in the hour or so before the rain began again. Better really to leave them spread over the chairs and wait for the fans to come on, but at least this way they would get a little sun, smell a little better. She could have done with an airing herself.

She grimaced as she wrestled with the heavy sheets. From the roof she could see along the irrigation ditches to the rice paddy. She could see Prabhakaran running along the levees, flapping his arms oddly like the irritable crows she kept scaring off with the flick of a wet towel. Shivaraman Nair has sent him to get more grass for the cows, she thought. And he is stealing a moment to play some private game.

They saw so little of him now. He was always away on his courier business. She hurried down from the roof, calling to the children, and they walked out through the grove to meet him.

When they reached the edge of the paddy they could see him more clearly, skipping his way between the terraces.

Something was wrong. Juliet could see now that the odd and erratic movements were not those of play. He appeared to be injured. They began to run as his weird cries reached them.

Precariously balancing on the narrow levee, Juliet folded him in her arms, terrified. He was sobbing and twitching convulsively, hysterically, shrieking incoherently.

"Hush, hush, hush!" Juliet begged. "What is it?"

The storm of his weeping increased.

"Come!" he sobbed. "Come and see!"

And they followed him across the paddy and through the forest.

"Oh my god!" Juliet moaned, stricken, when she saw Yashoda sitting still and trance-like on her porch. "How *could* they, how *could* they?"

∽

In a state of deep but controlled and deadly calm anger, David walked up through the grove to the Nair house.

Anand, agitated and despairing, came to meet him.

"I know, I know, Professor David. I also am most upset and angry. I was not informed. It was kept from me. I thought only that she would be sent to Palghat. My father and I...we have quarreled...he is in a rage because I have argued with him and accused him. He has ordered me from the house."

David nodded curtly and brushed past him.

The meeting with Shivaraman Nair was one of mutual hostility, formality, and chilly politeness.

"I know you are a man of religious and moral insight," David began. "In the temple, I saw that your spirit was large and generous. This action was not worthy of you. It violates your own principles of justice."

"You are a scholar, Professor David. You know that for us wrong actions must be expiated according to the laws of Manu. The penalty for fornication is severe."

"Fornication?"

"It has been proven. My daughter Jati has seen it."

"Seen what?"

"She has seen the man who brought you here after the bus accident. He has arrived in his car at night. Though you and your family were not at home, he has not left again for two hours."

It was as though a blow had been struck, and David reeled with disbelief.

But it could not possibly be true.

"You consider that proof? That is hearsay, mere speculation."

"It is sufficient. A woman's duty is to keep herself free of public speculation. Gandhi himself, Professor David, on his own *ashram*, commanded the head of a young woman to be shaven. Though she herself had done no wrong, she had by her carnal beauty caused lust and impurity to enter the thoughts of the young male disciples. Gandhi himself has seen the need to curb the carnal power of woman."

David stared at him, stunned. He is angry at his own sexual disturbance, he thought. He is shamed by his own bondage to the power of her beauty.

Oh! he realized. As I am! As I am! He felt the kindred hidden spring in the intensity of his own anger. There had been a gross violation of his private aesthetic pleasure. Of a remembered moment in time when he had been held bewitched in the aura of her presence, when he had combed her hair.

He felt disoriented, implicated.

Oh god, he thought wretchedly. She gave herself into my protection and I have failed her. I should have handled it differently. Yet what should I, could I, have done?

An age ago he had sent a letter to her father. There had never been a reply. Had her father frowned on foreign interference? Or had the letter never reached him?

He said coldly: "I am sending a cable to her father in Cochin. If any further harm should come to her...." It infuriated him that he was not in any position to formulate an effective threat.

"There will be nothing further," Shivaraman Nair said. "Expiation has been made."

They made *namaskaram* with frigid formality.

35

Prabhakaran had been sitting in silence beside Yashoda for several hours. She had passively refused to be moved. She had brushed away with nervous and abstracted gestures the entreaties and suggestions of Juliet. When Professor David came, she had covered her head and face with her sari. She did not speak. She seemed suspended, floating, in a state of almost catatonic indifference.

The boy had hesitantly touched her, stroked her hand. She had made no sign so he had left his hand there in compassionate contact, not moving. Hours had passed.

The rain had begun again, sealing them in their solitude, in their cave behind the waterfall that hurled itself from the eaves.

Yashoda shivered a little from the dampness and Prabhakaran went inside her house to look for a shawl. He draped it around her shoulders and sat down again beside her, taking his flute and putting it to his lips.

He played of ancient sadnesses, of burning and impossible loves. He played of a child's longing for a mother, of the adoration of a boy beginning to be a man. He sounded the notes of beauty and pain, the long haunting cadences of memory.

At last he saw her tears and felt the faint stirring of movement in her. He touched her hand again and she opened her arms to him. They wept together, his head on her mothering shoulder, his hand caressing the smooth bare kernel of her head with infinite filial tenderness.

It was then that his formless and inarticulate grief began to harden around a seed of purpose. He left her to go to the house of his master.

꙳

Shivaraman Nair's anger filled the house as heavily as the clouds of cloying incense that drifted about the brass *puja* lamp.

His wife and daughter hovered nervously out of sight in the kitchen. Anand had gone to stay with a friend at the university.

First his son. And then Professor David in intolerable questioning of his moral authority. And now a servant, a *peon*, a mere slip of boy whom he had saved from village starvation, a *sweeper* whom he had fed and clothed! This nothing, this pariah, this scum on the surface of earth had dared to look him in the eyes, to accuse him of unjust and private revenge!

Truly the world was in chaos. All proper boundaries were in dissolution. He was almost choking on his rage.

And his kinswoman! He dared not even think of her. When her face came unbidden to his memory, he was alarmed by the violent trembling of his body. Now that punishment had taken place he did not want to see that face. He would have her sent quickly to her father. He would never see her again.

Ritual purgation was indeed called for, to cleanse the family, to preserve society. His correct action within the family would be followed by his participation in tomorrow's *arat* festival, the ritual cleansing of the kingdom itself, the bathing of the temple deities by the Maharajah.

He was leaving the house to meet with the city and temple officials, to join in preparations for the civic and religious rituals of the next day, when the delegation of Harijan laborers forestalled him.

"Hah!" he said with bitter and explosive scorn when he had

heard their story. Now he was to be shamed by Untouchables, by the pickers of his own rice! "Hah! Your story does not surprise me! Anything can be expected of that woman! You are quite correct. She is a female devil, a *yakshi*. She has been punished, she will be further punished."

And in raging contempt he flung a handful of silver rupees on the ground in front of them.

As he walked away from their wild scrabbling he spat on the swept sand of his courtyard.

He would, after all, have her sent to Palghat. There could be no compromise.

36

"I know you both blame me," Annie said, pacing back and forth.

David sighed. "No, we don't. In any case this barbarity had nothing to do with – "

"All the same they wouldn't have been so prone to be outraged if I hadn't…I wish you did blame me. I might be able to feel a bit indignant instead of sick with guilt." She had bought a packet of Indian cigarettes and was chain-smoking. "What I can't bear is her abject submissiveness. She *consented* to it! How could she do that, how could she?"

"There's nothing we can do until her father comes. I'm sure he will when he gets my cable. And in the meantime no one's going to harm her. Shivaraman Nair promised."

David waited outside the house in the forest until Prabhakaran reappeared.

"Professor David, she does not want to see you."

David went to the closed door and called through it.

"Yashoda!"

There was no answer. He turned the handle, rattling it purposely, and pushed the door slightly open. There was a startled cry, a rushing movement, and the weight of her body slamming it shut again.

"Yashoda," he said gently, his forehead pressed against the

weathered wood. "I have cabled your father. I want to talk to you."

Silence.

He applied gentle but steady pressure to the door.

"No, no, no!" she sobbed through the opening. "I beg you, Professor David, I beg you. I would rather die than have you see me like this."

He stopped pushing but the door remained ajar, the fingers of her right hand clenched around its edge. He traced the outline of her fingers gently and her grip relaxed a little.

"Your father will come to take you home, Yashoda."

"No! I will not go! Can I let my father see me like this? Even for him it will be disgrace. I will go to Palghat."

"You will not be sent to Palghat. Shivaraman Nair has promised."

"Yes, I will be sent. I will ask to go. I do not want anyone to see me ever again."

His fingers followed the curve of her hand and wrist, caressing, like a father with a wounded child. He reached in behind the door. She did not move.

"Yashoda," he whispered. "You have the most beautiful face in India. Nothing can change that. Nothing. You have nothing to be ashamed of."

He stroked her arm, his shoulder curving through the door opening. She did not move.

"May I come in?"

"Oh Professor David," she faltered. She came to life now, taking his hand in both of hers, holding it against her cheek, out of sight behind the door. "You are very kind, Professor David, and I am loving you. But you do not understand. I am so tired, so tired. There is too much danger living between your world and the old world. I do not want to try any more. Please go away."

"This is called shock, Yashoda. It's natural to feel this way now. But it will go away. You will be happy again, I promise you. Even though you think it's impossible right now. I don't want to bother you. I'll go away now. But you must send Prabhakaran if you need me."

He pulled her hand gently through the doorway and kissed it.

"I want to talk to her father," David told Juliet. "It's impossible to say enough in a cable. I'm going to try to telephone him from the Trivandrum post office."

They all walked to Shasta Junction, the children trailing wearily behind. But the taxis had gone to the *arat* festival and they hitched a ride on a buffalo cart, jolting along dustily and uncomfortably. It would have been faster, but more tiring, to walk.

When they reached the post office, it was closed for *arat*.

"We might as well stay and watch the procession," David said gloomily. "It will take us hours to get back anyway."

The crowds began to surge forward onto the street where the sweepers and waterbearers were still running along sprinkling sand and water. The burning strip of potholed blacktop had to be cooled for the feet of His Highness the Maharajah of Travancore. It had not rained for three hours and already the ground was searing to the touch. Thousands of umbrellas were hooked over arms, hanging black and folded like bats in temple niches, waiting for the rain.

Police with *lathis* ran to and fro, beating people back from the roadway with indiscriminate blows as the elephants, fabulously decorated, lumbered gracefully by at the head of the cavalcade. In the midst of the festive chaos, a tiny wrinkled white-haired old man walked alone. Barefoot and barechested, he carried a naked sword vertically in his hands.

He looked like a fantasy creature from Middle Earth.

He was the Maharajah of Travancore.

And then the gods themselves were among them, tolerant gods demanding ritual but not dignity, wobbling along on their flower-strewn palanquins, swaying precariously on the uneven shoulders of the bearers.

And all around, pervasive and close as the humid air, the noise. The sound of India. Brass bands and pipes and Vedic chanting and cheering and laughing and shrieking and car horns and *lathi* blows and screams. The tumult of the people of Vishnu, who began now to defy all attempts to separate spectators from participants, who surged in the wake of the palanquins to follow them to the sea.

And on the way the rains began and the umbrellas went up like a disturbance of bats. It poured. Sluicing down like a cataract, battering umbrellas and shoulders, coursing around the feet. Relentless, sullen.

On the beach everything was in milling disarray. Elephants and people swirled in a rain dance, crowds huddled under the snake boat awnings. The deities were lined up at the edge of the ocean where the Brahmin priests surrounded them in a dedicated choral block, chanting the Vedas in sonorous counterpoint to the drumming rain.

They could barely see the Maharajah, who must surely have been shivering with age and wet and cold. It was his personal religious responsibility to bathe the deities one by one in the sea. Their ablution, signaled by a Vedic crescendo and the trumpeting of an elephant, seemed unduly perfunctory. A frail little figure, his wet *dhoti* clinging to gnarled and skinny legs, ran up the sands to where an official car waited. A sword trailed from one of his hands leaving an erratic line in the sand.

37

Smoke wisped upwards from the mosquito coils. The fans were turning and all the soggy clothes were spread out below them. With its lights on the house glowed like a beacon through the dripping and rainy grove. But they kept the oil lamps burning because the power ebbed and flowed so fitfully. The lights would flicker and dim, the whirring fan blades would stutter and rattle and stagger to a stop.

David and Juliet would remain sitting quietly in the semi-darkness traveling private paths. Without Annie's restless pacing the house seemed strangely hushed. She had seen Prem at the *arat* procession and had gone off with him.

When the fans stopped they could hear the breathing of the children asleep in the bedroom. Then the fans would stir sluggishly again and the light bulbs would wink and tease and flutter. They would wait for the surge of energy, the blaze of light, the breeze from above. They would see the lizards skittering across the ceiling and walls, heading for shadowy corners.

Juliet watched David staring into his memories and remorse.

"Should we leave her alone tonight?" she asked.

"Prabhakaran is with her. And Shivaraman Nair gave his word. Nothing more is going to happen."

It rained as though it would never stop.

The rains sloshed from the thatched eaves of the toddy shop near Shasta Junction. Around the oil lamps inside the men caroused and sang. It was a festival day and they were better fed than usual. *Prasadam* had been freely distributed to the poor at the temple. Besides, they had done well to inform Shivaraman Nair of the strange happenings on his estate. They had silver rupees to show for it. They had been assured that cosmic order would be restored. More toddy flowed. There was a general feeling of well-being and heightened revelry.

Perhaps, the thought drunkenly grew, they themselves should attend to the vanquishing of the *yakshi*. Salvation would accrue to them. Also, with reference to this particular and present incarnation, Shivaraman Nair might be moved to greater largesse. Courage burned hot and heady in their veins.

Into the night and the rain they stumbled, a band of high purpose and noble intent.

Prabhakaran sat in the doorway of Yashoda's house looking out through the twisting ropes of water that sluiced off the roof. He played his flute softly to himself. Inside Yashoda slept, a deep and exhausted sleep. The night star was beginning its long slow slide towards morning. Prabhakaran played to keep himself awake, on guard.

Muffled noises reached him through the rain and his own music. He paused to listen. Voices, shouts, noisy singing. He was instantly alert, running through the forest to the edge of the paddy.

A knot of men, stumbling and staggering, were crossing the terraces. They are drunk, he thought. They have lost their way. There will be trouble for them. At the houses they will not have been heard because of the rain and the lateness of the hour. Everyone is sleeping. But in the morning Shivaraman Nair will be very angry. The police with their *lathis* will be called. Bodies in drunken sleep will be found strewn about the levees. For everyone there will be more trouble.

The men weaved and wandered between the terraces, sometimes doubling back in confusion. It was difficult for them in their condition to negotiate the levees. Several fell into the water, thrashing and calling, spitting and coughing the paddy mud. Their comrades shouted encouragement but slipped and slid on towards the forest.

Prabhakaran began to be fearful. Surely they were only lost and drunk, surely they were not...? But they were coming towards him. They had a goal.

All his senses and nerve ends flared like the hood of a cobra, and with snake-like speed he returned through the forest. His heart was deafening in his ears. Yashoda seemed drugged, heavy, bemused with sleep. He was still dragging her, crying, pleading, when the handful of men, like a rabble of monkeys, came babbling out of the trees.

They seized that *yakshi* and her consort, who was also thin and slight as a spirit. They twisted and pounded and smashed out all that evil, purging the world.

David and Juliet found them in the morning.

Yashoda lay crumpled at the door of her house like a broken and discarded doll.

Prabhakaran was floating among the lilies, blue with death.

38

The little procession wound through narrow streets towards
the banks of the backwater that meandered sluggishly through
coconut groves to the Indian Ocean. Water dripped from the
thatched roofs with soft gurgling sounds but the rain had
stopped an hour ago.

Both the small bier and the larger one, rocking gently on the
shoulders of the bearers, were massed with jasmine and lotus
flowers. David and Juliet and the children had gathered them
from the forest and the pond.

At the cremation grounds beside the backwater scattered
fires smoked and smoldered. Keening figures sat hunched
beside some of them, their heads cowled, watching. Others
sifted through cold embers gathering bones and ashes in
bronze vessels for scattering in sacred places. The air smelled
acrid with death.

At an oval depression lined with coconut husks the bearers
carefully lowered their burdens. Through the strands of flowers, the silk funeral bindings could be seen.

Shivaraman Nair sprinkled the shrouds with sacred water
from the Ganges itself. For this much gold had been given to
the temple priests. Shivaraman Nair had spared no expense
for this funeral. The shrouds were of pure silk with a border of
embroidered gold thread. He sought to bleach the dreadful
stain of murder from his life. When he had seen the drowned

blue face among the lilies, and the broken flute caught in the pond reeds, he had become secretly afraid that Vishnu had appeared to him in the form of the child Krishna, and he had failed to recognize the Lord of the Universe. He sought expiation. He had ensured that the culprits, violent fools, were all arrested. The sacred water, costly and redemptive, fell from his hands.

An old Kerala proverb came to his mind: *Though the bitter gourd be washed in the Ganges, it will not become sweet.* He trembled. I have caused this, he thought. Even my son turns from me. I have been guilty of wrong actions.

Yet he could not tell where his wrong actions had begun. It was surely unfair that he should find himself unexpectedly guilty of murder. He felt that events and intrusions had mysteriously conspired against him. He had been unwise to allow an unchaperoned widow to live on his estate, yet he had simply been responding with generosity to the request of his kinsman by marriage, her father. How could he be held accountable for her waywardness, for the interference of the Westerners? Should he have acted more harshly earlier? He envied his Palghat kinsmen their certainties.

And the woman herself – she was surely guilty. How could he forgive her when he had so cherished her beauty and purity, when he had been so moved by it, had known so well how it would tempt men to lust that he had sought only to preserve and protect her from being sullied. Even now when he looked at that man, at that Matthew Thomas whose very presence here angered him, he could taste the bitterness of his outrage, stinging as bile.

Yet he had not, certainly he had not, intended her death.

And still he was responsible.

More coconut husks had to be piled over the flowers, over the bodies. The men moved quietly, carrying, placing. It was sad work. Jonathan and Miranda were trembling, shivering as though it were cold. Their eyes were red and swollen.

Think of his smile, Juliet whispered to them. Think of his

flute. She held their hands tightly.

The fibrous husks were piled in a low mound. The bodies and the flowers were no longer visible. Everything of the biers was hidden.

They all stood silently waiting for Shivaraman Nair to light the sandalwood flares.

Matthew Thomas swayed dizzily and leaned for support against Prem who stood beside him. I have caused terrible destruction, he thought. I have sinned against God and my family. I have caused even an innocent child to die. Yet I did not know what to do. Things happened so suddenly. I was not ready for so many changes. I am glad I will die before I can no longer recognize the world. Already it is difficult for me to recognize it. I am always bewildered.

Prem steadied the old man, supporting his arm. He knew now that there were other wrongs and other griefs besides hunger and poverty. He had not understood that a rich widow could be a victim too. And now Annie was going to leave him. So lightly. She would write, she said. Nothing seemed to fit within his scheme of things. His philosophy was not used to accommodating a private pain unrelated to land and class. He felt disoriented, alone, between all worlds.

I have to fly home, Annie thought urgently, marooned in remorse. I have to atone where I can atone, where I won't blunder into destruction when I'm trying to help.

By an effort of will, David kept his mind off the treadmill of unanswerable questions. He held his consciousness steadily on the image of Yashoda's face in the lamplight, on Prabhakaran arriving with milk, playing his flute. You failed to save them, the waiting funeral pyres accused him. You failed, you failed.

We are implicated, Juliet thought, hearing again the first haunting notes Prabhakaran had offered her as a gift long ago when the coconut grove was Eden to them, when the world was young and innocent, when good and evil were distinguishable, never as sharply as day from night, but discernible as twilight is from darkness. We are not innocent of these deaths. We are implicated.

If she could only formulate the indictment. The questions (Had they interfered too much or too little? Were they culturally arrogant or excessively hesitant?) were already settling into a litany, an end in themselves. As though she had been granted a moratorium on answers. Even partial answers. But the basic dilemma still needled her.

Where had indictable actions begun?

Yashoda had looked to them for help; how could they not have responded?

Prabhakaran was lovable; they had been unable to treat him as a *peon*.

That was the given impasse: intractable.

That could never have been otherwise.

She would start there.

Her hands that had become calloused, that were forgetting the motions of Canada (the wiping of frost from a window-pane, the closing of an oven door, the small precise movements across typewriter keys) were impatient for the heavy comfort of her stone pestle. She would sit on the floor of her kitchen, the granite mortar full of rice between her knees.

She would not leave the questions alone. She would pound away at them until she had ground out answers.

Shivaraman Nair put his torch to the pyre.

39

Somewhere all the world's waters met.

Juliet sat low in the catamaran dipping the bamboo paddle from side to side, alone in the Indian Ocean. (The fisherman had demurred but when she paid him well he had allowed his scruples to subside. What could be done, after all, about the peculiar impulses of western women?)

Seething in between the lashed and buoyant balsam logs, the blood-warm waves lapped her thighs like birth fluid. And then, she thought, watching them foam and gurgle back out of the boat, they will curl themselves into the womb of earth again. They will whisper and return, exploring by trial and error, advancing and retreating. Somewhere, some time, yearning after the moon, they will slip below southern landfalls and sidle up to the great Atlantic currents. They will shiver and head north and foam around Nova Scotia and mingle with waters that have flowed past Montreal.

And some time soon, she thought, I'll follow them. After the rituals of grief and atonement seem complete.

She felt she would know when it was time.

Just as Annie had known, by the private clock of her emotions, when it was time for her to leave. Which had been immediately, of course.

"I think," she had said to Juliet, "that I might possibly be cured of rash impulse. All these years I have started and ended relationships at whim, I have dallied with other people's happiness, I have begun and then abandoned courses, I have backpacked around the world, stayed on the move, dropped in and out of my life. Now I'm making my bid for responsibility and permanence."

"And you'll start," Juliet had been gentle but sardonic, "by leaving India on instant rash impulse."

"You're not taking me seriously. I'm going to stop bitching about the mysterious lack of stability in my life and I'm going to work at creating it. I'm going back to finish law school. I'm going to call the man I walked out on in Toronto and ask him if he will let me back in the door."

"You'll call him from the airport."

"Why not? This time I'm making a committed effort."

How oddly, Juliet had thought, embracing her sister in farewell, how oddly we diagnose our own flaws, how predictably we prescribe for ourselves. How wistfully well-intentioned is the pendulum-path of our resolve.

As Annie's plane had disappeared beyond the last green quaver of coconut palms, Juliet had seen in its sky-trail the long arc of a swing that would never be still. We both want to be both of us, she thought.

And here I am still – the Indian Ocean was caressing her thighs like a lover she could not leave – here I float in the juice of earth, my body seeping into the elements, my blood flowing slow as the ocean's pulse – and a small part of me, cerebral and perverse, skitters enviously along the trajectory of Annie's life. (What is happening in the cities that will receive her en route to her future and past, what is happening in London and New York and Toronto?)

Jonathan and Miranda waved from the sand and she paddled shorewards. The other child, the missing one, was part of the element surrounding her. His ashes had been scattered in the ocean to return to those beginnings from which he would be reborn.

She was not ready to leave him yet.

Each day she sat on her stone floor and hugged the mortar with her knees. The dull thud of the pestle, the soft, resonant throb of granite against granite, sounded oddly Gregorian. Low in her throat she hummed a lament to its accompaniment, her requiem for a lost child. *Let light perpetual shine upon him....* Even there, where he flows in the veins of Vishnu.

In the still evenings she found herself listening for the sound of a flute.

But at dawn, and sometimes during the day, the alluring hum of Montreal began to disturb her trance. A jazz beat, seductive.

From Yashoda's desecration and death, her mind still shied away.

David left the grove early each day and sat for hours in the university library staring unseeing at ancient texts.

He turned the frail pages of illuminated manuscripts where Radha, in gold leaf and lapis lazuli, moved languidly on her ivory swing, trailing beauty through the air. Yashoda, reproachfully, gazed at him from those almond eyes.

I am everywhere, she said. I am the idea of perfection and of flawed endeavor. I am unattainable beauty. I am the moment of opportunity forever lost.

She came to him ceaselessly in image, in poetry, in idea. He found he could not recall the actual feel of her hair, the silk of her skin. He found he had difficulty sustaining a belief in her death. Her ashes were part of the air around him, he could smell rebirth in the forest's decay. He was hemmed in by five hundred million people for whom dying was a brief journey between lives.

But something ugly had happened, he reminded himself. A dread and final thing for which he was partly responsible. By a sin of omission at the very least. Yet when he placed the grotesque event penitentially before his consciousness, when he tried to hold it there like a *memento mori*, like the maggoty skull with which Saint Jerome kept his morbid sense of mortality kindled, then its jagged and horrid edges became fluid and wonderful to look at. Something transfigured and transcendent emerged, a thing of art.

There is something monstrous about me, he decided. There is something defective about me. I cannot take tragedy or unhappiness or death seriously. I see them as occasions for art, for transformation, for the enduring triumph of the human spirit. I do not feel the mother's anguish, I see the *Pietà*.

You only keep one kind of evidence. It was something Juliet had said often enough – with affection, he had thought; with despair, he saw now. And what had he done to her, willfully blind all these years to her distress? Like the emperor with his nightingale, he had kept her in the jeweled cage of his version of their life together, in the prison of a small stultifying town. She could no longer sing.

There is about my life, he thought, a dreadful passivity. I am a scholarly and detached observer rather than a participator in events. My faculties for sifting all the evidence, for postponing decisions, are over-refined.

His convoluted caution had cost Yashoda her life. He had been engrossed in the inner debate of what he could or should do; it might have absorbed him forever – but there had not been time.

No time.

He felt all at once the gut panic that a dreamer feels on being wrenched from deep sleep by a fire alarm: I will lose Juliet. This was what hindsight, what Yashoda's death, showed him: small signs accumulate like pollen in springtime, each easily ignored or repressed; then harvest comes in an irreversible rush, and after that the fall.

It seemed to him that Juliet was charged with the high-pitched stillness of a fledgling eagle on the lip of an abyss. At any moment she would marshal sufficient reserves of will and daring to spread her wings and soar. While he watched with the helpless molasses-slow muscles of sleep, she would vanish from his world as irrevocably as Yashoda had done.

There must be something, there had to be something he could do to prevent this disaster. But what? He seemed to have lost, long ago, the knack of action, of initiating events. He would have to learn to intrude on the course of his individual history as a stroke victim relearns speech.

Would he, could he, uproot his own life? Could he hurl himself into the jangle and burl of cities, which he had always disliked? Would that avert calamity? (But this was not a simple solution: there were complicated matters of tenure, and of post-sabbatical obligations to his own university.) If he should urge her to go to Montreal now, with his blessing, and beg her to wait until…?

But he feared bereavement and change. Bleak visions came to him: of soaring falcons never returning to the falconer; of the gaunt bronze dancer from the second millennium B.C. escaping – or being stolen – from her glass case, being lost to the eyes of art lovers and history forever.

There was no guarantee, should he make an incorrect move, that Juliet would ever come back. Perhaps it would be simpler to do nothing.

No. This once he required of himself an act of intervention. Even if he bungled it. It stunned him, the sharp pain of impending loss, but it felt redemptive, bitter as atonement. Nevertheless as he walked towards Juliet through the grove of his penitence, hugging his act of contrition to himself like a millstone, it began to take on a stark and aesthetically pleasing outline.

He took his wife in his arms. We will move to Montreal, he said. Had planned to say. Had rehearsed saying. Nobly and sacrificially. Of course you will have to live there without me for a while; it will be at least a couple of years before I can.…

Oh but she would never be lonely in Montreal. The afterglow of that city had always come back with her like an aura. She would go there without a backward glance. And to whom?

He felt dizzy with fear.

He held her and was unable to speak.

In Juliet's dream, the swing was moving faster and faster, the arcs growing wilder. She and Yashoda clung desperately to each other and to the ivory ropes.

"Don't look down!" she gasped.

Below them, infinitely distant, were rock-strewn crevasses. They careened lightly as air, fast as light, suspended from nothing, nothingness below.

"I can't hang on," Yashoda cried. "I'm falling!"

Juliet felt the savage pull of a plummeting body, the damp slippage of hand from clasped hand. Alone, vertiginous, doomed. As the sickening sensation of free-falling entered her own body, she saw, rushing to meet her eyes, the bird of paradise mangled on the rocks.

Then impact. A ballet of fragments, pieces of her own body, her own life, floated before her eyes like atoms in space. She clutched at them, frantic to prevent the dispersal, as her muscles and nerve ends, reflexive, twitched and danced and braided themselves with the damp bedding.

How many days had passed, how many weeks? From the shaggy length of the children's hair, from the calluses on her hands, Juliet measured time. Between her blistered palms, the stone pestle drummed out tentative decisions, overruled them, reformulated them.

It was, ultimately, fatal to careen between worlds. She knew that now. Her life was as segmented as an orange, her fragments held together by the mere rind of her will. It was dangerous to go on brutally pruning back the irrepressible green shoots of her desire for more fertile soil: urban, intellectual, and political. But they had grown together for so long now, she and David. It would be a savage act, separating their tangled roots. The question was – and she *would* pound out a final answer – which cluster of losses was the more death-dealing?

By bicycle one morning an arbiter of sorts – an official-looking one, dignified by pith helmet and khaki uniform – came wending down through the coconut grove, and the mailman handed Juliet a letter. It was Jeremy's handwriting and the postmark was not Boston, but Montreal.

She stared at it as though it had come from another universe. Or from a civilization so distant, so buried under layers of cataclysm, that the archaeologist is baffled, unable to hypothesize a meaning for the found object.

She walked out to the paddy with it and where the lowest terrace trickled into the canal that wound through numberless estates to the ocean, she placed it gently on the brackish water, address upwards, and watched it begin its long journey. Soon the inked runes of her name and past would bleed into the fluids of the earth and mingle with the ashes of Prabhakaran.

David sensed the irresolute weather of Juliet's emotions as a massing of rain clouds. Tonight, he thought urgently, before it is too late, I will speak.

When the children were asleep they stood together in the cool night air beneath the palms.

"About Winston," he said. "Pulling up roots...it isn't easy for me. It will take time." And then quickly: "Suppose you were to live in Montreal, I could come every weekend, and as soon as it's possible...." He spoke sadly, as though he were a doctor intimating a prognosis that was somber though perhaps not terminal.

She said with a guilty eagerness, as though a great weight of decision-making had been taken off her shoulders: "Yes. Perhaps that would work." Then, warming to the suggestion: "I could leave in a week or so, with the children."

So soon. Instinctively he reached out to clasp her, to prevent her, but dropped his hand uncertainly. "I won't be able to stay here," he said. "The place will be too full of ghosts. Perhaps I'll go to Madras for a few weeks."

"Yes." She nodded sagely. She might have been agreeing to the merits of an experimental cure – an elixir of herbs or a taking of the waters. "We'll rent an apartment in Montreal for the time being."

For the time being.

"Do you think…?" He took both her hands in his. "Do you think you will…?"

He did not need to say "wait" or "reassess." It was understood.

We are like trapeze artists who swing away from each other, she thought. It is a delicate act, full of balance and hazard. For such a long time we have been skillful, never falling though never certain. Will we touch on the next inward arc? Or will we miss?

"Do you think…?" he asked again.

How can I know? she wondered. All we have between us is more shared years than I can remember, two children, a tragedy, an aching sense of the terrible limits of knowledge and understanding, and this vast tenderness. Just these few things.

"How can I know?" she murmured.

They held each other, frail beneath the moon and the palms, and kissed timidly, as frightened children do.

ABOUT THE AUTHOR

Born in Melbourne, Australia, in 1942, JANETTE TURNER HOS-
PITAL began her writing career in 1975. She taught school in
Australia until her husband's academic research took them to
Los Angeles, Boston, London, and South India.

She has an M.A. in English from Queen's University, her
research area being medieval literature. In 1974, she was
awarded a Canada Council Doctoral Fellowship.

The Ivory Swing is her first novel, but Ms. Hospital has had
numerous short stories and articles published in North America,
England, and Australia. Her work has appeared in such publi-
cations as *Saturday Night*, *Atlantic Monthly* (in which her story,
"Waiting," received an Atlantic First citation), *Chatelaine*,
Mademoiselle, *Queen's Quarterly*, and *The Malahat Review*.

Janette Turner Hospital lives in Kingston, Ontario, with her
husband Clifford, a Professor in the Department of Religion at
Queen's University, and their two children, Geoffrey and
Cressida. Although she now devotes most of her time to
writing, she continues to teach English literature.

She is currently working on a new novel.

SEAL BOOKS

Offers you a list of outstanding fiction, non-fiction and classics of Canadian literature in paperback by Canadian authors, available at all good bookstores throughout Canada

The Mark of Canadian Bestsellers

THE MANAWAKA SERIES
by
Margaret Laurence,

Canada's most celebrated novelist,
Winner of the Governor-General's Award

The Manawaka stories, set in the most famous fictional town in Canada, offer a clear-eyed vision of Canadian land and people.

This skilled story teller balances humor and pathos as she portrays the human condition through characters struggling to come to terms with themselves and with the world.

☐ 01645-X	**A JEST OF GOD**	$2.75
☐ 01679-9	**THE STONE ANGEL**	$2.95
☐ 01695-0	**THE DIVINERS**	$3.50
☐ 01706-X	**A BIRD IN THE HOUSE**	$2.75
☐ 01720-5	**THE FIRE-DWELLERS**	$2.95

Seal Books are available in paperback in bookstores across Canada, or use this handy coupon.